Desperate

Nicki Monroe & Jessica N. Barrow-Smith

Desperate

Desperate

Nicki Monroe

Jessica N. Barrow-Smith

NEVAEH
PUBLISHING

www.nevaehpublishing.com

Nevaeh Publishing, LLC
P.O. Box 962
Redan, GA 30074-0962

Cover Design: Alex Johnson III
Editor: Dwan Abrams

ISBN-13: 9780983918769
Library of Congress Control Number: 2012937498

Second Printing: November 2012

Printed in the United States of America

Alex and Nia, all my love

~Nicki

To Jonathan Smith, with love

~Jessica

Acknowledgements

First and foremost thanks to God for giving me the gift to write.

Thanks to Alex for giving me the space to write and getting on me whenever I slacked off. Thanks to Nia for being so doggone funny and such a mommy's girl.

Thanks to Ireana for making me feel like the best big sister in the world, and to my niece, Carrington, for loving her tee-tee so much!

To my mom and dad—I love and appreciate you. You mean the world to me.

To Belinda, Garet, and Grant—I love you!

To Pittershawn—you are such an incredible woman. You've had such a positive impact on me. Thank you for being so generous and selfless. You are in my heart.

To Elissa—you're a dynamic woman, and I'm proud to call you my friend.

To Shana—my sister in literary kinship. Too often women are accused of not helping each other. You've proven that nothing could be further from the truth. Thank you for giving me such an amazing opportunity.

To Carol—you are truly the definition of a phenomenal woman. I'm honored to know you. Thank you for adding *Desperate* to the Black Expressions Book Club line up. To the staff at Black Expressions—thank you for being so professional and an absolute pleasure to work with.

Many thanks to all of the book clubs that have and will select *Desperate* as their book of the month.

A special thanks to all my literary sisters who have encouraged me along the way to complete this book.

Peace & Blessings,

Nicki Monroe

To God—I appreciate the gift you've blessed me with.

To Dad—thanks for coming to me in my dreams and giving me a hug when I needed it the most.

To my husband, thanks for letting me have an affair on you with the laptop.

To my kids—Kaniyah, Seven, and Canaan—my mom, my brothers and sisters, Hollie "No Middle Name" Capers—thank you all for the unconditional love and support.

To my biggest fan, Ronda Neal, who constantly nagged me and said, "Girl, when are you gonna come out with another book?"—I needed that; read and enjoy, Ronda.

And to that special author who gave me a chance when everyone else just passed me by…words aren't enough to show you my gratitude.

Last but not least, to those I didn't mention by name, charge it to my head, not my heart; for you, too, are appreciated.

~Jessica N. Barrow-Smith

Prologue

"Dad, what are you doing here?"

"I came to see you. Can an old man come to check up on his only son?"

"But you're dead."

"You don't think I know that by now?" Charles patted his leg on the step and laughed like it was the funniest joke he ever heard. His eyes crinkled at the sides from his laughter. "They say a dead man can't tell no tales. So I came to tell you the truth. But you better listen up. 'Cause I can't stay long."

"I'm bugging," Chris said aloud and rubbed his eyes, certain that when he looked at his father again, he wouldn't be there anymore. Chris had just left his best friend Melvin's house and he'd had one too many drinks. He knew it had to be the alcohol playing tricks on his mind.

"It ain't the alcohol," Charles said and held out his hand. "Touch me. I'm real."

Chris looked at his father's extended hand, but made no move to touch him. He blinked continuously, but no matter how much he blinked, his father would not disappear.

When Chris was fifteen years old, a sophomore in high school, he came home one day and found his father sprawled across the living room couch, the front of his face blown off, brain matter stuck to the wall behind him, and so much blood that from that day forward, Chris despised the color red. Chris was now thirty-two years old. His father had been beneath the ground for over a decade and a half. Skin and organs that were in his body when they placed him in his grave had decayed and deteriorated a long time ago. The man was nothing but bones and just a few teeth—the few teeth that didn't get blown out his mouth when he pressed the gun to his jaw and decided to end his life. It had taken some time, but Chris had come to terms with his father's death. Had he forgiven him? Somewhat. Had he let go of the pain and devastation? Some days were better than others.

But whatever the case, his father was dead. That's why, for the life of him, he couldn't understand why his father was sitting on his front steps, wearing the same plaid shirt and white-washed jeans that he'd been wearing the day he died. The only difference was his face wasn't hanging off. He looked healthy, vibrant. Taut, tanned skin, teeth that had browned a little from years of alcohol, cigarette smoke, and poor hygiene habits, and his perfectly trimmed goatee, never a hair out of place. His twinkling brown eyes and his handsome smile that had made many women swoon and was undoubtedly the culprit of his failed marriage. He looked to be about forty-two, the same age he was when he died.

"Sit down beside me, son; let's talk."

Just as Charles said those words, Chris's wife came soaring into the driveway, her convertible stopping just inches from hitting the house. Chris and his dad both looked questioningly in her direction. Angelique jumped out of her pastel pink convertible and all but pulled Christopher out of the car, rushing toward the house.

"He has to pee," she explained to Chris as she hurried across the lawn with Christopher, Jr. already unbuttoning his pants. "He almost pissed in my car! All that time we spent at the school rehearsing for that play, and you would've thought he'd have the decency to relieve his bladder there. But *no-oooo*! He wants to wait until he gets in Mommy's leather seats and not say a thing about having to pee until we've passed every convenience store in the state of Texas! Christopher, Jr. if you pee in your pants, I'll skin you alive."

"Hurry, hurry, Mom! I can't hold it no more!"

As she fussed, she hurried up the steps, all but dragging Chris's son behind her, and the two literally walked through Charles as he sat there with his chin propped in his hands and a

2

wistful smile on his face.

Angelique continued walking, unaffected by passing through a ghost. But Christopher, Jr. paused momentarily and turned around and looked at his grandpa with a smile. Charles waved at his grandson and Christopher, Jr. chuckled and waved back before Angelique yanked him in the house and raced to the bathroom.

"You spit him out," Charles said, once Angelique closed the door behind them. "Handsome little rascal. He's gonna go far in life. Do some great things."

Still unsure about the situation, Chris eyed his father warily. "He looked at you like he knows you."

"He does know me. I come to him all the time, him and all my grandbabies. They still have their innocence. They can still see the other side."

"So what are you supposed to be? Some kind of angel?" Chris smirked. "I know that's a lie. If you kill yourself, you die and go to hell. So what are you, a demon or something?"

Charles exhaled loudly. "I'm just your father. Nothing more, nothing less."

"Father?" Chris guffawed and leaned against his car. "Because you bust a nut in my mother and made four kids by her does not make you a father." Chris couldn't believe that he was talking to a ghost, but there was so much bottled up in him that he was thankful for this opportunity to get it out. "You bailed out on her," Chris said, clenching his jaw. "*I* became the father. *I'm* the one who held her when she cried. *I'm* the one who raised my three sisters. Times got hard, and your sorry ass just checked out on us. Did you have to do it in the house? We still had to live there, you know? You could've went and drowned your ass in a river or something. But no, that would make too much sense. That would be too easy on us. And you could never make things easy on us."

Charles pushed up from the top step and his knees creaked. Chris found this surprising. Everything about him seemed so realistic, from his creaking knees to the piece of lint sticking to the side of his curly hair. He couldn't possibly be a ghost, could he? But he had to be. He was dead. Chris had seen the aftermath of the suicide with his own two eyes.

"I ain't get it all right," Charles said, sighing heavily. "I messed up time after time after time. I could give you excuses, but that's all they'd be. Excuses. I could apologize, but it don't take away the pain. Millions of times I've asked God—literally—if I can go back and do it again. But He said nah, it don't work that way. You make your bed, you gotta lay in it. It's consequences to everything. You gotta understand that it ain't just your life. When you make decisions, they don't just affect yourself. You understand me?"

"Why are you telling me all this? What does it matter now? Just like you said, you can't go back and change a thing. Why are you even here? Go back to heaven or hell or wherever you came from."

"Chris, you're gonna die."

Chris shrugged his shoulders. "You ain't telling me nothing new. All of us got a number. We all gotta go one day."

"Yeah, but sometimes you speed up your time. It's all about choices—"

"Which is what you should've thought about when you took the coward way out."

For the first time, Charles raised his voice. "Won't you listen to me, Chris? I'm trying to save you and I ain't got much time left. I came to warn you."

It was then that Chris noticed that his father was fading, flickering like a flame that someone was lightly blowing on. Ignoring his father, Chris popped the trunk and began taking out the $100 worth of groceries that he had purchased from Womack's IGA store. With ten bags in each hand, he walked through his father and felt a cold chill come over him as he passed through Charles's body.

"Don't be like me, Chris. Don't be stubborn. Don't be—"

Chris used his foot to kick the door shut on his father. As far as he cared, the man could crawl back in the wooden coffin that he had slithered out of, and choke on his own embalming fluid.

Inside, the house was warm, uncomfortably warm.

"Baby, did you turn the heat on?" Chris called out.

From somewhere upstairs, Angelique called down, "Yeah, I did. When I got on the steps, it suddenly got so cold. Like the temperature dropped or something. I got goose bumps. Did you pick up the ground beef from A-Pointe?"

"Yeah, I got a few other things too," he called back, and quickly went in the kitchen to unload the bags before Angelique came downstairs.

She hated when he shopped at Womack's IGA store. The IGA store sold primarily knock-off, generic brands of food, and she considered the place the "poor people's grocery store." He had no problem shopping there and felt that he got three times the food with the same amount of money than shopping at A-Pointe. Moving fast, he unloaded the goods, balled up the grocery bags, and stuffed them into the bottom of the trash.

He moved over to the deep freezer to pack in the frozen food items he'd bought, and nearly jumped out of his skin when his father suddenly appeared at the kitchen table, sitting in one of the cushioned dining chairs.

"Dammit, Daddy," he whispered fiercely. "You'll have to chill out with that shit before you make me have a heart attack. Go away! Isn't there some rule that if I tell you to go away, you have to disappear?"

His father was already fading so much that Chris could look through his body and see the beautiful mounted bronze butterfly art piece behind him on the wall that Angelique had paid nearly a fortune for.

"I can't go until I warn you, son. I came for no other reason but to warn you. If you chase after her, you will die."

"Chase after who?"

Now, not only was his father fading visually, but his voice was fading as well. It sounded as though he was speaking to him from the other end of a fluted cone. His voice was tiny, barely audible.

"Pay attention to the man…"

"What man?"

"The man in the shadows… He'll be in the shadows…"

Irritated, Chris flung the frozen veggies into the deep

freezer, then turned to face his father. Instead of facing his father, he was face to face with his wife, and she was looking at him like he needed to be admitted to a mental ward.

"Who in God's name were you talking to?"

Chris shrugged his shoulders. "Myself."

Angelique didn't seem convinced. She rolled her eyes and walked to the table, then picked up some canned beans he'd bought. "PorkaPorkin' pinto beans? Really, Chris? You've been shopping at that cheap store again?"

Chris pecked his wife's lips. "Babe, you know this is my week to buy groceries, and money is tight. I still have to put gas in the car."

"Well, you should've just said something. I would've given you the money—"

"I don't need your money."

"It's not *my* money, it's *our* money."

"Yeah, well, I don't need 'our' money," Chris retorted with plenty of attitude.

Angelique sighed as she washed her hands at the sink, then popped open the package of ground beef. As she seasoned the meat, she asked, "How's your job search going?"

"It's going."

"Your breath smells like liquor. Let me guess, you went to the bar with Melvin."

"Maybe."

She huffed. "What's up with the attitude?"

"Long day," he called over his shoulder as he swept his shirt over his head and raced up the stairs to take a shower. "And I'm not hungry. I already ate."

In the bathroom, his father appeared once again. But this time, he was so faint, he was more like a mist sitting on the toilet than an actual person. This time, his father didn't budge or even look up from the tiled floor. Just before he disappeared entirely, he looked up at his son with forlorn eyes and whispered two words: "I tried." Then he vanished.

Shaking his head at the absurdity of the whole situation, Chris stepped into the warm spray of the shower and made a solemn vow. "I'm retiring from drinking."

After that day, he still took a few drinks here and there, but nothing heavy. He never saw his father again. Not on the steps, not at the table, not in the bathroom. But he never forgot his father's warning. And he never went a day without paying attention, very close attention, to anything that moved in the shadows.

One

"Melvin, do you see dead people?"

"Hell yeah, every day. You ever seen those women walking around with that foundation on that's two shades too light? Face look like Olay and neck look like Oh-no. I call it funeral makeup. Look like they supposed to be in a casket."

"Melvin, I'm being serious."

"I'm being serious too." Melvin chowed down on a sprinkled, chocolate-iced donut—which was his sixth donut in the past ten minutes—then said with his mouth full, "I've been working on this joke. Tell me what you think about it."

Without sparing his friend a glance, Chris continued to vacuum the passenger floor of the black and chrome Cadillac Escalade, pressing the lever to squirt out a layer of foamy Rug Renew before sucking it up with the angled vacuum head. He had just finished the passenger carpet and was moving over to the driver side when Melvin pulled the plug on the vacuum.

"Man, what you do that for?"

"That vacuum cleaner might be loud, but it ain't that loud. You heard what I said."

Chris pointed at the three other sedans and the two SUVs that they hadn't even touched yet, the ones that had been repossessed a few days ago and were still full of trash, crumbs, and other debris. "Do you see how many cars we still have left to do? And I got to leave at two for an interview. Save your jokes for another time and let me do my job."

"An interview! You ain't tell me nothing about an interview," Melvin said, walking over to his friend and giving him a heavy thud on his back. "So what kind of job is this? You're gonna be a computer IT, or some shit like that? Somewhere where you're making a little more money than the chump change I'm putting in your pocket?"

And he wasn't lying when he said "chunk change." He paid Chris forty dollars per detailed car. On a good week, like this one, that meant a total of fifteen to twenty cars and a measly check for $600 - $800. Eight hundred dollars wasn't enough to pay a quarter of the mortgage on his two-story, cobblestone and paneled French country house. Six to eight hundred dollars a week, or roughly twenty-five hundred dollars a month, seemed like a slap in the face when just two years ago, he was bringing home monthly paychecks that always had three zeroes behind the leading double-digit number.

After investing seven years of his life into TCP Robotics Research, and coming up with several technological advances that had landed the company numerous international contracts that stretched from Toronto, Canada all the way to Sydney, Australia—then to be called into the office and fired because they had to cut their staff in half? To go from being a computer engineer specialist to a...to a car detailer in his best friend's backyard? It was more than embarrassing for Chris—he'd rather have two baby nuts and a pinkie for a penis than to deal with this bull.

"So what kind of interview is this?"

Chris's eyes dropped to the vacuum cleaner in his hand and he pretended to be completely engrossed by the black and orange lettering on the 500 watt machine. "I'd rather not talk about it. If I get the job, then I'll tell you. If not, then it really doesn't matter, does it?"

Melvin looked at him strangely, realizing that it was something more going on with his friend than what he was letting on, but he decided to let it go. "Anyway, so let me tell you this joke I've been working on—"

"Melvin, on the real, I'm not trying to hear another one of your tired ass jokes." As soon as he said the words and saw the hurt expression flash across his friend's face, Chris quickly said, "I'm sorry, man. I didn't mean it like that. Say the joke. And I swear this shit better be funny."

Melvin held the orbital polisher and leaned against the burgundy PT Cruiser, one of the worse-for-wear cars that they hadn't even begun detailing. He performed a magical feat and stuffed the last chocolate donut in his mouth, downing it with just two chews. Then he cleared his throat, which meant that he was getting into character for his comedian act.

"A'ight, so a man walks in the bar and sees a gorgeous woman sitting alone, sipping on a martini. He asks her if she'll sleep with him, and she says, 'How much you offering?' So he tells her that 'cause of the recession and shit, he just lost his job and he's a little hard up right now. She calls him a scrub and tells him to keep it moving. So he sits at the bar beside her and watches three other men try to get at her, but they're all hard up on cash too. Finally, they're the only two at the bar and she asks him what time is it. He says it's a quarter to eleven. 'Eleven?' she exclaims. 'I'm usually in bed by this time. But if I ain't in bed by midnight, then fuck it, I'm going home.'"

Always the one to crack up on his own jokes, Melvin doubled over the car, clutching the hood while his large belly jiggled with every laugh. It took Chris a minute to get the punch-line, but once he understood it, he simply lifted his eyebrow and gave Melvin a half-smile—one that was more pity than humor.

"Shit was funny, right?"

"It was all right, man." Chris gave his friend dap. "But keep perfecting your art. The worse thing to do is to take the stage, tell a punch-line, then hear the crickets chirp."

"Yeah, like what happened last time, right?"

"Right," Chris said with a nod, recalling the last time that Melvin begged to be the opening act at a concert only to receive bored stares, a chorus of boos, and the persistent request to "Get his fat ass off the stage!"

"I've been trying to hone my skills, you know? Steph got me this gig at a sport's bar that she's gonna be bartending at this weekend, and I really wanna make a lasting impression. You coming to see me in action, right?"

"You know I got your back. But here's what I recommend."

"What's that?"

"One thing that tends to go pretty well with a crowd is to make fun of yourself. All the great comics have done it. If you're short, crack jokes about your shortness; if you're ugly, crack jokes about how ugly you are; and if you're fat—"

"Mu'fucka, you calling me fat?"

"—then crack jokes about your fatness. It's a way of letting the crowd know that you got this flaw, and instead of them laughing at you, they can laugh with you. You feel me?"

"My dawg."Melvin did an about-face, then saluted his friend. "See, that's what I like about you. You seem to know the solution to everything. So tell me this; what's the solution to getting Stephanie to like me how I like her? I ain't just trying to smash, either. I'm really feeling her. I want to tell her, but…I don't know how to deal with rejection—which is something your pretty-boy, muscle-packed ass don't know nothing about."

Chris shooed his friend's accusation away. He got that a lot, being called a pretty boy. Maybe it was because of his toasted-almond complexion, or his jet-black long eyelashes and eyebrows that were naturally arched. Some said it was his low-cut hair that had more waves than the oceanfront. Others said it was something about his lips, his almost naughty smile. And then, of course, it was his 6'2" frame that housed not an ounce of body fat, and was covered from neck to calves with defined muscle tone. He knew he was a handsome man—back in the day, he used to be a bit of a ladies' man—but he never considered himself a pretty boy.

However, he had to admit that he was a bit surprised that Melvin was feeling Stephanie like that. The kind of women that Melvin usually tried to talk to were women with low self-esteem: overweight, unattractive, missing teeth, old enough to be his mama—the distasteful list was seemingly endless. But Stephanie? Stephanie was built like a brick-house with an hour-glass figure, light brown eyes, and a flawless bob haircut that fit her heart-shaped face perfectly. Though she oozed feminine beauty, she had a classy tomboyish demeanor that kept the drooling men at bay. She was the type of woman who could kick it with the fellas and easily fit in.

Up until this point, Chris always thought that Melvin found her attractive but assumed he had placed her name at the top of his unattainable, never-in-this-lifetime list.

"Kiss her."

Melvin's eyebrow shot up high. "What you mean, kiss her?"

"Kiss her with confidence."

The way Melvin was looking at Chris, it was as though he was speaking a foreign language. "Of course, she's going to slap the dog-shit out of you. But she likes you, Melvin. She likes your personality. You make her smile; she even laughs at your corny ass jokes. And if you kiss her with confidence, controlling the kiss and coercing the kiss, that's your unspoken demand for her to recognize you as something more than just a friend."

Though he was standing a car's length away, Melvin seemed to be on another planet as his eyes took on a faraway look and his lips perked up, giving practice kisses to the air. His tongue darted out, whipping around in a circular motion that made Chris cringe and force back a gag.

"No tongue," Chris added. "For first kisses, tongue is tacky. Just lips, your hand on her chin, holding her face still, and your body close to hers, but not touching—not touching unless she steps forward and flattens her breasts against your chest."

"Damn," Melvin whispered, still lost in his fantasy world. He shook his head, shaking himself away from the imaginative stronghold of his thoughts. "No wonder Angelique is so crazy over you. You know your shit."

They exchanged dap again, then Melvin turned on the polisher and Chris plugged in the vacuum. As he finished vacuuming out the Escalade, Chris couldn't stop thinking about Melvin's words: "No wonder Angelique is so crazy over you." Boy, if Melvin only knew the truth. But he hadn't let Melvin in on the ugly reality of his marriage.

The truth about his marriage was that the shit was falling apart worse than wet tissue paper. Chris had no doubt that financial woes were to blame. Every place he put in an application, he heard one of two things: either they weren't hiring, or he was overqualified. It had gotten so bad that he'd even put in out-of-state applications online—and actually got an interview that offered him the job on the spot, under one condition: they'd have to move to North Carolina. Of course, Angelique had refused to relocate, saying, "No one wants to move to that country bumpkin state. That's where people go to retire and babe, I still have a year before I turn thirty... I'm staying right here in San Antonio, Texas." So he'd turned down the job and continued to search for employment, while she continued to do the same. It didn't take long for the unemployment they had been living on to run out; and then suddenly, they had to start figuring out how to turn twenty cents into twenty dollars—it had went to hell in a gasoline-drenched hand-basket from there.

Angelique had stubbornly refused to downsize her lifestyle, even though they both had lost their jobs during one of the hardest economic times in years. He had recommended that they let the house go, suffer the loss, and move in with his mother or one of his sisters until they could get back on their feet. But when he made that suggestion, she reacted as though he had cursed her out. She was determined to live in their posh neighborhood where each home was either a French country house, or had a Mediterranean or Italian flare. She still wanted to keep their luxury vehicles, and continue to shop at the top-notch stores and bombard their son Christopher with new toy after new toy—regardless of the price. She was determined to continue keeping up with the Joneses, despite their hardships. And for that reason, she made Chris feel inadequate. Luckily, she was able to land a sales representative job at an insurance company where she was making almost the same amount that she had been making at Delta Airlines. With that weekly paycheck, she alone paid every single bill—the mortgage, the car notes, the insurance, utility bills. Any time they went out to eat, she picked up the tab and left the waiter a gracious tip.

And though she tried to make it seem like footing all the bills and having a "broke" husband didn't bother her, her actions and behavior screamed otherwise. The Angelique he'd known before getting fired was never short-tempered or belligerent. The Angelique before the termination was his personal freak: she gave him the cookie anytime, anywhere, and any place. He didn't even have to ask for it; all he had to do was give her that look and she was wet and ready. Now, he couldn't even remember the last time they'd made love, or even had a quickie for Pete's sake. She was always too tired or too sore; her period was on, or she had to get up early the next morning, or she just wasn't in the mood. She never had a short supply of excuses.

After he finished vacuuming the car and using the compressed air blower to remove any leftover dirt and grime from the carpet, cushions, and the crevices in the vinyl and burled walnut wood trim, Chris returned the tools to Melvin's garage-shed. He washed his hands in the grit-covered garage sink, then donned his black blazer and gray and black plaid newsboy cap.

"You gone already?" Melvin asked as he sprayed down a coupe that was in dire need of a wax and polish. Chris kept walking and gave him the deuces sign. "I'm only paying your lazy ass for two cars. That's eighty dollars. Unless you come back after your interview and help me knock out a few more of these babies. You know I gotta have these things ready for Old Man Henry by tomorrow."

Old Man Henry was basically Melvin's boss. He was a little white-haired old man who owned R&R Cars, an auto shop that sold refurbished, confiscated, and repossessed cars. All the man did was sit in his office and play his guitar. Chris was sure that once Old Man Henry passed, he'd probably let Melvin take over his business since he didn't have any living children.

"No, they're all yours," Chris called out as he ducked into his black on black, customized Infiniti G. "I gotta go."

"Aye, man, why'd you ask about dead people?" Melvin called out as Chris started up the car.

Chris rolled down his window and yelled back, "'Cause my dad was sitting on my porch steps yesterday when I got home. We actually held a conversation."

"But your dad's dead."

"I know."

Melvin just stood there a moment, unblinking, then said, "Fool, I knew you was crazy. Get out my yard, and you better get that job!"

Chris hoped he got the job as well; and based on how desperate the manager sounded when he called Chris in for the interview, he was pretty sure that the job was his. However, there was no way in hell that he'd tell his wife that he'd finally landed employment as a night-shift stocker at Womack's IGA store. He decided that if he got the job, he'd tell her that he worked there, but as a security guard, not a stocker. And that would be the first outright lie he ever told his wife since the day he stood before his family and hers and said, "I do."

He felt some kind of way about lying to Angelique. His intentions weren't to deceive his wife; however, he was at a point in his life where he felt like his well of options was running dry. He had become a man who was distressed and despaired; but most of all, he had become a man who was downright desperate.

Not wanting to think anymore, he blasted his music and rolled down the windows, then out-sang the newbie R&B artist on the radio, singing at the top of his lungs the whole ride to his interview.

Two

"And now I introduce to some, and present to others…Miss Butterscotch."

I heard the DJ call my name, and no matter how much I pinched and rubbed my nipples, they wouldn't stay hard. In a last ditch effort, I grabbed my chilled bottled water and rolled it across my flat nipples. They perked up and stood at attention like two missiles. Satisfied, I put on my shiny black vinyl top and hurried out on to the stage. The DJ winked at me as he put on a slow, sensual song, and I smiled my appreciation.

With an alcohol-drenched towel in hand, I did something that my boss absolutely abhorred. I thoroughly wiped down the stripper pole—got to be sanitary—then tossed the soiled towel to the DJ. As I looked around the crowded club at the white men dressed in suits, conducting "lunchtime meetings," I licked my lips and tried to choose which one would offer the most money for a lap dance. I preferred dancing for this crowd because I didn't have to bend over and touch my toes. There was no droppin' it like it's hot. These guys liked big titties, not big asses. But one thing they paid well for was for me to squat over their laps and gyrate my ass all over their hard little sticks. Or, their personal favorite: straddle them and suffocate their reddened faces between my fun bags—boy, did they get off on that. And it suited me just fine, especially since my breasts were natural triple Ds.

Finding the beat of the music, I winded my body while massaging and jiggling my breasts. Dollar bills littered the stage. But I wanted more than flimsy, washed up George Washingtons—I wanted to see some Benjamins. I could tell the men were captivated by me because they stopped talking and their eyes followed my every move. Some of them drank liquor while others leaned back in chairs and discreetly touched their groins. I felt like a goddess, and I imagined every man in the place as my slave. They had to worship at my feet. The thought almost made me laugh, so I bit my lower lip and loosened my vinyl mini-skirt, slowly dragging it down my toned legs.

Prancing around the stage, I showed off my flat stomach, small waist, and apple bottom. I made eye contact with some of the patrons before slinging my blonde wig side to side. I continued making seductive gestures before spreading my legs into a V, then flipping upside down on the pole while I slid down into a slow split. The men went wild. They whistled and clapped. More money littered the stage. At the edge of the stage, I bounced my booty until I felt someone slide some bills between my crack. Only then did I reach behind me, undid my bra, and flung it across the stage. I ran my fingers between my ample cleavage and gave a naughty grin. I knew every guy in the club wanted to do me. Being the object of so many men's fantasies made me feel even more powerful and sexy. I liked being in control.

One man in particular was screwing me with his eyes. So I descended the steps of the stage and walked over to him and swallowed his face with my boobs. While I wiggled and jiggled my breasts, his penis grew harder by the second. He stuck a wad of money into my garter belt, and the bills felt good pressing into my thigh. After him, I moved over to another man and slow-winded my ass in his lap. He grinned like an old, balding pervert and filled my garter belt with even more bills.

Noticing that the song was about to end, I returned to the stage and gave everyone a final showdown as I wrapped my long, slim leg around the pole and swung my body around until I slid down to the floor in a provocative position. The song ended, and I collected every crumpled dollar and gathered my clothes off the floor before leaving the stage.

I went straight to the dressing room to count my money. Some of the other dancers were in there touching up their makeup, styling their hair, and adjusting their costumes. I counted out fifteen hundred dollars and stuffed it in my Prada bag. Not bad for four hours worth of work.

Quickly, I changed into a pair of tight jeans, gold top, and open-toed, high-heeled, rhinestone sandals. When I went to pay the DJ, he grabbed my arm and whispered, "You need to stop playing and let me get your number, Butterscotch. Your husband can't wax that ass like I can."

He always did this; try to flirt with me, even though he knew his flattering attention was headed down a dead end street. The only time he tried to talk to me was whenever our boss was not around; but when Dexter was present, the DJ would jokingly whisper, "Let me leave you alone because there goes your boyfriend."

I don't know why he called Dexter my boyfriend. My relationship with my boss was strictly about the business; even though he was a piece of dark-chocolate eye candy…and you know what they say about dark chocolate. It's good for the body.

"I'll see you tomorrow," I said to the DJ, handing him his cash. "And find me another song like the one you just played. I liked that song. You see how it had me grooving."

"Girl, you had me so hard watching you dance…"

I ignored him and said bye to everyone, put on my designer sunglasses, and left the club. I couldn't be late picking up my son from kindergarten.

As soon as I got in my Lexus, I flung my purse on the beige leather passenger seat. I felt free as I rode down the highway, thinking about my place in life. Seven years ago, I graduated from Texas A&M University with a degree in International Business. Chris and I got married a year later. Not long afterward I landed a job as a marketing executive at the airport. I loved my job, and I worked there for five years. Then the recession hit, and I got downsized out of a job. The timing couldn't have been worse because my husband got downsized too. We had some savings, the equivalent of six months of our salaries in an emergency fund, so we thought we'd be all right until we found other jobs. The problem was that we didn't find other jobs.

A year had passed, our unemployment had run out, and neither of us had landed new jobs. Not the kind of jobs we were used to. The final straw came when we were unable to afford our mortgage. Never in a million years would I have thought we'd be in that situation. We were hardworking people who stayed on the right side of the law, paid our taxes and our bills on time. The thought of losing the home we had worked so hard to get made me feel like a failure.

Stripping was my last resort. I tried other avenues first, like trying to sell our house. But the housing market had crashed as well, and there was no way we could sell our home without incurring a loss. Chris wanted to downsize, but we couldn't qualify for a new home without either of us having any proof of income. And if we allowed the house to go into foreclosure, it pained me to think about how many years of suffering we'd have to endure while trying to rebuild our credit scores. When he suggested moving in with his mom or his sisters, I just looked at him like he was crazy. I had not come this far in life to allow the mat to be yanked from under my feet. Time was of the essence, and since my husband wasn't stepping up to the plate, I worked my way into the adult entertainment business and did what I had to do.

At first, I felt ashamed of my profession. Even now, I wouldn't brag to anyone about being an exotic dancer. But over the past six months, to my surprise, I've come to like being a dancer. I don't work at some sleazy, graffiti-covered hole-in-the-wall. Instead, I landed a job at an upscale gentlemen's club. Besides the money, I liked the flexible hours. I worked only three days a week: Monday, Wednesday, and Friday from 10:30 a.m. to 2:30 p.m. That worked well for me, especially since I never took home less than three grand a week.

Unlike some of the other girls I worked with, I didn't need to drink alcohol or do drugs to get me in the mood to dance in front of a bunch of strangers. Most of the time I thought about making love to my husband, or how much money I stood to make just for being sexy; that made me wet real quick. Something about getting paid to be hot resonated with me. I felt like a model or an actress. Like them, I put on a show, and gave the customers what they wanted.

Unbeknownst to my husband, he actually gave me my stage name. He often commented that my golden-yellow skin felt as soft and smooth as butter, yet tasted as sweet as butterscotch. Butterscotch just has an exotic sound to it; that's why I picked it. Plus, it goes along with my Puerto Rican and black heritage.

Working the pole came with ease. Long before I had ever thought about dancing professionally, I put a pole up in my bedroom and took a pole-dancing class with a few of my closest girlfriends. I knew how to work it. I just hated keeping this part of my life a secret from my husband, family, and friends. Rather than telling them the truth, I told them that I got a job in sales. That wasn't a complete lie. Technically, I was in sales. I sold fantasies to men.

Regardless of how messed up all of this seemed, telling lies didn't come easy for me. It pained me to my core. Lying goes against my moral fiber. I think I'm a decent person…at least I try to be. Even though I understand my reasons for becoming a stripper, I fear the judgment that'll come if anyone I know and love ever found out, especially my husband. He'd be disappointed in me. That's putting it mildly. He'd be so disgusted that he'd probably divorce me and seek full custody of Christopher.

And my father, he's probably turning over in his grave. Never in this lifetime would he have thought his sweet baby girl would be doing something so naughty. My mother, if she ever caught wind of it, probably wouldn't even be surprised. She wouldn't hesitate to drag my name through the mud and utterly destroy my character. The quote came to mind: *It takes twenty years to build a reputation and five minutes to destroy it.* That's why I strive so hard to keep my professional and private lives separate. I don't want people to confuse what I'm doing with who I am.

Enough with all the negative thinking; I'm giving myself an anxiety attack. I can't focus on stuff that hasn't happened. Chris doesn't know, my father is deceased, and my mother is non-existent, so what am I so worried about? I refuse to be consumed with intense fear, worrying about what ifs. For now, I'm going to roll with it…whatever *it* is.

Three

"Chris, are you playing or are you serious?"

He wasn't sure which bothered him more, the sound of her voice when she said it, or the disgusted look on her face as her eyes searched his for an answer. A parent seated directly behind them shushed them for the third time. Chris had half the mind to turn around and tell the middle-aged brunette to shut the hell up and quit acting like they were sitting in the movie theatre instead of sitting in a sparsely seated auditorium, watching a kindergarten "Reasons for the Seasons" skit that none of the parents were truly interested in except for when their child took the stage.

"That woman behind us is really starting to piss me off," Chris said under his breath. "If she shushes me one more time—"

"Don't try to change the subject, Chris. I just asked you a question."

Instead of replying, he shushed his wife and pointed at the stage, then stood with his phone turned to "camcorder" mode. Their son Christopher was standing front and center on the wooden stage, dressed in a dark gray storm cloud costume. In his hands, he tightly clutched a bright yellow bolt of lightning made from cardboard, which Chris had helped him construct the week before. He thought it would be a nice touch to the storm-cloud outfit.

"I am the storm," Christopher said in his soft voice, while keeping his eyes focused on his parents. Chris mouthed the words with his son. "I happen mostly in the spring. I bring rain and wind. When I come along…" He paused, scratching the side of his head while he looked at his father for the answer.

"When I come along," Chris said in a loud stage whisper,

"kids can't go out and play."

"Oh yeah! That's right, Daddy!" Christopher exclaimed, and the parents in the audience let out a uniform chuckle. "When I come along, kids can't go out and play. But I'm only passing by; I'm never here to stay."

Angelique clapped and grinned, showing all 32 of her procedurally whitened teeth as she cheered for their son. "You did great, babe!" she yelled out before retaking her seat. Once the next kid took the stage, dressed as a bumblebee with hands full of golden fluff, which Chris assumed was "pollen," Angelique leaned over and said, "So you mean to tell me you're going to be working as a security guard at the IGA store? And you're not joking?"

Chris sighed then shook his head. "No, baby, I'm not joking. And you shouldn't sound so upset about it. It's just something for now, okay? I'm still putting in applications elsewhere. This, along with the detailing job, will hold us over until something better comes along."

Angelique pinched the bridge of her straight and narrow nose, then moved her lips as though she was counting down from ten in order to remain calm. "How much does the job pay?"

Chris knew that question was coming. He sighed, then told her the truth. "The starting rate is eight dollars an hour—"

"Eight dollars an hour!" Angelique said entirely too loud. Every parent in the auditorium glared at them with narrowed eyes and pursed lips. Chris heard one parent murmur, "So disrespectful," and another mutter, "And they're supposed to be the adults."

Angelique and Chris both apologized, and they took an unspoken truce, remaining quiet for the rest of the event. But Chris knew that the conversation was far from over. Instead of reacting to his wife's pouting, Chris focused on the children on the stage.

Christopher had made him so proud with his performance. The little girl up next was a blond-haired, blue-eyed kindergartner. Dressed in a rainbow costume that must've been too heavy for her because she walked leaning to the side, she sang the words to her rainbow song and looked and sounded unbelievably cute. Chris had always wanted a daughter. Angelique and he had tried numerous times to get pregnant again; they'd both mutually agreed that once she got pregnant with their second child, she'd become a stay-at-home mom until the kids reached school-age. But that plan had flopped miserably. As soon as the recession hit and they lost their jobs, having another child became the ultimate no-no. Children cost money, and that was something that they could no longer afford.

After the play ended, they took Christopher to Fun World to celebrate the great job that he'd done with remembering his lines. He wolfed down slice after slice of cheese pizza—the only topping that he would eat; everything else, he picked off—then played every game in the place before becoming obsessed with playing bumper cars. He seemed completely oblivious to the thick tension that had grown between his parents.

Angelique had resorted to giving Chris the "silent treatment/cold shoulder" combo. Any conversation that he tried to start with her, she quickly shot it down.

After Fun World, they took Christopher to get ice cream. Chris remembered a time when they'd always buy two ice cream cones—one for Christopher, and one for them to share. And they'd lick that ice cream down until the only thing left were their two cold tongues; and then they'd lick down each other, which always tasted so much sweeter than the ice cream itself.

Chris asked Angelique if she wanted to get a cone to share, which she answered by simply giving him the "Puh-lease" look.

When they finally turned into their driveway, Christopher had worn himself out so much that he was knocked out in the backseat with his mouth cocked wide open. Chris carried his son into the house and undressed him to his boxers before pulling on a night shirt and tucking him into bed. He kissed his son's round cheek and lingered in the room for a few seconds more, thinking of how lucky he was to have fathered such an amazing son.

He thought back to his own father—or should he say "sperm donor." His father had spent the majority of his life denying Chris and his three younger sisters as his own children, even though they all resembled him much more than they did their mother. Even without their father's help, his mother had raised her four kids to be smart, successful, and full of love. She had always told them to follow their heart in life; she loved to use the contradictory saying that "if you follow your heart, you won't always get it right, but you'll never get it wrong. I promise you, you'll never get it wrong." Chris didn't know how true that was. She had followed her heart and ended up with a man who could've won the Sorriest Husband & Most Pathetic Father of the Year Award—so obviously, she hadn't gotten it right.

Chris had made up his mind that come hell or high water, he would never be like his father. He wanted to give his son a positive role model to use as an example in life. When Christopher, Jr. looked back on his childhood days, Chris wanted his son to remember him as being a loving, caring, supportive dad who was always there, who never let him down. That's another reason why not being able to support his family the way he should hurt him so much. The man should be the primary breadwinner; the man should be taking care of home—not the other way around.

Deep down inside, he felt that by remaining jobless, he was teaching his son that it's okay for a woman to run herself ragged in order to take care of a grown ass man, fully capable and able of taking care of his own self. Here was his wife, bringing in the money—a sales representative working at…well, he didn't know where she worked at; but wherever it was, he knew that they paid her damn good. And here he was, deceiving his wife, making her think that he was a security guard when he was nothing more than a lowly stocker working at a store that sold primarily generic products, and making only seventy-five cents more than minimum wage.

The sound of an ignition turning shook him out his reverie, and he pulled back Christopher's bedroom window curtain and glanced outside at the cars coated in blue moonlight. Wasting no time, Chris rushed downstairs to see what was going on. He hurried outside only to find his wife in the driver seat with the car in reverse.

"Wait! Wait!" he yelled out, chasing the car down. "Where you going?"

She put the car in park and rolled down the window. "Tori

and I are going out tonight. I told you earlier; did you forget already?"

Tori was her childhood best friend, the sister that she never had a chance to have growing up. Chris faintly remembered her mentioning the outing, but that was beside the point. If she left to go out, who would be at home with Junior when he left for work?

"Really, Angie? Didn't I tell you that my first night working is tonight? I have to be to work in…" He glanced at his wristwatch. "…in less than two hours."

"You call that work, Chris? Eight dollars an hour and you have the balls to call that work?"

Chris worked his jaw but didn't say anything.

"Baby, let's just be real, okay? You working at the IGA store, it's embarrassing. I don't even shop there, and you know that, Chris. Here's what I suggest." She flipped down the visor mirror and checked her lips, then added another coating of lip gloss. "I suggest you call Womack's and tell them you've had a change of heart. Tell them to find someone else to fill the position. And you keep looking for a *real* job, while I keep working this sales job. I'm making enough money for both of us right now, okay? So why even waste the gas to drive down to that…to that cheap, dirty-looking store to embarrass our family name?"

Unsure of what to say, Chris just stood there, staring at his wife's mesmerizing lips and breathing in deeply the delicious scent of the vanilla-based perfume she was wearing. God, she was so alluring, so sexy. He just wanted to lean back the driver seat, climb on top of her, and take her on the ride of her life.

"It's been two whole months," Chris said, and leaned into the car, kissing the underside of her jaw and lightly squeezing her large breast. "I swear it'll only take like two minutes." His voice dropped another notch, and he couldn't restrain a groan. "Just two minutes, baby. Junior's sleep. Please, baby. Please?"

"Maybe when I get back, if you're still up."

"I'm going to be at work, Angie. Don't make me beg—hell, I don't care if I have to beg. Please, baby? I need you."

Instead of replying, she rolled the window up, giving Chris no choice but to step away from the car. He watched Angelique back out the yard before speeding down the driveway, the cellphone already up to her ear.

Feeling stilted, Chris rubbed his hard penis through his pants, then wobbled back into the house—unable to walk straight because of the size, length, and pressure of his throbbing erection. In the bathroom, he lathered his man with Vaseline and straddled the toilet, going to town with his hand. With that sexy image of his wife tattooed in his mind, just like he promised her, it barely took two minutes for him to bust into the toilet.

Afterwards, he sat down on the commode and put his chin in his hands. Something was up with Angelique. Exactly what, he couldn't put his finger on it. There weren't any dead giveaway signs, like keeping her phone locked or coming home late. Besides withholding sex from him or that constant condescending stare of hers, nothing much had changed in their relationship. Yet and still, Chris found himself wondering why whenever they were in the same room with each other, sitting side by side, it still felt as though they were light-years apart. Or maybe he was just tripping and over thinking the situation—maybe these thoughts were just an unexpected symptom of sex deprivation and depression.

Chris glanced up at the bathroom clock and realized he needed to put a move on it. After he cleaned up, he called Melvin and asked him to house-sit until Angelique came back from her partying. As though he actually had something better to do, Melvin fussed and whined, but finally promised that he was in the car and headed over.

By the time Melvin arrived, Chris didn't have a minute to spare. He thanked his friend, promised him that he owed him one, then jumped in his car and sped over to Womack's, punching the clock right on time.

Four

"A'ight, so a man walks in the bar and sees a gorgeous woman sitting alone, sipping on a martini…"

As soon as the words left his friend's mouth, Chris's spirit dropped. He spread his fingers across his forehead and looked down at the table, lightly swirling his Scotch and watching the chunks of ice clink against the glass. He knew he had vowed to never drink again, but that was one promise that he was struggling to uphold. So instead of entirely giving up his prescription-free, golden stress-relief medication, he self-imposed a strict limit of two glasses and no more. He was still nursing his first glass, taking tiny sips to make the alcohol last. Just as he expected, half the crowd didn't get Melvin's joke, and the ones who did let out a small chuckle seemed to be having mercy on the failing comic.

"It's not going good for him tonight, is it?" Stephanie invited herself to Chris's lonely table and tossed her bartending towel over her shoulder.

She was wearing a tiny strapless black dress that dipped low in the back and didn't even come to mid-thigh, along with a pair of six-inch stilettos that had silver heels almost as thin as a syringe needle. He had no idea how she stood behind the bar all night in those heels, or how she worked the bar without stopping every five seconds to pull down the hem of that dress. But he had to give it to her, she was wearing that dress and she looked hella sexy in it.

Back in his day, he would've been all over Stephanie from day one, regardless of the fact that he was involved with Angelique, and regardless of the fact that Melvin was crazy over her. Angelique had considered him a whore, but he had considered himself a connoisseur of fine-ass women. But that was a part of his past, a part that he wasn't overly proud of, but a part that had nonetheless shaped him into the respectable man he was today.

It took finding a true relationship with God to realize that he was not only hurting these women and hurting his fiancée at the time, but most of all, he was hurting himself. It was no overnight process, but staying constantly in God's presence had eventually delivered him from the stronghold of lust. Now, when he saw a beautiful woman, he could appreciate and respect her beauty, instead of undressing her in his mind and smashing her senseless. But he had to admit. The more his wife withheld sex from him, the harder it was getting to stay faithful to her, both in body and mind.

"Naw, he's not at his best," Chris admitted and sat back in his chair, crossed his arms. "Even his fat jokes flopped. He used all the ones that've already been overdone."

Stephanie sighed. "At least this crowd is compassionate. No boos yet."

Keyword, Chris thought, *yet.*

They sat and watched Melvin move on to his next series of jokes that actually got genuine laughs out of the crowd. He began talking about his car detailing business and how some people are just nasty as hell with their cars. Then he moved on to talk about repossession.

"I always know when the repossessed car I'm detailing belonged to a brotha. For one, it's either a Buick Regal, a Chevy Caprice, or a damn Challenger all setting on rims 'bout this high—" He leveled his hand just above his nose to show the height. "How the hell you gonna have a nice ass car setting on nice ass rims, parked in front of a Section 8 apartment? You got enough money to afford a whip like that, but you pay your rent with a voucher. Don't make no damn sense. Black folks gotta do better."

The crowd nearly fell out laughing. Their laughter was contagious and it didn't take long for Chris and Stephanie to start grinning too.

On a roll, Melvin continued, "Women nasty with their cars. You get a car repossessed from a woman, that shit is full of napkins

Nicki Monroe & Jessica N. Barrow-Smith

and baby pampers, drive-thru food, bills, shoes, toys from the kids, empty tampon boxes. Now, the inside of a brotha's car usually be clean—maybe some ashes here and there, but that's about it. So that tells me that overall, brothas are cleaner creatures than nasty ass females."

The men clapped and cheered, rooting loudly, but the women were shaking their heads with their lips twisted to the side. A woman from the crowd responded to that accusation, to which Melvin replied, "Don't hate boo boo, I'm just calling it like I see it. Don't make no damn sense! Now brothas, the only thing you gon' find in their car is ashes and roaches—and I ain't talking about the bugs hiding in your kitchen cabinet."

Again, the crowd roared with laughter. Melvin was laughing too, his big belly jerking up and down with each laugh. He said through his laughter, "If a brotha don't smoke, only thing you gon' find in his whip is gold Magnum wrappers—and if they got little willies, like myself, you gon' find Durex and Lifestyles. I'm just being real. See, I carry around the gold pack 'cause it's a status symbol. But if I put this thing in a Magnum, it's like having sex with a trash bag on."

That joke did it for him. When Chris looked around the dim sport's bar, all he saw was teeth and smiling faces. People were beating on the tabletops, some hanging out their chairs, some holding their sides and looking like they were in pain from laughing so hard.

"Yes!" Stephanie whispered loudly and touched fists with Chris. "I knew he could do it. He got 'em now. All he has to do is stay on track and work the crowd."

"Bitch! When did you start working here? Get up and give me a hug, boo!"

Chris and Stephanie both whipped their heads around at the same time. A tall man, immaculately dressed in a blazer, form-fitting jeans, and a pair of snakeskin dress shoes approached the table and all but pulled Stephanie out her seat. The man was taller than Chris, but much slimmer, dark-skinned with a tapered black out, both hair and beard. He walked like a straight man, dressed like a straight man, even had a voice heavier than Chris's. But the

29

gray contacts, his choice of words, and the feminine inflection in his voice gave it away. And when he hugged Stephanie, he hugged her like they were going home tonight and would practice making a baby all night long. To the onlookers, they probably thought the guy was the luckiest man in the world. And Melvin, who had been on a roll for a hot minute, began to stumble as he observed the hug too. Not to mention the peck-on-the-lips kiss that followed.

The man invited himself to sit at the table and Stephanie introduced him as Giovanni, her baby brother. Instantly, the man took on a masculine swag and shook Chris's hand, which put Chris a little at ease. Then Giovanni returned his attention to his sister. "Bitch, I've been calling you for like the past two weeks."

"I know and I'm sorry. I always call you back, but we end up playing phone tag. And I don't work here. I still work at Limelight, but I'm outsourcing, picking up extra cash when I can. So what's up? What's been going on?"

The man choked up and placed his pinkie finger beneath his eye as though he was about to catch a tear. "Me and Tony broke up."

Stephanie's mouth fell wide open. "But I thought…I thought y'all was gonna get married and everything."

"We were until the bitch found out I was an escort and started tripping. I mean, he was wondering where I was getting all this money from, and you know I'm making like five to ten thousand a month. So this little bitch got a private investigator, one of those homewreckers from *Cheaters* or something, and he busted me while I was escorting this woman. I mean damn, I only escort women, and you know me; I don't do cuts, okay? Strictly dickly."

Chris was torn. Part of him wanted to get up and run from the table. He didn't want to hear a man crying over a breakup with another man. He didn't have anything against homosexuals. His motto was: "Whatever floats your boat." But yet and still, he didn't want to hear that nasty shit. But then again, on the flipside, he was intrigued by the fact that this man was an escort. And he was making five to ten grand a month? That wasn't bad, concerning the nature of his "job."

Hating to butt in, but burning with curiosity, Chris asked,

"So you work for an escort business and you don't sleep with the women you escort?"

"Exactly!" Giovanni exclaimed. "I *don't* sleep with the women I escort. I've never slept with a woman in my life, and I put that on my grandmother's grave. But sometimes these women want to suck me off, and I'm like, okay, sure. What man in his right mind would say no to oral sex? And plus, when they're doing it, I close my eyes and pretend like it's Tony's mouth—'cause nobody can suck me off like Tony. I swear to God."

Chris felt some vomit come up in his mouth and he quickly swallowed it down with the last swig of his Scotch. But he wasn't feeling a buzz, and after that uncomfortable conversation, he definitely needed a buzz. "Steph, I need a…" He held up his glass. "And no ice this time, please. Just straight Scotch."

Stephanie nodded, took the glass, and quickly headed to the bar, leaving Chris alone at the table with her brother.

The silence stretched between them, and in order to fill in the awkwardness, Chris cleared his throat and asked, "So what escort company do you work for?"

"*Worked* for. I *used* to work at Diamond-Elite. But I quit that bitch to show Tony that I care about him more than I care about money. Tony is the only man I've ever met who didn't fuck me in the ass and then fuck me over, you feel me?"

Chris struggled to swallow, but nodded. "Yeah, I feel you."

"He shouldn't judge me because of how I make money. Hell, I could understand him being so pissed if I was a stripper or a prostitute or some shit like that. All I do is escort these women and get paid out the ass for doing so. Five to ten thousand a month."

"Five to ten G's?" Chris repeated after the guy.

"Yes, boo; that much money. But you know what?" The man went into his wallet and pulled out a handful of Diamond-Elite business cards and tossed them on the table. "I'd be willing to give up all that shit, all that money—" his eyes filled with tears "—just to be with Tony. I love him, and I want us to be together and be happy and share our life until death do us part. He is my air, he is my lung, he is my—"

Stephanie returned to the table and she sat down Chris's

drink, then pulled her brother into her arms. "Come on," she whispered in his ear. "Let's go to the bathroom. I don't want people seeing you break down like this." Holding his hand, Stephanie led her brother toward the even dimmer hallway that led to the restrooms.

By now, Melvin had walked off the stage and all but ran over to the table. Usually, he always asked, "How'd I do?" first, but this time, he said, "So you just gonna let dude take my girl like that? What, they went to the bathroom to hook up?"

"Probably, if she's into incest."

Melvin frowned. "What you mean by that?"

"That's her brother, Melvin."

Skepticism filled his brown eyes. "You swear?"

"I swear."

"Her blood brother or her play brother? 'Cause chicks will give up the panties to their 'play' brother in a hot minute."

"From what I grasped, they're real brother and sister. And even if they're not, he's gay—not bisexual, but gay. They went to the bathroom because he's crying over a recent breakup with some other man."

Melvin's face twisted up with disgust; then he shrugged it off. It seemed like a weight literally lifted off of his shoulders as he dropped onto the same seat that Giovanni had just occupied. "So how'd I do up there?"

"You started off weak, came in strong, then tapered off 'cause you were more concerned with what was going on over here than keeping the audience's attention. But I'll admit, you did a helluva lot better than I've ever heard you do before. I'm proud of you."

Melvin touched fists with Chris, then helped himself to Chris's Scotch. He nodded his head at the stage. "They're having open mic night. You should get up there and sing something. You remember how you used to do that R&B shit when we were kids? Singing all them love songs, making the girls' panties wet. A swagger brotha with a killer voice, you used to pull them all. I thought you was gonna grow up and be the next R. Kelly—the R. Kelly before he was accused of pissing on little girls. Why'd you stop singing?"

Smiling while reminiscing on those days, Chris shook his head. He hadn't sung in years, besides singing in the shower and singing along with the choir whenever he did go to church. "Singing don't pay bills," he said, then added, "and you're gonna pay for that drink too, dawg."

Melvin shrugged. "If you ever decide to play around with that singing shit again, just let me know. I got a homie who owns his own studio. He owes me favors too, so all I gotta do is speak the word and he'll give you studio time."

Chris shook his head. He wasn't about to waste his time with that mess. Singing was just a hobby of his, and hobbies don't pay the bills. But that escorting gig…

Chris slipped one of the business cards into his pocket, then tuned back in to Melvin, who was talking about how nervous he was about kissing Stephanie tonight. "I'ma do just what you said, dawg. I'ma put my arms around her little waist, stand on my tiptoes—'cause you know she tall as hell with them heels on—and I'ma kiss her with everything I got."

"One arm, not both." Melvin lifted an eyebrow at his friend, so Chris clarified, "Just put one arm around her. And when you do, press your hand into the small of her back—don't feel on her ass either; that's tacky. And don't lean forward either. Wait until she tips her lips toward you or until she moves into the kiss."

Melvin gulped Scotch and nodded, gulped and nodded. It didn't take long for Stephanie and her brother to come out of the bathroom. Besides his eyes being bloody red, no one could tell that he had been crying. As Stephanie began introducing Melvin to Giovanni, Chris replaced his tweed hat and told Melvin that he'd catch him later.

The entire drive home, the only thing Chris could think about was that escort business and the amount of money Giovanni said that he was making a month. He wondered if Giovanni was being honest or exaggerating the salary. Five to ten thousand dollars a month was a nice hunk of money. With that amount, he could tell Angelique to keep her entire paycheck to herself, or spend it on shopping sprees or going out to eat with Tori. He would have more than enough to pay every single bill in the house and still have money left to play with. He could shower his wife with tennis bracelets and imported necklaces heavy enough to put a crick in her neck. But then again, Chris thought as he made the left that would lead him directly to his neighborhood, what kind of lie would he tell her this time? And better yet, would the money even be worth having to live a double life, a constant lie?

Chris pulled into their driveway and turned the car off, but he made no move to open his door. Angelique was there because her convertible was parked right beside him. She had worked late today, so he knew she was tired and probably already in bed with her hair wrapped and her mind deep in REM sleep. Waking her to try to get some would be like trying to invoke life into a zombie—completely pointless.

Biting his lip in indecision, he pulled out his phone and removed the business card from his pocket. Hesitation and anxiety caused his fingers to linger over the number buttons for quite some time. He looked up at the curtained window of their bedroom, which was dark except for the light orange glow from Angelique's reading lamp. He looked at the steps where his father had sat. Thankfully, the spot was empty. Despite the streetlights looming above, Chris noticed that his house was enshrined with shadows. He flicked on his headlights to combat some of the darkness.

Finally, he dialed the number on the business card and listened to the automated system: "If you're calling to utilize the services of a female companion, please press 1 now. If you're calling to utilize the services of a male companion, please press 2 now. If you're calling because you're interested in working for this company as either a female or male companion, please press 3 now. If you're calling for any other reason, please press 0 to speak to the operator."

His heart beat so loud, he was surprised that his wife couldn't hear the pounding, even from the confines of his car two floors below her. He half expected to see the room light turn on while Angelique wondered where in the world was that thumping sound coming from.

In gentle slow circles, he rubbed the spot over his heart to try to calm the erratic muscle. Then he touched his temple, trying to get the colliding thoughts in his head to be still so he could think clearly. He gnawed at his bottom lip, suspended in indecision.

The automated female voice repeated the options again. Chris took a deep breath, slowly released it, then pressed 3.

Five

I woke up to find Chris staring at me. I used to think it was cute. Now, it's just plain old annoying. The look in his eye let me know that he was in the mood to get some. I wasn't feeling it, so none would be got.

"Aren't you tired?" I asked as I flipped back the covers to get out of the bed only to discover my man's member was harder than Chinese arithmetic. I looked away, trying to act like I didn't notice. If Chris knew I noticed, he'd make me feel obligated to do something about it. "You didn't crawl into bed until two something this morning. You know you're still sleepy."

"I am," he assured me as he stroked himself. "But never too tired for that."

Careful not to look in his direction, I made my way into the bathroom and took a tinkle before brushing my teeth and splashing water on my face. As I pat-dried my face with a towel, I felt something poke me in the behind. Frustrated, I stopped leaning over, threw the towel on the vanity, and turned around.

"What are you doing?" I tried not to sound like I was full of attitude, but judging by the dejected expression on Chris's face, I hadn't done a good job of hiding my feelings. Seeing him look so pitiful reminded me of Valentine's Day, two months ago, when I offered him some sympathy sex.

* * *

We had woke up on Valentine's Day morning, and Chris

had placed a crystal vase filled with a dozen long stem red roses, heart-shaped balloons, and a card on the night stand on my side of the bed. I had softened my tone and said, "We've got about fifteen minutes before we have to wake Christopher up for school. Do you think we can be done by then?" I had to ask, because Chris tended to get carried away. He's like the Energizer Bunny…he keeps going on and on and on and on. Not necessarily a bad thing, but when I have stuff to do, or things on my mind, I need him to hit it and quit it.

A slow smile crept up on his face, so I knew I had his approval. Judging by the size of his woody, I had gotten his undivided attention too. I started peeling off my pajamas and tried to make it back to the bed so that I could wrap myself up in the comforter, but Chris stopped me. He grabbed me around my waist and pulled me back into the bathroom. He picked me up and plopped my naked behind on top of the cold granite countertop. Before I could protest, he thrust himself inside of me. The only thing coming out of my lips were moans and groans. I tilted my head back as he gripped my hips and pulled me closer to him and went deeper inside of me.

Chris shifted his weight and raised my legs until they rested on his shoulders. I could feel him in my stomach. He felt so good that I didn't want him to stop. I started talking dirty and saying stuff like, "Don't stop," "Tear this *cho cha* up," "It's all yours, big poppa." All of which made him go deeper, harder, and stronger. I could tell that my words excited him to the point of ejaculation. He pumped faster and faster and then slowed down as he released a high pitched sound that sounded like a call of the wild that let me know he had bust a nut. He shuddered and became limp for a moment before withdrawing himself from me.

I couldn't help but smile at him. No matter what problems we faced, Chris never disappointed me sexually.

He had handed me a warm wet washcloth as he washed himself off in the sink. I slid down off the counter and washed up in the other sink.

Chris kissed me on the cheek. "I'll make little man's breakfast," he had said.

He surprised me, especially since cooking breakfast and getting Christopher ready for school had always been my responsibility. Maybe I needed to start giving him some leg in the morning a little more often, I thought.

* * *

I stopped reminiscing and snapped back into the present. I couldn't deny that Chris satisfied me sexually, but here lately he hadn't been satisfying me emotionally. Romance had packed up and left our marriage, leaving frustration and arguments in its place.

Chris changed into a pair of relaxed fitted jeans and polo shirt and made his way downstairs to fix breakfast. That's when I heard a text message come through on my cell phone. I wondered who it could be at six o'clock in the morning. I hurried up and checked. Didn't need Chris questioning me.

I read the text from Dexter, the owner of the club where I worked. He wanted to know if I could fly to Miami this weekend to strip for a private celebrity birthday bash at another upscale club that he owned. He stated that he'd pay for a first class flight, accommodations at a five-star hotel, and a car and driver to take me around. He also promised that the compensation would be bananas.

How could I say no to that? I couldn't, I surmised. Biting my lower lip, I wondered what I was going to tell Chris. He'd never believe that my insurance job would have me traveling out of town on such short notice.

Swallowing the lump forming in my throat, I texted back that I was down and for him to email me the itinerary. My heart raced with excitement and fear. I had heard about those celebrity parties and knew girls who walked away with tens of thousands of dollars in just one night.

Today was Thursday, and if I was going out of town this weekend, I had a lot to do. I needed to get in with my hairdresser, get a mani, pedi, massage, facial, a full Brazilian wax, and eyebrow threading. I touched my legs and they were baby bottom smooth. Thank goodness for laser hair removal. One less thing to be concerned about.

Still thinking about all that I needed to get done, I threw on a pair of sweats and went into Christopher's room with toy trucks, cars, blocks, and a football scattered on the floor, and woke him up. Yet another thing to add to my to-do list: clean Christopher's room.

Rubbing sleep from his doe eyes, he yawned and got out of bed. I kneeled down and gave him a big hug then kissed him on his chubby cheek. I followed Christopher into his aquarium-themed bathroom complete with cobalt blue tiles surrounding the lower half of the room to give an instant under-the-sea effect. I had had the bathroom hand-designed by one of the most expensive interior design companies in Texas; every time I walked in the bathroom, I smiled because I felt that I'd gotten my money's worth—even though Chris thought it was over-the-top spending and downright ridiculous.

Christopher used the bathroom and took off his jammies. Since he had taken a bath last night, all I had to do was wipe him off. I would've helped him get dressed too, but he was going through an independent stage and insisted on dressing himself. I didn't like it; it hurt my feelings. Made me feel like he was growing up too fast. Next he'd be acting disgusted by my kisses and wiping off his cheek every time I gave him a kiss. I stared for a moment, a wee bit sad that my baby wasn't a baby anymore.

Shaking off the sadness, I wiped his face off last and reminded him that his underclothes were waiting for him on his dresser, and his uniform hung neatly on his door. I went down the hall to let him get dressed in private while I figured out what lie I was going to tell Chris.

I racked my brain trying to come up with a plausible explanation for why I had to leave town quick, fast, and in a hurry. One thing about Chris, he wasn't stupid. He pondered over information until it made sense. If he caught any inconsistencies in my story, it would be a wrap. I thought about my girlfriends, trying to figure out which one of them would make the most solid alibi. Tori was the only one who came to mind.

Before I could get my story straight, I heard Chris yelling for Christopher to come and eat. Christopher met me in the hallway and we went downstairs together. He looked so cute in his creased khaki pants and crisp white shirt.

Once we reached the bottom of the stairs, the smell of scrambled eggs and sausage assaulted our nostrils. The food smelled delicious, but I'm not a big breakfast eater. A protein shake would suit me just fine.

As soon as we turned the corner, Chris cast a furtive glance over his shoulder, then abruptly ended his phone call in a hushed tone.

"Morning, little man," Chris said to his mini-me as he slipped the phone into his back pocket and motioned in the direction of the plate of food on the table that he had especially prepared for his son. He gave me a winning smile as he pulled out a chair for Christopher.

Christopher took his seat and recited the blessing he had been saying since he was two years old then ate.

"Who was that on the phone?" I asked with curious eyes.

"The job. Just some paperwork they want me to come in and fill out. You working from home or the office today?" Chris asked, catching me off guard.

I hated when he asked me point blank questions like that. What should be a simple answer always turned into an outright lie. If I say I'm going into the office, he's going to expect me to dress in a professional manner. Then I can't run around like I need to without feeling stuffy. If I tell him that I'm working from home, he's going to expect me to work...or at least look like I'm working. He may even want a quickie.

"I'm not sure yet." I avoided making eye contact and started preparing my protein shake. "Want one?"

"Sure."

My phone rang. It was Dexter.

I glanced at the screen of the phone, then looked over at my husband who was staring at me intensely. I felt like he suddenly had X-ray vision and telepathic abilities. Part of me wanted to send Dexter's call to voicemail, but that would definitely pique my husband's interest. Then I thought about answering the call but walking off; however, that would be a dead giveaway. Praying that I was making the right decision, I turned my back to Chris and took the call using my most professional tone and carefully choosing my words.

Invisible steam left my ears when Dexter said, "I'm just calling to make sure you check your email. I just ordered the plane ticket online, and they're going to send the confirmation via email."

"Okay, thank you for informing me of the situation. I'll get to it shortly." A simple text message would have sufficed and saved me the hassle and the mini-heart attack. "That was my boss," I said ending the call. I went to the counter and finished stirring my protein shake.

Chris sighed. He looked at Christopher, who was sipping his orange juice, and then grabbed me by my wrist. Not too hard, but enough to get my attention, forcing me to look at him. With a serious tone, he said, "Is there something I should know?"

Every time he took a stern stance with me I felt invisible fingers tickle my insides, causing me to release a nervous giggle against my will. His nostrils flared, but I tried not to let that faze me.

"I don't know what you're talking about," I said between giggles and wriggled my wrist free. "That was my boss. Why are you tripping?"

"I'm finished," Christopher said and got up from the table.

"Go brush your teeth," Chris told him, and he did what his daddy said.

As soon as Christopher was out of earshot, Chris cornered me.

"What's your problem?" I snapped. "Back up off me!"

"Just chill," he said and gently held both of my wrists. "I need to talk to you about something." His demeanor had changed; his voice had softened, some of the tension had left his shoulders, but he was licking his lips repeatedly—something he did whenever he was nervous or anxious about something. "I got this job offer in Las Vegas," he continued, and instead of looking at my eyes, he looked at my throat. "The interview is this weekend, and if I get the job, we don't have to relocate. It's a part-time job that pays a full-time rate, and I'd only have to fly to Vegas on the weekends—

at least two weekends out the month."

Never in my life had I heard of such a position. "And what company is this?" I asked.

He picked his protein shake off the counter and downed half of it before replying, "It's called Diamond-Elite Business Solutions. They oversee all the, uh, computer systems of the…the, uh, casinos. And my interview is Friday, tomorrow. So I'd have to fly out there to the interview. And if I get the job, I'd have to stay the whole weekend."

Relief whooshed through me like a gust of air from a tropical storm. "Well great," I said, clapping my hands together. "Good for you! Much better than that security guard crap you were doing at Womack's. Now, we'll just have to secure a baby-sitter over the weekend because you'll be in Vegas, and I'll be in Miami. You think your mom would be—"

"Miami?" Chris took a step back. "What the fuck do you mean you're going to Miami this weekend, Angelique?"

"I got a message from Tori this morning, and she wants me to go to Miami with her this weekend. That's why I'm working from home today, okay? I'm going to try to get all of my work done this morning so I can spend the rest of the day getting ready for the trip."

Out of all my friends and associates, I picked Tori because she's like a sister to me. Neither of us has any blood sisters, so when we met back in the sixth grade, we've been play-play sisters ever since. I can always count on Tori to have my back. Plus, her first ex-husband was a dentist and the second a plastic surgeon. She got broke off in both divorce settlements. She doesn't think anything about getting up and taking spontaneous trips.

I frowned at Chris. "Why are you looking at me like that?"

"Because you've lost your damn mind. We didn't talk about this."

"Don't even go there," I said with plenty of attitude. "You didn't touch bases with me before deciding to suddenly up and take a trip to Vegas."

"It's not some random trip!" he yelled. "I'm trying to get a *real* job so you don't have to be ashamed about your husband working at the IGA store. I'm trying to get a *real* job, so I can keep your ass laced in Jimmy Choos and Dooney & Burke handbags."

"Oh, so now this is about me?" I tossed back, feeling tears stinging my eyes. "You are taking this completely out of proportion and you need to calm down."

"Don't tell me to calm down," he huffed. "What's going on in Miami anyway?"

"What difference does it make?" I tried to keep my voice down so that Christopher couldn't hear us even though I knew that was a mute point considering that Chris was yelling loud enough for the both of us.

"Are you serious?" He smirked. "You sure you wanna stick with that answer?"

I felt backed in a corner and desperate to tell him something. "She's thinking about buying a condo there and wanted me to go with her to check it out." The way this lie fell into place amazed me. Now all I had to do was fill Tori in.

"A trip to Miami costs money." He lowered his voice.

I was so sick and tired of Chris rambling on and on about my spending and what we couldn't afford. The very reason I've never watched that syndicated 70s sitcom, *Good Times,* is because I couldn't understand why any woman would marry an uneducated man who couldn't keep a job, and then have three kids with him and happily raise her family in the ghetto. Just didn't make sense to me. I never wanted to be with a guy who had to tell me, "We can't afford this," or "You can't have that." In my mind, Chris had turned into that guy, a buster.

"Don't worry. If I can handle all the bills here, then I'm sure I can handle a little flight to Miami, even though your trip to Vegas might break you." I regretted the words as soon as they flew out of my mouth. I didn't mean to sound like I was boasting. I could see the sadness in his eyes, and my heart broke for him. I pressed my hands together like I was about to pray and touched my mouth with my fingertips. "That didn't come out right. I didn't mean it like that."

I reached for Chris, fixing my mouth to apologize. He jerked away from me. Without saying a word, Chris left me alone in the kitchen. The stone-cold look on his face stopped me dead in my tracks and sent a frosty chill up and down my spine. I'll never forget the dark look in his usually loving eyes. What had I done?

Six

"Man, I hope you get the job, and I hope you screw every woman you escort. And record the shit too, 'cause I wanna watch. Maybe you can teach me a thing or two."

"Really, Melvin? And what about my wife?"

"What about her?" Melvin smacked his lips. "Man, I don't even know what you married her for anyway. That's why you had to basically drag me to the wedding—me and yo' mama. Ain't neither one of us wanna be there, smiling, clapping, pretending like we happy for you. She don't care nothing about you; it's always been about the money when it comes to Angelique. I told you from day one—"

"Melvin—"

"No, hear me out. Let me talk."

Chris rolled his eyes while he held the phone to his ear and waited for Melvin to finish smacking on whatever he was gulping down. Chris assumed it was a bacon, egg, and cheese biscuit from Grandma's Kitchen. And knowing Melvin, it wasn't one biscuit; more like four or five with a couple of hash browns to go along with it—this undoubtedly contributed to his ever-growing Santa Clause gut.

"When did you meet Angelique?" Melvin continued.

"You already know. Seven years ago when we went to that club."

"And what were we going to the club for?"

Chris sighed and rolled his eyes again. "We went to celebrate me landing my job at TCP Robotics."

"Exactly. She met you the night you got hired at the most

high-paying job in your life. Chris, you and me both know that we grew up broke, busted, and disgusted. Dawg, we grew up in the same projects, our apartment buildings side by side. But being broke ain't faze us. We learned how to live with just enough and be okay with that shit. Then you meet this high-maintenance, boogie-chick, and all of a sudden, everything you do, you gotta do it big. That ain't even you, Chris, and you know it."

"What's so wrong with having nice things?"

"When'd you hear me say that? Ain't nothing wrong with having nice things. But something's wrong with a person only wanting to be with you 'cause you got nice things."

"If she was only with me 'cause of what I got, then she would've been left me, Melvin. I ain't had a job in two years. My funds are dried up. And she's still with me."

"You keep thinking that. Chris, she ain't with you. She's over in Miami doing only God knows what with only God knows who, and when her shit comes to the light—'cause trust, it always comes to the light—you gonna be the one sitting there looking like BoBo the Clown."

"Chill out about my wife, okay? She's not perfect, but who is? You're misunderstanding the situation."

"How so?"

"I'm not doing this escorting job to get a free ticket to screw any woman that I desire. I'm taking on this job because I *want* to be the provider for my family. My wife shouldn't be responsible for paying all the bills. And your little detailing business ain't cutting it for me—"

"Don't call my business little—"

"Then don't call my wife a gold-digger. See that's the problem with men like you. You don't understand the fundamental difference between a gold-digger and a go-getter."

"I insist you explain the difference to me," Melvin requested with sarcasm dripping off his pathetic attempt at donning a British accent.

"The difference is that a gold-digger is about one thing and one thing only—money. Nothing else matters. But my wife…"
He shook his head, smiling as he thought about her. "My wife sets

goals and goes for them, and she doesn't let nothing or nobody stop her. My wife is educated and perfectly capable of taking good care of herself with or without my help or financial assistance. She doesn't need me, she desires me. There's a difference, Melvin. And she didn't marry me to complete her; she married me to complement her."

"Well isn't that lovely?"

"Kiss my ass, Mel."

"I will not. But what I will do is tell you what Stephanie told me about Angelique last night, after we finished having sex—"

"You tapped that?"

Melvin didn't miss a beat. "Naw, man, I didn't. I wanted to, but she wanted to cuddle. We laid in bed all night, kissing and touching. Cuddling with her was better than boning any chick I've ever smashed in my life. Man, I think I'm falling in love with her already—"

"Okay, so what did she say about my wife?"

"Boy, you better sit down for this one."

Chris felt his heart palpitate. "I am sitting down."

"Basically, Stephanie told me—"

"Mr. Hines," the secretary said politely, "Mrs. Whitmeyer is ready to see you now. Please follow me. Do you have the wardrobe selection that you were asked to bring?"

"Uh, yes, ma'am, I do." As badly as Chris wanted to find out the dirt on Angelique, he told Melvin he'd call him later and quickly followed the secretary to the back with his wardrobe bag in hand. "Mrs. Whitmeyer?" Chris asked, drying his suddenly sweaty palms on the seat of his pants. "I was under the impression that I was meeting with a Mr. King. Dexter King."

"Oh, he had to take an out-of-state emergency trip. So you're going to meet with the top woman in charge." She smiled at him and tossed her jet-black curly hair over her shoulder. "No worries though. She can be a bit intimidating, but I'll let you in on a little secret." She dropped her voice to a whisper and gave his arm a flirtatious squeeze. "You already got the job."

"Seriously?"

"Seriously." She kept her voice low as they walked down

47

the long corridor lined with large framed photos of relaxing landscape scenes and pillars topped with greenery. Her heels clicked against the marbled floor. "The pics that you sent us, Mrs. Whitmeyer has already photo-shopped them and posted them onto the website. And she's already added your name to the gallery of male escorts."

"My real name?"

"No."

He exhaled his relief.

"She's given you the name Solomon. She said she likes the strength that exudes from your physique."

"Wow." Chris wasn't sure if this news made him more or less nervous. Sometimes, people looked a lot different in person than they did in pictures. What if he didn't live up to the pedestal that this woman had already put him on? What if she took one look at him and the light in her eyes dimmed and her shoulders slumped?

Thankfully, the secretary didn't say anything more as she led him down the seemingly endless hallway. They finally came to a stop in front of an office with the gold-plated name Whitmeyer attached to the door. A glance at his watch informed him that it was exactly eight o'clock. One thing was for sure: Diamond-Elite might be run predominantly by black folks, but they were definitely prompt.

"No worries," the secretary said softly. "You'll do fine." She rapped on the door, and a voice made raspy by years of heavy cigarette smoking beckoned them to come in.

The receptionist pushed the door open for him then made her departure. Still rather anxious, Chris repeatedly wet his bottom lip as he stepped into the spacious office that had a skyline view of the Vegas skyscrapers. Mrs. Whitmeyer's wooden oak desk took up nearly a fourth of the room. Besides her overly large desk, there was nothing more in the room but a water dispenser with cone-shaped cups. The water machine gurgled as Chris walked over to the desk with his hand outstretched. The woman stood to her full height to greet him, and Chris was taken aback by her stunning beauty despite her age.

Unlike many cigarette smokers, this woman had aged well. Like a black curtain framing her face, her hair fell in layers; it was longer at the back, shorter at the front, and not a strand of gray hair in sight. Her peanut butter brown skin was smooth and taut without a single blemish or imperfection—no crow's feet at her eyes, no wrinkles around her lips, no loose skin at her neck. The top of her head came to his shoulder, and her pink and gray plaid skirt suit only accentuated the curves of her breasts, small waist, and shapely thighs. Behind a pair of thin-framed glasses that sat high on her long narrow nose, her cat-shaped eyes searched him from top to bottom and shined their approval.

"Well, well, well. Your pictures do you no justice," she said, and gave him a wide smile that had an uncanny resemblance to his wife's smile. Perhaps it was the brightness of her whitened teeth.

He shook her hand and allowed her to kiss both his cheeks. "So that's a good thing, right?"

"Indeed it is," she said and retook her seat, giving him a coy smile. She crossed her legs behind the desk, exposing a rather generous portion of her stocking-clad upper thigh. Chris politely averted his eyes.

"And you've never modeled before?" she asked, still watching him with eyes that were almost calculative.

Chris shook his head. "No. Never."

"Where'd you get all those amazing pictures that you sent me?"

"I did a photo shoot about a year ago. There was a local photographer that was paying for models to pose for his portfolio. Just a way to get a little extra cash on the side. I was going through some tough times financially—still am, if I'm being honest. Then a guy mentioned your escorting service—"

"What guy?"

"Uh…Giovanni."

"Escorting isn't his only talent." She sat back in her seat, allowing her skirt to rise even more, and nibbled on the tip of her fountain pen. "He should try his hand at the big screen; he's a marvelous actor."

Confused, Chris frowned. "Ma'am?"

"Never mind me. Just thinking out loud." She lit an extra long Virginia Slims and pulled on the cigarette before speaking through the smoke. "You don't have to call me ma'am. That makes me feel old."

Chris smiled his apology, then watched in amazement as she placed one leg atop her desk and kept the other planted on the floor, giving him a full shot of her waxed bikini line and silk red panties. His eyes quickly darted up to hers, which wore a rather naughty smile.

"How does your wife feel about you working for me?"

"She doesn't—" Chris frowned. "Wait. How do you know I'm married?"

She pointed at his left hand, which bore his gold wedding band, and blew a stream of smoke out the side of her lips. "I hope you don't plan to wear that while you're working." She shook her head and scrunched her face. "Not a good look."

He slid off the ring and pocketed it before allowing his eyes to roam around the room, trying to figure out where to look besides between Mrs. Whitmeyer's legs. She had sex appeal, and she knew it too; probably had a lot to do with how she fell into such a prominent position. It was not a secret that many women decided to suck and fuck their way to the top.

His eyes finally settled on the view behind Mrs. Whitmeyer and zoomed in on the black, mirrored skyscraper that sparkled as it reflected the sun's morning rays. Then a question came to his mind. "How does your husband feel about you owning an escorting business? *Mrs.* Whitmeyer."

Her eyes narrowed into slits. "Never question me, Mr. Hines. That's rule number one, you understand? Keep my husband's name out your goddamn mouth."

Slightly taken aback by her venomous words, Chris replied in a calm tone, "I can do that, Mrs. Whitmeyer, but on one condition. Don't bring up my wife again. She doesn't know anything about what I'm doing, and I desire to keep it that way."

"Understandable." A long silence stretched across the room, and Chris found himself wondering if he had messed up the job before he even got in good. And then she added, "Well, I'll cut to the chase." She closed her legs daintily before standing to her feet and dubbing out the cigarette in a crystal ash tray. "You got the job if you want it. And you start today, assuming you accept the position. Your first client will be Ms. Raleigh Parker. She's staying at the Bellagio Hotel in order to attend a wedding tomorrow, and she has requested the company of a male companion. You're supposed to meet her at two this afternoon. She's already paid the donation in full so—"

"The donation?" Chris asked.

Mrs. Whitmeyer frowned and crossed her arms. "So obviously, you haven't read the manual I emailed you."

"I, uh, I started on it but—"

"Shut it up."

"Excuse me?"

"Sit," she said and pointed at the swivel chair behind her desk.

Every fiber in his being was telling him to walk out the door and never come back. He didn't like how this woman talked to him, he didn't like how she looked at him, and he didn't like the negative tension mounting between them. Yet and still, the money enticed him. Tentatively, he took a seat in her chair and turned to face the computer screen.

"Read the rest of the manual, Mr. Hines. And when you finish, Griffin, our photographer, is going to take you into the shoot room and get some more pictures of you. After that, I need you to complete this paperwork," she said, pointing to some stapled papers that bore a yellow sticky-note with his name on it. "And then, you are ready to begin your first adventure. Talk to you shortly." She paused, then turned around and leveled an icy stare at him. "And don't try to nose through my shit either. My computer programs are password-protected. Understand?"

"Yes." Chris didn't realize he was holding his breath until the moment she left the room. He exhaled a whoosh of air and felt lightheaded after doing so. That woman was truly something to reckon with. He didn't care how good the money was, Chris couldn't see himself working for her long. She had too much attitude for him, and she walked around like her shit didn't stink as bad as everyone else's.

Chris quickly scanned the escort handbook, only half paying attention to the wealth of rules and information. He focused on the paycheck portion of the manual, though. Each employee would be paid their "donation" directly from the client and pay Diamond-Elite ten percent of their earnings. For clients who paid in advance online, Diamond-Elite would deposit half of the money in the employee's account prior to the meeting, and the other half in the account upon completion of the "date." That meant that if he took on this client today, Diamond-Elite would drop twenty-five hundred dollars in his account and then another twenty-five hundred dollars Sunday, minus their ten percent fee. Chris smiled so hard, his face hurt. The first thing he'd do with the money is pay his tithes; secondly, he'd buy his wife a diamond-studded necklace, bracelet, and earring set. He was certain that once Angelique saw the jewelry set, her panties would hit the floor and those sexy legs of hers would be wrapped tight around his waist. The thought alone gave him a hard-on, making it difficult to focus on the task at hand.

Before he could finish browsing the manual, Griffin knocked on the door and beckoned him to come. The shoot left him feeling rather uncomfortable since the majority of his shots were taken in his boxers only, and the cameraman was flamboyantly gay. The most difficult shots were the ones taken completely nude with nothing covering his precious jewels but the corner of a white fluffy towel. Relieved that the shoot was over, he returned to the office and finished the stapled paperwork.

Finally, about two hours later, Mrs. Whitmeyer sauntered into the room and questioned him about the manual. Thankfully, he had read just enough to pass her "pop quiz."

"Well..." she said, crawling on top of her desk and taking a seat directly in front of him with her legs spread in such a way that he sat directly between them. Her skirt had rode up her thighs and bunched at her crotch area, and Chris could smell the Victoria Secret bath wash she'd bathed in. "Welcome to Diamond-Elite Escorting Services. Glad to have you on board."

"Glad to be on board," Chris answered in a level tone, keeping his eyes on hers as he tried to figure out her strategy.

"So your first client is Ms. Raleigh Parker. You do understand that you are not required to sleep with her, correct?"

Chris nodded. "I read the manual, Mrs. Whitmeyer."

"Of course you did, honey," she said, and patted his head like he was a good dog. "You're a good husband, Mr. Hines. But I'm wondering. What do you do after escorting Ms. Parker all day, treating her like a queen—which I have no doubt that you will—and then this woman who has paid five thousand dollars—*five thousand dollars*, Mr. Hines—decides she wants to take you back to her hotel room and sample your goods? And judging by the lump in your pants, you, my dear, have been blessed with quite a big…stiff…" Her eyes dropped down to his crotch, and she licked her tongue across her bottom lip before saying, "Cock."

Amused by her blatant come-on, Chris gave her a half-smile.

"You mean to tell me that you'd leave poor Ms. Parker in her hotel room all by her little lonesome? After all the money she's paid? She'd feel cheated, Chris. Your integrity toward your wife is touching. But I'll be damned if I'll allow your 'integrity' to give my company a bad look. I'll be damned if I allow your 'integrity' to leave one of my clients feeling cheated out of her thousands of dollars."

Realizing where this was going, Chris shushed her by placing a finger against her lips. First, she looked surprised, then let out a small gasp when his hand dropped from her lips and stroked her thigh. "Mrs. Whitmeyer, have you ever had a man make love to your mind?"

"What do you mean?" She sounded breathless and closed her eyes as his finger trailed up her thigh and twirled circles against her silky pantyhose. "See, the body is controlled by the mind. So if I can get into your mind, it makes my job that much easier when you allow me to hold you close and get inside your body. Open your eyes; I want you to see what I'm doing to you."

She did, and by then, Chris had stood to his feet and was leaning over her, his body not quite touching hers, his lips close enough to hers that if either one of them moved, their lips would undoubtedly brush against each other.

"Mrs. Whitmeyer, has your husband ever looked at you with such fire—"

"—I told you not to mention him—"

"—with such intensity, such passion; his eyes feel like fingers caressing your body, and you swear that he touched you, even though he's hovering over you, his lips just a breath away?"

Again, she moaned, and he placed his finger against her temple.

"It's because he touched you here." He tapped her temple, then slid his finger down her high cheekbone, and followed the curve of her neck, causing her to shudder uncontrollably. Then he leaned forward and said, "And has your husband ever placed his lips against your ear, just like this. And you felt the hairs in his mustache tickling the tender skin on your neck. And when he speaks, his register is so low, his timbre so smooth and mellow, that his voice travels down your spine and reverberates between your legs. And all you can think about," he moved his lips over hers, pausing centimeters above her opened mouth, "is how his lips feel, and how sweet the kiss would taste, and how badly you want to feel the pressure of his mouth on yours."

He heard her moan and ran his thumb over her bottom lip before slowly pulling away.

"And then he pulls away and you're burning up with passion, Mrs. Whitmeyer. And he leaves you to yourself, feeling sensual, feeling sexual. You touch yourself—and you're wet, throbbing, aching; you imagine him on top of you, his weight crushing, but not hurting, his stroke deep, but not rough. And you wake up in the morning, still feeling like a woman instead of a one-nightstand; your dignity still intact, and enough memories to last you a lifetime. Would you feel like you got your money's worth? Or would you feel…cheated?"

"Mrs. Whitmeyer, Griffin said his proofs are…" The secretary held open the door and looked from Chris to Mrs. Whitmeyer, who quickly hopped off the desk, looking rather embarrassed. The secretary gave them a knowing smile. "His proofs are ready, Mrs. Whitmeyer." She closed the door softly behind her without asking any questions.

Chris looked over at Mrs. Whitmeyer who still seemed rather shaky. "You okay?"

Her response was breathless. "I need to go to the bathroom."

Chris grinned as he watched her walk away, thoroughly convinced that he had proven his point.

Seven

I arrived in Miami looking like a celebrity and feeling like my shit don't stink. Wearing an all white top, white belt, and white pants that fit so snug they could've been painted on, my body looked like milk, as the rapper Ludacris would say. Between the champagne, tasty gourmet food, seats so cushy I thought I was lost in a cloud, extra pillows, and enough leg room that I could stretch my long legs without touching the seat in front of me, I stepped out of First Class convinced I'd never fly coach ever again in life.

In true Dexter fashion, he hadn't missed a beat. When I strutted into the terminal, I didn't have to wonder where to go. A uniformed driver greeted me with a sign that had my name on it and escorted me to baggage claim to pick up my newly purchased Louis Vuitton luggage.

I caught a few people staring and pointing and even overheard some people asking each other who I was. I just grinned, tossed my shiny, silky natural hair over my shoulder and kept it moving. My Dominican hairstylist had hooked my hair up with a ceramic flat iron. No complaints here.

We stepped out into the elements, and I marveled at the clear blue sky and perfect temperature. Everything seemed brighter in Miami, like switching from a regular TV channel to hi-def. To me, it was that noticeable.

The driver opened the limousine door and ushered me inside before loading my luggage in the trunk. I inhaled the coconut scented interior and ran my hand over the butter-soft leather seat. If this was a dream, no one had better wake me up. I could count the number of times I had ridden in a limo: my prom, my wedding, and my uncle's funeral.

I noticed a wet bar and an assortment of nuts, chips, and Godiva chocolates. The driver took his seat behind the steering wheel and told me to help myself to anything I wanted. Hearing those words made me tingle all over. I can't remember the last time a man said those words to me. Aside from the rapper T.I.'s song, *Whatever You Like,* nothing came to mind.

"*Permanecerá en la Estación de Playa de Internacional de Triunfo,*" the driver said.

I couldn't contain my excitement. Was he serious? Dexter had been tight lipped about which hotel I'd be staying; even still, I knew it would be nice. But The Trump International Beach Resort nice? He had raised the stakes to a whole other level. I had to tell somebody.

I got on the phone and called Tori. She answered on the second ring.

"*Hola, chica!* I just wanted to let you know *que yo estoy aquí en* Miami."

"Well, I am so glad you had a safe trip, Miss Thang." She sounded suspicious. "Now are you ready to tell me what's going on? Why you got me lying to Chris? Better yet, why are *you* lying to Chris?"

"It's not what you think." I stuck a stick of gum in my mouth and chewed.

"If it's not what I think, then tell me what it is. And don't tell me bullshit 'cause I can smell it from a mile away."

I pondered the thought of confiding in Tori. Through the years we had shared lots of secrets. We had enough dirt on each other to ruin reputations and relationships. If I couldn't trust her, who could I trust? Besides, I didn't want her thinking I was having a secret rendezvous. I put on my big girl panties and told Tori the truth, the whole truth, and nothing but the truth, so help me God.

After an uncomfortable silence that lasted maybe 30 seconds in real time, but felt like 3 minutes in phone time, Tori finally spoke. "What the hell?"

"Don't judge." I wrapped a strand of hair around my index finger.

She let out a chuckle. "Who? Me? Judge? Child, puhleez. All the shit I've done and am still doing, who am I to judge you?" Her tone turned serious. "You just be careful. Remember that you can't trust everybody." I heard her sigh into the phone. "I know you're not a real drinker, so don't accept drinks from people and definitely don't leave your drink unattended. People are crazy. They'll have you doped up and taking it up the ass somewhere. For real."

I took her words to heart. I had no doubt that she had genuine love and concern for me. "I'll be careful. I promise."

"Are you the only girl dancing, or did Dexter invite some more dancers?"

Now that, I didn't know. I couldn't believe I hadn't even thought to ask. Though it would be nice to be the only dancer so I wouldn't have to split a dime with some other bitch, Tori had me thinking. I was miles and miles away from anyone I knew, and you could never underestimate people. What if this party got a little out of hand? It'd be nice to have another girl there to help me regain control of the situation. I made a mental note to call Dexter and ask him if I'd be dancing with company.

But, to calm Tori's nerves, I said, "Yes, girl! I'm dancing with three other chicks, so chill out."

"Just be careful," she reminded me again. "On a different note, you're about to see some real ballers. Don't get stars in your eyes and let the glitz and the glamour fool you," she warned. "Chris is a good guy. He's cut from a different cloth. Just because a man has money don't make him any better than the man you got at home." She paused and then added, "Don't let anybody mess your stuff up."

"I won't," I assured her. "You know Chris and Christopher mean everything to me."

"I know how much they mean to you. But I also know how much you never wanted to be poor. We grew up in B'more together, remember? Neither one of us came from money. Hell, we used to come home from school and our lights would be turned off." She gave a stoic laugh. "Sometimes we couldn't even afford toilet paper. That's why you and I vowed we'd never marry, or have babies with broke men."

Speaking of broke men, I told Tori about Chris's promotion from being a security guard at the IGA store to possibly being a computer IT for Diamond-Elite Business Solutions.

"Where the hell is that?" Tori asked.

"It's located in Las Vegas—"

"Las Vegas?"

"Tori, chill," I told her again. "We're not moving to Vegas. If he gets the job, he'll only have to work over there two weekends out of every month. Working part-time, but bringing home a full-time check. You can't beat that."

We talked for a few minutes more, and she made me promise to check in with her on a regular basis. I agreed, and she promised to cover for me if Chris called again. We got off the phone, and I replayed our conversation in my mind. Sharing my secret with my best friend made me feel so much lighter. What a relief.

Outside the tinted window, cars cruised by at a leisurely pace. Though the air conditioned limo felt amazing, I wanted to feel my hair blowing in the wind. Also, it wouldn't hurt to let passersby catch a glimpse of who was being escorted in this luxury ride.

My hair flowed like a delicate curtain as I rolled the window down. I glanced up and caught a glimpse of the driver's dark brown eyes in the rearview mirror as he told me in Spanish that we were almost there. Another surge of excitement zapped through me.

When we arrived at the resort, I had to remind myself to breathe. It was breathtaking. The place looked like a tropical paradise complete with palm trees, swimming pools, and fountains, all along the oceanfront. The hotel itself reminded me of a skyscraper.

My driver helped me out of the car and loaded my luggage on a cart for the bellman to take inside. He gave me his cell phone number and let me know that he'd be available to take me anywhere and everywhere I needed to go. I thanked him and gave him a tip. He grinned and tilted his hat at me.

Inside the resort, class, elegance, sophistication, and charm oozed from the walls, the fixtures, and the people. I could've lived in the lobby. That's how spectacular it was. At check-in, the clerk acted exactly the way I expected her to—professional and courteous. She did everything with a smile and flare. Impressive.

Though I tried not to gawk at my surroundings, I couldn't help myself. I felt as though I had been warped into a rich lifestyle, and that's where I wanted to stay. Being there felt good...like I belonged. A girl could get used to this.

I held my breath as I stuck the card in the door and entered my one bedroom suite. The bellman carried my luggage inside, and I tipped him, too, then he left. Contemporary furnishings, marble bath, and a private balcony overlooking the ocean—I inhaled deeply as my eyes danced around the room.

Lying on top of the luxurious bedding was a vinyl bustier pant set and a pair of 4-inch clear heels with a note that read:

I hope you find everything satisfactory. Wear this to the club tonight. I picked it out especially for you. I'll bet you'll look like fire. ~Dexter

I smiled as I thought about how Dexter had gone all out for me. Then again, had he really gone all out? I mean, Dexter had long ends, and I'm not talking about hood rich either. Dexter earned plenty of money from his upscale gentleman clubs in Dallas, Miami, and Atlanta. I had even heard a rumor that he produced adult entertainment films as well. A weekend getaway like this would've broken Chris, but to Dexter, I'm sure it was mere play money. I could only imagine the type of money he stood to make this weekend.

I checked my watch and realized that I had four hours before I had to head out to the club. I yawned. The travels seemed to be catching up with me. At least I had enough time to take a nap. But before I did, I needed to call Chris and let him know that I had a safe trip.

I called Chris's cell phone, but he didn't answer, so I left a message. Then I hung up my clothes and unpacked my toiletries in the bathroom before clearing off the bed and taking a nap.

Two hours later I awoke to find that I had missed a call and a text, both from Dexter. He didn't leave a voice message, and his text served as a reminder for me that the driver would be here to pick me up at 9:00 p.m., and for me to be dressed in the outfit he had selected just for me. I simply typed back: K.

I sat the phone on the nightstand and nestled back on a pillow, feeling a little down. Chris hadn't called me back. What was he doing? I wondered. Had he gotten the job? Was he already working? Or was he still pissed off at me?

I didn't have time to stress over Chris. I'd have to deal with him later. So, I got my butt out of bed and started getting ready for tonight—starting with a relaxing milk bath.

After my bath, I sat on the bed and rubbed a combination of lotion and baby oil all over my body and followed up with body shimmer on my chest. I heard sexy knocking and decided to let her in.

Still naked, I went into the bathroom, put on my makeup, complete with an appealing smokey eye, and wore my hair parted down the middle hanging straight down. By now, I was on sexy overload. I'd never admit this to anyone, but seeing myself nude turned me on.

I then flossed, scraped my tongue, brushed my teeth with an electric toothbrush, and gargled. Had to keep my breath minty fresh. Couldn't be sexy with a rank mouth. I checked myself out in the mirror as I applied a couple of coats of pink glitter lip gloss.

"Butterscotch is here," I said to no one in particular as I went into the other room to get my outfit.

My wedding ring glared at me from the dresser. I picked it up and locked it in the room safe, then put on my clothes. I must admit that I hated not wearing my wedding ring. It made me feel as though I was being even more deceptive than I already was. But that was part of the business. I had to create the fantasy, the illusion that my patrons actually stood a chance of getting with me. Even though nothing could've been further from the truth.

It was 8:55, so I decided to go downstairs and wait in the lobby. No sooner than I stepped out of the elevator, my cell phone rang. Dexter was on the other end telling me that the car was waiting outside. Not a breeze ruffled the still night air as I hurried outside and saw my driver standing beside the limo with the door open. I know it sounds silly, but I felt like Cinderella going to the ball.

"*Muchos gracias,*" I said as I crawled inside.

To my surprise, Dexter was sprawled across the backseat, dressed in his customary dark suit and expensive silk tie. He had so much swagger that he wore sunglasses at night. And his scent…masculine with a hint of fruit to it. The dark blue of his suit accentuated his flawless deep brown complexion, and he pulled at his goatee as he displayed his perfect smile. I'll bet if I looked up the words sexy or swagger in the dictionary, I'd see Dexter's photo smiling back at me in both places.

"Come on, baby girl." He motioned for me to sit next to him. "I won't bite…unless you want me to." He laughed.

I ignored his latter comment and made myself comfortable. The driver closed the door behind me. I suppose "baby girl" was going to be my nickname for the rest of my life. The youngest of six, all five of my brothers still call me some deviation of girl. With baby girl being the most popular, I get the occasional young girl, little girl, big head girl, hey girl, and sometimes just plain ol' *girl.*

As the limo pulled off, Dexter popped the cork on a bottle of Pol Roger Brut champagne and offered to pour me a glass, but I declined. He filled a flute glass and placed the bottle back in the silver bucket.

Dexter took a sip of the vintage fizz and said, "Baby girl, this is one of the finest, most expensive champagnes you can get." He licked his lips and the movement of his tongue momentarily mesmerized me.

He placed his hand on my thigh and gave it a little squeeze. "Aren't you the least bit curious as to why I invited you, out of all the girls at the club, to come to Miami?"

So I guess I was dancing solo after all. And quite frankly, I didn't care. I just wanted to make some extra money. And as long as he was coming along with me, I felt some measure of security. I shrugged my shoulders. "Hadn't thought about it," I admitted.

He took another sip of his drink. "I like you, baby girl…a lot." He sat his drink down. We coasted along so smoothly that his drink didn't move. "Probably more than I should. I've tried to shake the feeling, but I can't." He wrung his hands together. "I want you to be my date this weekend. What's your story?"

His date? "What do you mean? I'm not...I'm not stripping for a birthday party?"

"No, baby girl," he said, shaking his head. "That's just what I said to get you to come along. I didn't bring you down here for a birthday party; I brought you down here for me."

Suddenly, my throat dried up and I felt like I needed a drink after all. I knew Dexter tended to flirt with me a lot, but I never thought it was anything more than a little harmless flirting.

"You married, got any kids?" he asked.

I didn't believe in giving people a whole lot of information about me right up front. The fact that I was born and raised in Baltimore, I had a natural distrust for people. My defenses went up, but I didn't let it show.

"I've been married for six years, and we have a five-year-old son."

His eyebrow shot up like the joker. "Oh, for real? I never would've guessed you'd given birth. I couldn't find a single stretch mark on your body. And believe me, I've looked you over from head to toe."

I was still at a loss of words. As bad as I wanted a drink, I refrained from asking for one. I didn't like to drink under stressful situations. That's how a lot of people develop drinking habits. "Dexter..."

"Shh..." He placed a finger against my lips. "Before you say a word, I'ma keep it one hundred with you. I want you." Stroking his goatee, he said, "This is the only way I could think of getting you to myself so I can get to know you better." He squeezed my thigh again. "I'm not trying to sleep with you. I mean, if you want to go that route, we can. I just want to spend a little time with you and spoil you. As fine as you are, you deserve to be spoiled. Baby girl, I've been to Brazil and back, and I haven't met a woman who's even half as attractive as you are. And that's saying a lot."

His compliment made me blush. He lined my cleavage with

his finger, and I brushed his hand away. "Dexter, this isn't..." I shook my head and inhaled sharply. "I'm married, and you're my boss. I just feel like—"

"What does your husband do?"

I knew where he was going with this line of questioning, and I resented it. I started to tell him that it was none of his business, but I didn't want to seem defensive, like I was ashamed of my husband. So, I told him what he used to do. "He's a computer engineer."

Nodding his head, he said, "That's what's up." I could tell he hadn't been expecting that answer. "Does he know what you do?"

I sighed. "I'd rather not talk about my husband."

"Cool." He licked his lips again and the sight made my *cho cha* wet. "I respect that."

Somehow I doubted that.

He leaned over and whispered in my ear, "I'd do anything for you, baby girl. All you have to do is ask. Let me spoil you like you deserve to be spoiled." He caught my earlobe between his teeth and nibbled it.

I nudged him away. "You need to slow your roll. I've already told you that I'm married and I'm not trying to go that route with you. If you can't respect that, then maybe we need to cut this trip short—"

"Okay, okay." He backed up. "I'm sorry. I was out of line. I swear to you, I'll keep my space. I'm not going to do anything you don't want me to. Just spend the weekend with me. We can hang out, chill, get to know each other. What's so wrong with that?"

A lot was wrong with that. It was bad enough that I'd lied to my husband about coming down here for a house-seeing, and now I was coming down here to spend the weekend with another man? Common sense told me to turn down the offer. Common sense told me to hop my happy ass back on the plane and high-tail it back to Texas. But something kept me rooted to the backseat, sizing Dexter up with my eyes. He had promised to keep his distance, and he had requested to spoil me. After all I'd done to take care of home and Chris, didn't I deserve a chance to be spoiled? It wasn't like I was going to have sex with him or anything.

Dexter must've picked up on my indecision, as well as the fact that I was leaning more toward a yes than a no. He reached in his coat pocket and handed me two cards.

I looked at the cards. One looked like an American Express Black Card and the other like a room card. "What are these?" I asked.

He took one of the cards out of my hand. "This one is the key to my penthouse on Miami Beach." He handed it back to me. "And the other one is a Black Card."

My jaw dropped.

"You do know what a Black Card is, don't you?"

Hell yeah, I know what a Black Card is, I wanted to say. It's the ultimate status symbol! Instead, I said, "Why are you giving these to me?"

He shook his head. "Because I want you to have them. Use them when you're ready to start rolling with the big boys."

I looked him in the eyes and said, "I don't think so."

I tried to hand the cards back to him, but he refused to accept them. "Seriously, keep them. You never know when you may need them."

I turned my head and stared out into the darkness for a moment. Truth be told, if I weren't married, I wouldn't even think twice about getting with Dexter. What's not to like? No doubt he's hot, successful, and rich. He was a bit dark for my taste, but it was an enticing darkness—the blacker the berry, the sweeter juice. Not only was he sexy and rich, but he was sophisticated and well-mannered. The perfect package.

"You all right?" he asked.

I looked at him. "If you're offering me your room card, why didn't you just let me stay at your Penthouse instead of the resort anyway?"

Behind Dexter's head I could see bright lights and knew we had arrived at the club. The driver slowed down and made a right turn.

With a serious expression on his face, Dexter said, "Would

you have stayed there with me?"

The way he looked at me seemed so intense…I could feel his passion. Goodness, if I allowed him between my legs, I knew he would take me to heights I'd never reached before. He aroused something within me, awoke something that had lay dormant for a long time. My *cho cha* throbbed for him, like she was trying to speak to him from my panties. I needed some fresh air. I had to hurry up and get out of that car and put some distance between us. There was no denying that Dexter wanted me, and I didn't know how much longer I could pretend like I wasn't feeling him too—married or not.

Eight

According to the weather app on his cell phone, it was seventy-seven degrees in Vegas, but people were dressed like the mercury on the meter had reached one hundred plus. Some women wore bikini tops and booty shirts that showed their perfectly rounded buttocks; others were dressed in tiny, backless and strapless dresses that they had to keep rearranging every other step. Vendors selling everything from hotdogs to Freddy Krueger gloves beckoned for passersby to come and buy. Though lunchtime traffic was still a half-hour away, cars sat bumper to bumper in the road and irritated drivers took turns honking their horns. People filled every inch of the sidewalks, and all of them seemed like they were in a rush, just seconds from missing their scheduled appointment.

However, Chris was very much in time for his scheduled appointment. Afraid that he wouldn't be able to locate the Bellagio Hotel, he had caught a cab and arrived an hour early. When he walked into the hotel, he felt like he had walked into a royal palace. The marbled floor gleamed so brightly, he could use it as a mirror if he wanted. The foyer was spacious with high-tech looking furniture, a rushing waterfall in the center of the hotel, and 96-inch mounted flat screen TVs everywhere he looked. He disappeared inside the spacious bathroom, changed into a navy blue shirt, a pair of fitted jeans and comfortable loafers, then splashed some Paul Sebastian on his neck and dabbed it behind his ears.

In order to pass the time, he went walking down the strip, initially just to do some sightseeing, and ended up buying Ms. Parker a single yellow rose from a thieving vendor who charged him twelve dollars for the flower. Another vendor was selling authentic jewelry and called out to Chris, but he quickly walked by, still pissed about the twelve-dollar rose.

"A phenomenal sale, only today! By one pair of earrings, get another pair half off," the vendor called out.

This brought Chris to a momentary stop. He hated to pass up a good deal, and this definitely was one. After perusing the impressive selection for nearly fifteen minutes with the stinking breath seller breathing down his neck and watching his every move, Chris finally settled on a pair of yellow diamond teardrop earrings and hanging pearl earrings. Angelique's jaw would drop once she saw these exquisite earrings. He hadn't bought his wife an expensive gift in a while, and he knew it would be a pleasant surprise for her upon his return. He forked over the three hundred dollars, but struggled to release the money into the man's gritty hands. Part of him wanted to renege on his decision, but finally he gave in. Angelique was worth way more than three hundred dollars; she deserved to be spoiled sometimes, and at least he finally had the means to do it.

Back inside the hotel foyer, he sat down in one of the three sitting areas, intentionally choosing the red, black, and gray sitting area that was the closest to the revolving entrance. Instead of sitting in the reclined seat and putting his feet up on the ottoman, he chose to sit on a small square-shaped seat that was half hidden by the low hanging leafy branches of a décor tree. He had a picture of Raleigh and hoped to catch a glimpse of her; he wanted a chance to observe her without her realizing that she was being observed. Especially since he would be spending the night with this woman. For all he knew, she could be a serial killer or a devil-worshipper. The world was crazy nowadays; one couldn't put anything past anybody.

The first twenty minutes passed without much action. Chris had an opened newspaper to his face, but he wasn't reading the news. Instead, he lifted his eyes over the top of the newspaper every time he heard footsteps approaching. Quite a few people came in and out of the revolving doors, but not a single face matched the one in the picture.

Chris glanced at his watch and noticed it was five minutes to noon. Just as he flipped the newspaper page, the nearby elevator door opened and he heard heels click-clacking across the marble floor. Chris peeked over the newspaper again, and a smile lifted the corner of his lips. It was her. Raleigh Parker. She was a lot thicker than she looked in the picture—not fat, but thick. Large hips, large thighs, small waist, big chest…but she was way overdone compared to the picture in his wallet. Everything about her screamed too much. Her face was nearly hidden in a huge bush of curly hair that looked as though it was hiding a few birds and maybe a robin's egg or two.

She had on enough makeup that he could have scooped her foundation off with a spoon and she would still have plenty left to cover every blemish or scar she'd ever acquired in her lifetime. Her eyes were red, and he wasn't sure if it was because she had been crying, or if her eyes were burning from the heap of blue and black eye shadow that she had packed onto her eyelids. And that bright red lipstick slathered across her lips was the ultimate no-no. And then her eyebrows? Lord, help her Jesus. She had drawn them on with a kohl black pencil and arched them so high that no matter how she changed her facial expression, it always looked like she was going, "Wha'? Wha' happened?"

Then there were her clothes. She had a voluptuous body and an ample bosom—but there was a big difference between sexy and slutty. Her breasts were pressed up high with a wonder-bra that was working overtime at creating wonders. Her white flowy blouse was cut so low that her breasts seemed as though they would tumble out of the shirt, and her brown areolas were almost visible. Her flat belly had a silver hoop laced through her navel, and her hip-hugging jeans sat low on her hips—so low in fact, that her pelvis bones showed prominently, and he knew that if she bent over, the whole world would see the crack that separated her butt cheeks. Her pants were low-rider skinny jeans; the pants hugged her ankles and showed off golden stiletto heels and toenails that nearly blinded him with the gold glitter nail polish. She looked a hot mess—a failed attempt at high-class sophistication. But the potential…Chris was certain that the potential was there. If only she'd tone it down a notch and shave off a few excess layers of goo.

Raleigh walked around the foyer, gnawing her thumbnail

to bits as her nervous eyes swept the room. She looked out the revolving door for the fifth time, then went to the receptionist desk and asked if a man had come in looking for her.

"No, ma'am," the young attendant told her with a shake of his head. "Not to my knowledge."

"Because he's not coming," a woman said, sauntering over to Raleigh. The woman was shorter than Raleigh, but they favored so much in the face that Chris was sure they had to be kin. However, the woman was much slimmer than her counterpart.

And then another woman walked up, also favoring Raleigh, but she had to be a size four or five at the most. "The family already knows that you invented this man, Leigh," she added. "Do you really have to carry through with these shenanigans? You know that man—who is nothing more than a figment of your imagination—is not coming to the wedding with you. He does not exist, Raleigh. Why are you down here searching for a fantasy?"

The other lady held up her hand and the two women high-fived each other before falling out laughing.

"Couldn't have said it better myself, Raja," the first woman added, still laughing. "So why don't you run upstairs and eat a donut, sis. I'm sure it'll make you feel better."

Raleigh's bottom lip trembled and her red eyes welled with tears. "He is coming. Maybe his…maybe his flight had a delay or something. Maybe…"

"You are so pathetic!" the first girl cried out. "Solomon does not exist. You made him up to save face, and who can blame you? If I had to attend a wedding in which my baby sister was marrying my ex-fiancé, then I'd try to save face too—"

"Raleigh, baby, is that you?" Chris asked, keeping his eyes solely on Raleigh's as he walked between the women. Her eyes expanded at first, and he saw the breath catch in her throat as her hands began to tremble.

"Excuse me, ladies," he said to the other two women as he pulled Raleigh into his arms and hugged her tight against his body. She felt soft all over and warm, and her body smelled baby powder fresh. Without releasing her from the hug, he whispered into her ear, "Just go with it, okay?" and then found her lips and kissed her with unbridled passion until she moaned into his mouth and melted into his arms. Had his arm not been behind her, offering her support, she probably would've hit the floor.

When he finally broke the kiss, he pressed the rose into her hand, then stood behind her and hugged her waist with both arms as he stared at the two ladies whose mouths looked like perfect Os. He kissed the side of Raleigh's neck, then asked, "Who are these two beautiful ladies, baby?"

The first lady quickly found her composure and held out her hand and gave him a false smile. "I'm Raja, her oldest sister. And this is Rachel, our other sister. And you must be Solomon."

"In the flesh," he said. He first shook Raja's hand before placing a kiss on the back of her hand and then did the same to Rachel. "I've heard so much about both of you."

"Really?" Raja's perfectly arched eyebrow soared high. "Sad that we can't say the same. To be honest, we didn't know you existed until a few days ago. It almost seemed as though you materialized out of thin air." Her eyes narrowed as she stared at Chris beneath her lashes. "For Raleigh to be so in love, I find it odd that we hadn't heard about you sooner than now. Don't you, Rachel?"

Chris cleared his throat and squeezed Raleigh's waist tighter. "Pardon our clandestine relationship, but we prefer to keep our relationship low-key. I'm the type of man that when I find a woman whom I adore, I like to guard her and our love. You never know when there are vultures around, waiting to strike."

The expressions that materialized on the two sisters' faces were a definite Kodak moment.

Quickly falling into her role, Raleigh said, "We'd love to stay and chat, but..." she hooked a finger through Chris's belt loop, "...it's been a while and we have a lot of catching up to do—a *lot* of catching up. So come on, baby," she said, giving him a peck on his lips. "I know we got all night, but I want to get an early start."

"And I willingly oblige," Chris added, allowing her to lead him to the elevator by his belt loop. He couldn't help but glance over his shoulder and savor the jaw dropping looks covering her sisters' faces.

Once the elevator door closed, Raleigh threw her arms around his neck and gave him a real hug. He was surprised to feel her hot tears rolling down his neck, burning a path into his skin. "I'm so glad you came," she said through a hiccup. "I really didn't think you would show up. I figured...I figured...I'm just kind of used to getting stood up." She wiped her nose in her hand, then apologized for doing so. "I guess that was kinda gross, right?"

"It's natural," he said with a shrug. "It happens."

She looked down at her toes and wiggled them, suddenly going to great lengths to avoid looking at his eyes. "You are a *lot* better looking than your pictures—not to say your pictures are bad or anything, but I just...I didn't expect you to look so...so attractive." Quickly, she added, "And I don't expect us to go to my room and have sex or anything. I know I'm not the best looking thing in the world, and I know you only kissed me to prove a point to my sisters. I really appreciate that. And I know I paid five thousand dollars for your services, but you don't have to kiss me anymore since I'm sure it makes you uncomfortable—"

"Who says it makes me uncomfortable?"

Her head shot up and she looked at him as though her ears had deceived her. Instead of responding, Chris simply caught her hand and laced his fingers through hers, then held on tightly. Her hand felt so tiny and small, dwarfed by his much larger one. He almost felt like her protector, her savior; as though she was Cinderella and the two ladies downstairs were her wicked stepsisters. Her vulnerability, the way she wore her feelings on her sleeve, intrigued him.

"I like you already," Chris told her softly. "You have a beautiful spirit."

She smiled and her eyes shimmered. "Thank you. No one's ever said anything like that to me before."

The elevator dinged and hand in hand, they stepped onto the fourteenth floor.

Nine

The night at the club exceeded my expectations. Crystal chandeliers hung from the ceilings, girls danced in cages, and all the waitresses looked like models. Plus, there was no shortage of athletes, rappers, and top-notch hip hop producers in the building.

When Dexter and I walked in, he acted like he owned the place, and everyone treated him as such. The confidence he exuded, and the respect he commanded became intoxicating to me. We sat in the VIP lounge overlooking the entire club and watched all of the festivities. We ate Maine lobster with clarified butter and green salad.

The true ballers went beyond making it rain; they created storms. I started to go down to the main floor and pick up some of that free money being tossed on the main stage and into the audience, but Dexter stopped me. He told me that as long as I was with him, I'd never have to scrounge for money.

I later discovered that the club had collected over a million dollars that night and had to hire an armor truck with armed guards to come pick up the nightly drop. However, out of that money, Dexter gave me $50,000 in cash and told me he'd take me shopping the following day.

I had never possessed such a large sum of money at one time. I knew one thing for certain…there was no way I'd spend that much money on shopping. Not even close.

I felt nervous having all that money around me, so Dexter locked it in his office until we left around two o'clock in the morning. We then walked along Haulover Beach and talked about Dexter's empire, his plans for the future, and his desire to settle down with the right woman.

Dexter seemed sincere as he shared his vision and poured

his heart out to me. He reminded me of the old school rapper, Master P. Not in the sense of being southern; Dexter hailed from New York. Rather their business acumen and being somewhat of pioneers. I respected that about Dexter.

Afterward, he took me back to the resort. Before I got out of the limo, he caressed the back of my neck and told me that he hoped I slept well. In his eyes, I could clearly tell that he wished I wasn't sleeping alone. The desire to kiss his luscious lips nearly overwhelmed me. I didn't realize I was staring at his lips until he whispered, "I don't mind if you kiss me. Actually, I want you too."

His words interrupted the magic of the moment. I immediately backed away from him. Guilt panged me in the stomach like a menstrual cramp. Never in my life had I wanted to kiss a man who wasn't my husband as badly as I yearned to kiss him. I hurried out of the car and went up to my room, alone.

Saturday morning I snacked on fruit and a cup of decaf coffee for breakfast. I had to hurry up because I had overslept. I didn't get out of bed until 9:00 a.m., and Dexter was supposed to pick me up at 10:00 for a few hours of shopping and then fun in the sun aboard a private yacht.

I put on a pair of skinny jeans, a gold low cut top, and Camilla Skovgaard gold-tone stilettos. For the boat, I packed a Brazilian triangle string top made in holographic silver shattered glass with a matching string thong. Made for ogling, not for swimming. I also carried a toothbrush, toothpaste, deodorant, sun block, and $5,000. I put the rest of the money in the same safe that housed my wedding ring set.

Shouldering my oversized bag, I slid my designer sunglasses in place and met Dexter downstairs. This time the limo had been replaced by an Aston Martin. I couldn't help but smile my pleasure. I threw my bag on the back seat and slid in.

"Morning, baby girl," Dexter said as the driver drove off. "How'd you sleep?"

I wasn't about to tell him that I tossed and turned all night with thoughts of him. The internal dialogue had become so combative that I had to pray. I prayed for the strength to keep my desires only unto my husband and not succumb to temptation.

"I slept just fine," I lied. "Thanks for asking. What about you?"

He placed his milky smooth brown hand on top of mine. "I thought about you all night. I wondered what it would be like to lick your sugared almond and make your love juices flow."

I swallowed hard and squirmed in my seat, fantasizing about him pleasuring me with his mouth and tongue. Feeling sexually frustrated, my body craved sex. I silently reprimanded myself for allowing my mind to go there. I cleared my throat and pulled my hand from underneath Dexter's and sat it on my lap.

He chuckled. "All right. I'll stop." He poured us mimosas.

I sipped on the mimosa and looked out at the palm trees, the endless beach, and scenery. We arrived at the Aventura Mall and the driver dropped us off where we blended in with the crowds of people littering the streets. We visited several stores. I purchased souvenirs for Chris and Christopher. I even purchased a new pair of pumps and a handbag for myself.

We took a break and ate a seafood and steak lunch at Ocean Prime Restaurant. We opted to eat on the outdoor patio terrace. The service was unsurpassed, and the atmosphere was electric, sexy, and sophisticated.

Dexter kept gazing into my eyes. "Are you having a nice time?"

"The best," I said, and I meant it.

After lunch, we went to Bal-Harbour Shops and stopped in Cartier where Dexter brought me black diamond teardrop earrings with a matching tennis bracelet. The jewelry cost so much that we had to take out insurance on it.

"Me consientes mucho," I said to Dexter.

"I don't know what you said, but that sounded sexy." He laughed. "Let me hear you call me *papi*," he joked.

I laughed too. "I said, 'You're spoiling me too much.'" Then I paused and continued. *"Papi."*

He roared with laughter. "You deserve it all and more, baby girl."

I checked my watch and the time was 4:00 p.m. Where had the time gone? We then headed to the marina and boarded a 54-

foot Sea Ray. I changed into my bikini and slathered sun block all over. As soon as Dexter saw me, he licked his lips and shook his head.

"You look…amazing," he complimented.

I thanked him and handed him the bottle of sun block. "Would you please put some on my back?"

"Sit down," he instructed me, and I took a seat on the upper deck. He paused before untying my top. I grabbed the strings before my "twins" were exposed. He grabbed the bottle and poured the lotion in his hands. In slow circles, he rubbed the cream on my back.

His strong hands felt good.

"There you go," he said when he finished.

"Would you please tie my strings back?" I felt his warm, peppermint smelling breath on the side of my neck. His hands slid around front and cupped my breasts as his lips kissed my neck. I jumped up, exposing my breasts. I don't know why I rushed to cover myself up; it's not like Dexter hadn't seen me butt naked many times on a regular basis at the club. Even still, I felt unacceptably naked. "Dexter, that was inappropriate," I admonished. "You can't keep disrespecting me and my marriage this way."

He threw his hands in the air. "I apologize, baby girl. It's just that when I'm this close to you, I can't help myself. We'd be so good together and you know it."

"Even if I thought that were true, there's nothing I can do about it," I explained. I looked into his ebony eyes. "If I were single, it wouldn't be an issue. But I'm not single, so being with you isn't an option." I said that more for my benefit than his.

He sighed. "I just hope he's worthy of you."

His words stopped me dead in my tracks, rendering me speechless.

"Let me help you with that," he said as he grabbed my bikini strings and tied them.

For some reason I couldn't stay upset with Dexter. Plain and simple, I liked him. Even when he crossed the line, I didn't feel threatened.

We sat back down and looked out into the endless turquoise water. The ocean had a calming effect on me. I felt so peaceful, like I didn't have a care in the world.

My cell phone rang, startling me. It was Chris. Oh, so now he calls me? An entire day later after my plane had touched the ground. I hit the decline button. Not even a minute later, he called right back, so I pressed the silver button sending him straight to voicemail.

"Your husband?" Dexter asked.

I nodded my head. "I'll call him later."

"Does he make you happy?" His tone sounded serious and his eyes showed a hint of concern.

"Marriage isn't just about happiness. Honoring your vows is important."

"I get that, but life is too short to be unhappy."

I felt myself getting defensive. "I'm not unhappy. Can we drop this?"

"That's fine with me, baby girl. I'm easy like a leaf blowing in the wind."

And with that, we enjoyed the tranquil waters in silence.

I got back to the resort at 8:00 p.m. and called home so that I could say good night to Christopher. Tori asked me how did the stripping go. Instead of telling her the truth, I played along and told her that I'd made hella cash shaking my ass, and the men were all as well-behaved as could be expected. We didn't talk long because I could barely keep my eyes open. I took a shower and crawled into bed. As soon as my head hit the pillow, I was fast asleep.

Three hours later I shot up in bed. Screams stuck in my throat threatened to strangle the life right out of me. My heart pounded so hard I felt like I had just run a marathon. I couldn't stop crying. I had the most horrible nightmare about Chris getting his *pene* sucked and having sex with another woman. The worst part was that he appeared to be enjoying it.

The dream seemed so real and vivid. I got out of bed and paced the floor, tears still streaming down my cheeks, hands shaking. I couldn't get the image out of my head. Out of all the years I had been married to Chris, he hadn't given me any reason not to trust him. Plus, I've never had a dream like that about him before.

Feeling unnerved, I tried to figure out what it all meant. Could it have been my guilty conscious projecting on to Chris? I didn't think so. Then I remembered when Chris and I first got together, when we were just dating. Chris was the king of cheating; he knocked women down like Dominos. Every time he cheated on me, I always knew because it showed up in my dreams. I recalled one particular dream that was so detailed that I even saw what the girl looked like—it was a bitch who I recognized from his job. I woke him up and confronted him. He didn't have time to think of a lie, so he confessed.

Ever since then, I've learned to trust my dreams. I remember Tori saying that a man is either cheating, about to cheat, or just finished cheating. I didn't want to agree with her, because I was certain that there had to be some men who didn't cheat, although I didn't personally know of any. Every boyfriend I ever had, including Chris, cheated. My own daddy used to cheat. It was as simple as this: Men cheat because they can.

I didn't want to believe that Chris had started cheating on me again, but I couldn't shake this feeling. Intuition told me that my husband had betrayed my trust in the worst way. I felt like getting on a plane right then and there and choking the life out of Chris. Could he really have used his trip to Las Vegas as an opportunity to get in a 'free smash' with another woman? I grabbed my phone and called him. His phone went straight to voicemail. Son of a bitch! I hung up and flung my phone onto the bed. My neck tensed up as my hands uncurled and curled into fists.

I can't explain it, but from the deepest depths of my soul I knew without a shadow of a doubt that Chris had betrayed me. My hurt quickly turned to disappointment, jealousy then anger. Tori and I have both lived by the creed: "I'm faithful to you as long as you're faithful to me, and not a minute longer."

Chris's monkey ass had crossed the line, and I'd make sure he lived to regret it. Two could play this game.

Ten

"So how did you two meet?" Rashida asked, delicately lifting her fluted wineglass to her lips. Rashida was the baby sister out of the four girls, and the one who would be marrying Darryl at exactly ten o'clock the following morning in the East Wing of the Bellagio Hotel.

Like Raleigh's other sisters, Rashida favored Raleigh in the face, but she was the most petite one of the four—both in size and height. She stood five feet even, and though she was twenty-eight years old, just three years younger than Raleigh, she was often mistaken for being a child. It probably had a lot to do with her face, which resembled a baby doll's, with her chinky eyes, dimpled cheek, and plush lips. She embodied the phrase "cute as a button." Not only was she the smallest of the four, she was also the brains of the family. Raleigh had informed him that Rashida was so intelligent, she skipped two grades in high school and graduated summa cum laude from Princeton.

Her husband-to-be sat to her right, dark-skinned and immaculately dressed in a suit and tie that probably set him back a couple of thousands. Two men sat to his left: his best man and his only groomsman. To Chris's right, Raleigh toyed with the linguini pasta on her plate—she hadn't taken a single bite of anything besides a nibble of lettuce and a sip of ice cold water. Seated to the right of her, Raja and Rachel took turns exchanging flirtatious looks with the best man and groomsman.

"It's quite interesting how we met." Chris didn't stammer or stutter as the lie flowed from his lips. Raleigh and he had rehearsed every detail in the room, so he knew everything he was supposed to say, and knew exactly when he was supposed to say it. "We met at a therapist office—I was walking in and she was walking out."

"Therapy? When did you take therapy?" Rashida asked her sister with a concerned expression.

"It's something she chose to partake in about two months after she caught you and Darryl screwing in her bed—"

Darryl choked on his wine and went into a horrible coughing fit. Rashida patted his back, and Raleigh reached under the table and hit Chris's thigh hard enough to leave a bruise. He gave her an encouraging smile, but she still looked like she was about to jet from the table at any given moment.

"Look," Rashida said in a soft voice, after Darryl had excused himself from the table, "I know I look like the bad person here, but I'm sure Leigh didn't tell you the whole story. She only told you what you wanted to hear."

"Really?" Chris twisted basil linguini around his fork tines, then brought it to his mouth. "Then what's the whole story?"

Raleigh stood, attempting to excuse herself from the table, but Chris caught her wrist and asked her to sit with his eyes. Hesitantly, she retook her seat.

"I actually met Darryl first. We work at the same hospital together and have been working together for three years now. I'm an OB-GYN, and he's a heart surgeon. What happened with him and my sister was a—it was a one nightstand gone wrong. She ended up pregnant; he felt like he needed to do the right thing, so he popped the question. And then she..." Rashida swallowed and looked away. When she started talking again, the tone of her voice had changed, softened. "...and then she lost the baby, and he wanted to be...to be free of her. But she didn't want to let go."

Raleigh had told him a lot of things. But she hadn't told him about being pregnant or miscarrying Darryl's child. Again, Raleigh tried to stand, but Chris held her thigh, keeping her seated. He leaned over and whispered in her ear, "You've gotta stop running from your family."

Darryl returned to the table and everyone commenced eating, albeit carefully avoiding the huge white elephant sitting at the table.

Finally Rachel cleared her throat and said, "So, Chris, you say you two met in therapy. If you don't mind me asking, what were you in therapy for?"

"Sex."

"Sex?" Rachel, Raja, and Rashida all said in unison.

Chris slid his arm around Raleigh and leveled his gaze with Rachel's. "I was addicted to bedding beautiful women; couldn't quite control myself."

Rachel didn't miss a beat. "Well obviously, therapy worked well for you. Even if you're still addicted to sex, you're definitely not addicted to beautiful women anymore."

Raleigh flew up from her seat so fast that her wineglass fell into her plate and shattered. Chris tried to reach for her, but she ran out of the dining area, her face shielded by her hands.

Chris snatched the napkin from around his neck and tossed it on the table. He glared at her sisters, one by one. Then he said to Darryl, "I'm sorry, man, that you're about to become a part of such a cruel, inconsiderate, heartless family—or maybe I shouldn't apologize, since you fit in rather well with them."

"It's just an unfortunate situation for us all," Darryl called after him, but Chris didn't pay him any attention. He had already cleared the dining area and was speed-walking down the hallway, yelling Raleigh's name. But she was nowhere to be found. Chris took the elevator, willing it to move faster, and hurried to their hotel room, but she wasn't there either.

Chris's heart ached for her. No one should have to go through that kind of embarrassment and ridicule. It pained him that her family treated her like a black sheep, like an object of scorn rather than a human being. For the next thirty minutes or so, Chris searched the hotel for Raleigh, but his quest was futile. She wasn't in the pool or the spa room, wasn't on the balcony, wasn't in the bar. Unsure of what to do next, he walked down to the foyer and retook a seat on the rectangular chair near the revolving doors.

Within minutes, he saw her emerge from the stairwell, breathless from descending so many flights of stairs. Pieces of her curly weave stuck to the sweat shining on her forehead. Chris stood and called her name, and though she looked right at him, she kept walking and slid into the gold-plated revolving door. Not wasting a second, he slid in behind her, still calling her name. She continued to ignore him and stepped out into the warm night air, shouldering her purse and walking amazingly fast in such thin heels.

Chris jogged to keep up with her. "I'm sorry about back there," he said to her back as he dodged pedestrians and ignored vendors who called to him. "I should've let you leave when you first tried to go."

"Don't worry about it," she called over her shoulder without breaking her pace. "And you don't have to follow me. I'd rather be alone right now."

"Raleigh—"

"Leave me alone, dammit!"

"Raleigh—"

She stopped so abruptly that Chris knocked into her and she fell on the sidewalk. "Oh God, I'm so sorry," he said and helped her to her feet.

Her palms had scraped against the pavement and were turning red. Her face scrunched in pain, and he noticed that she tenderly kept her weight off her left ankle. Once she had regained her balance, she yanked away from his touch and gave him a glare icy enough to freeze an ocean.

"I think you've done enough," she said through gritted teeth.

He didn't say a thing as she re-shouldered her purse and half-walked, half-limped away from him. Chris stood and watched her bushy curls disappear in the crowd, and he dug his hands into his pants pocket, feeling like the world's biggest idiot. His intentions had been noteworthy, but they'd backfired in his face. He felt like a failure, a feeling he hadn't felt since the day TCP called him into the office and told him that his services were no longer needed. But what fascinated him the most was that he was feeling this way about a woman who didn't even know his real name.

His cell phone rang. The caller ID displayed the word:

Wifey. Instead of answering her call, he pressed ignore, pocketed the phone, and took off after Raleigh. His phone started ringing again. This time he answered it without glancing at the caller ID. "Hey, baby," he said breathlessly, "let me call you back in about ten minutes. I'm kind of in a rush."

"This is not yo' baby, fool," Melvin said while chuckling. "And what you so in a hurry for?"

"It's a long story. I'll tell you later."

"Well I gotta tell you something now. And I hope you ready for this shit. You need to know the truth about yo' sorry ass wife."

Eleven

"Another Scotch, no ice."

Chris swayed on the stool as he slid his empty glass across the bar. The bartender seemed hesitant to take the glass from him. "This is your last one for the night, okay, buddy?"

Chris shrugged his shoulder. What he really wanted to do was tell the bartender to shut the fuck up and pour his drink. He was a grown ass man with pockets full of cash—and most of all, he could hold his liquor. This would make his fifth Scotch, and though he was definitely buzzing, he felt like he needed at least two more to seal the deal.

As the bartender took his glass as well as a few other orders at the bar, Chris turned on the stool and looked out at all the scantily clad women in the club. It was a four-story club with dancing on each floor, and the club was so packed that Chris was sure it was just one or two people away from meeting capacity. He had visited the three upper floors, searching in vain for Raleigh, and had finally given up, returning to the first floor to drown his frustrations in his favorite amber liquid. Hundreds of clubs littered Vegas' strip; the strip was the haystack and Raleigh was the needle. Finding her was next to impossible—unless she wanted to be found.

The first floor of the club was having karaoke night, and every ten minutes or so, another tone-deaf singer would take the stage and belt out a Whitney Houston or Celine Dion song. A heavyset woman with two necks and a belly held in by a belt that threatened to pop at any second took the stage and cued the live band to play Aretha Franklin's "I Never Loved A Man."

Surprisingly, her rich, soulful voice sounded a lot like Aretha's; so much so that people began to gather around the stage, transfixed by her voice and compelling stage presence.

As Chris sipped his Scotch and watched the man on the guitar play it as though the music was coming from his fingers instead of the strings, Chris thought about what Melvin had said on the phone: "Stephanie said she saw Angelique at a gentleman's club butt naked on the stage. Said she was shaking her ass for that cash. She told me not to tell you, but you my dawg, so you know I had to look out for you."

No, Stephanie had to be wrong. The Angelique he knew would never do something like that. She was too classy, too sophisticated for something so low and degrading. What woman who had a college degree and who could fluently speak five different languages—Spanish, Italian, German, French, and English—would willingly partake in such a degrading job? Not only was she beautiful and intelligent, she was a faithful wife who he was willing to trust his very life in her hands. And her mothering skills? He couldn't handpick a better mother to his son. Stephanie had to be wrong about what she'd seen. There was no way she could be right about Angelique stripping. But…but what if she was right?

Head tilted back, he chucked down half of his freshly poured drink. Chris listened to the woman sing the lyrics to Aretha's song so beautifully, with so much power behind her big voice. Even though Aretha was singing about a no-good man, he related every word to his trifling, sorry-excuse-for-a-wife. If what Stephanie had seen was true, then what else was Angelique lying about? She paid the bills every month by selling her body. What should've been sacred and reserved for his eyes only, she was willingly exposing to any man who had the right amount of green in his hands.

Chris finished his Scotch in two gulps and staggered off the stool, heading over to the crowd that had formed around the well-lit stage.

When the woman finished her song, the crowd begged for her to do another, but she shook her head and said that her throat was bothering her and she needed to save her voice. The MC asked if anyone else would like to sing, but no one wanted to take the stage after that fireball.

Chris hadn't been on a stage in years. The last time he'd taken the stage and sang was during a talent show his senior year in high school. He'd won first place, and Melvin, who had done a few stale jokes, had gotten booed off the stage and picked at for the rest of the school year for being so damn corny. Chris thought his singing years were behind him, but suddenly he felt a song in his spirit and he had to get it out.

Before his courage could fail him, Chris took the stage and cued the band to play Donnell Jones's "Where I Wanna Be." Thankfully, the bright white lights shone directly on the stage blinding him. He couldn't see any faces in the crowd—everyone looked like shadows against the backdrop of the bright lights. That suited him just fine. Chris let the music flow through every fiber of his being, and when he heard the music break, cueing him to come in, he sang the words as though Angelique herself was sitting on the stage and he wanted her to know how badly her lies had hurt him. Emotions mixed with adrenaline and five glasses of Scotch had taken him to another level. He moved over the whole stage, singing as though he was already a superstar and he was dedicating this song to everyone who had ever been hurt in a relationship, and who were sick and tired of the lies, the frustration, and the pain.

When the song ended, the applause and cheers from the crowd nearly deafened him. Chris felt drained, as though someone had pulled a plug on him. He heard the crowd chanting, "One more! One more!" but he couldn't sing another song if he tried. He didn't realize he had been crying until he made it outside the steaming club and the night air blew his sweat and tears dry.

Keeping his eyes averted from the crowd of people walking up and down the strip, Chris made his way back to the Bellagio Hotel. In the hotel lobby, Chris disappeared into the bathroom and dialed his wife's number at least ten times, but she didn't answer any of his calls.

Chris took the elevator up to the fourteenth floor, half hoping that Raleigh wouldn't be in the room. He'd already made up his mind that he'd write her a letter apologizing for causing more harm than good; he'd also made up his mind that he was going to return half of the fee to her since he'd only done a half-baked job at being her "companion." But his hope was short-lived because as soon he approached their hotel room, she opened the door, dressed only in a thin cream night slip.

Making no move to enter the room, he said, "How's your ankle?"

She smiled. "Better. It doesn't hurt at all."

Still remaining in the hallway, he said, "Look, I understand that you hate me right now. So we don't have to spend the night in the same hotel room. I can just—"

She touched his arm gently. "I want you to spend the night."

"You sure?"

She nodded and opened the door wider for him to come inside. He took a deep breath and entered the room, tossing his tweed hat on the dresser before sinking into the King-size bed and pulling his shoes off.

Raleigh sat on the bed beside him, albeit far enough away that two more people could've sat between them. Her voice soft, she said, "I didn't know you could sing like that. It was so much... so much pain in your voice. Pain and passion. It was...it was amazing, Solomon."

Chris paused in taking off his other shoe. "You were there?"

She nodded. "I saw you when you came in. I was sitting at the far back. Déjà Vu is one of my favorite clubs to go to when I come to Vegas. I love the first floor—the karaoke floor. The creativity there inspires a lot of my drawings."

"You draw?"

She shrugged and looked off. "Yeah, little drawings here and there. Pencil drawings. It's nothing to brag about. I'm not a Picasso or Van Gogh or anything—"

"Why are you always downing yourself?"

Again she shrugged and looked off.

"Can I see something you've drawn?"

"I'd rather not."

Chris unrolled his socks and stuffed them in his shoes, then went into the bathroom to piss out the five Scotches that had his bladder screaming for mercy. He stripped naked and climbed into the hot stream of the shower, washing the day's funk down the drain. The water felt so good, he could've stayed in there all night. But the hot stream eventually went from lukewarm to cold; his signal to get out. He dried off and secured a towel around his middle before returning to the room.

When Raleigh's eyes landed on him, he sensed that she felt uncomfortable. Her face and ears had turned bright red and she quickly turned on the TV and flipped through the channels. Once Chris had slipped on his boxers, he said, "Chris."

"Huh?"

Chris sat on the bed beside her, sitting so close that their thighs touched. Though she tried not to look, her eyes scanned over his arms, his chest, the thin line of hair that trailed from his navel and disappeared in the waistband of his boxers. "My real name is Chris, not Solomon."

"Oh."

Again, the room grew quiet. The only sound was the newscaster on TV predicting a rainy forecast for the next day. Chris wasn't sure of what to say. To be honest, the only thing he could think about was sex. Raleigh was looking delicious in that little thin night slip. She wore no bra, and the chill of the air conditioner had her nipples straining against the silk material. He wanted to suck one in his mouth and see if it tasted as lovely as it looked. Through the night slip, he could see the red panties that hugged her perfectly rounded butt. She still had on a lot of makeup though, and he wondered if she was going to sleep in all that gunk and goo. He also wondered how she would react if he kissed her; pressed her back onto the bed, slipped that night slip off of her, and kissed her from head to toe, maybe even sucking on her toes.

"She really hurt you, didn't she?"

Her words pulled him away from his thoughts of a sexual tussle in the sheets. His eyes questioned her.

"The only way you can sing like that is if you're hurting

or you've been hurt, and the pain really hit home." She picked up his hand and held the brown side of his fingers up to her face. She rubbed the spot where his wedding ring should've been. Instead of a ring, there was a brown band that six years had permanently branded into his skin. "Divorced? Widowed?"

He laced his fingers through hers and looked down at her juicy lips. "Let me taste your lips again."

Her eyes fell closed and he could feel the bed shudder from her body. He didn't wait for her answer, simply leaned over and kissed her, closing his lips over hers, covering them fully. She groaned into his mouth, and the groan caused his erection to harden even more. Holding her chin, he delved his tongue into her mouth, tasting her sweet lip gloss and reveling in the feel of her tongue against his. This time he groaned, wondering why this kiss tasted so much sweeter than the one they'd shared in the lobby only hours ago.

The Scotch already had his brain swimming, and the scent of her body, along with the feel of her nails lightly scraping his upper arms, was sending him over the edge. Out of the six years he'd been married to Angelique, he'd been completely faithful to her—but after what Melvin had told him, he felt like he had a right to lay with Raleigh. If she could sneak around and do her dirt, then hell, why couldn't he?

With these thoughts urging him along, he climbed atop Raleigh, slowly pressing her back against the bed as he kept his mouth securely on hers. He slid his hand up her slip and gently plucked one hardened nipple, and her back arched in the bed. Chris couldn't believe how well their bodies meshed together. As his hands roved over her curves, learning their shape and structure, her body responded to his every touch. His hands dropped between her legs, and he stroked her soaked panties. Her sensual response made him growl, and Chris knew he wouldn't be able to restrain himself much longer.

"I want you so bad," he whispered into her ear. "Can I have you?"

"Yes," she whispered—and then as though snapping out of a dream, she tore her lips away from his. "No," she said, shaking her head and pushing at his chest. "No, please. Get off me. Let me up. Please."

"What'd I do wrong?"

"Please, Solomon—Chris—whatever your name is. Please get off me. This is wrong."

Sighing deeply, Chris rolled away and let her up. "What's wrong, baby?"

"Don't call me baby." She climbed off the bed and rearranged her large breasts to fit into the night slip. "I'm not your baby. You don't even know me. I don't even know you. I'm paying for you to be here. If it wasn't for that, you wouldn't even know I exist. You don't want me, but because I paid that large lump-sum, you have to act like you—"

"I *do* want you," Chris assured her. He gestured at his penis, which was sticking out like a pole. "Can't you see how badly I want you?"

She glanced at his erection, but looked away. "That's not for me. That's for your wife."

Her words struck home for him. As much as he didn't want them to be true, he felt like she was right. Angelique and he hadn't had sex in over two months. He couldn't get it from his wife, and then he come to Vegas and simply touch a woman, who despite her loads of makeup and big hair, he was very much attracted to; and from that one simple touch, her panties became drenched for him. He wanted Raleigh; but as bad as he wanted her, he knew it wouldn't be fair to her to use her body as a replacement for Angelique's or as a balm to heal his hurt pride.

"And besides," Raleigh added, "I'm ugly anyway. Without this makeup, I look like a troll."

"Why would you say something like that?"

"Because it's true."

She sat on the edge of the bed, and when he asked her to look at him, she refused to do so. Chris stood to his feet and went to the bathroom, wetting a clean rag. "Come here, Raleigh," he called, but when she didn't appear, he called her name again; this time more as a demand than a request.

He heard her soft footsteps padding across the floor as she

came to him. He sat her down on the toilet stool and knelt between her legs. Then he began to wipe her face.

"Wait! What are you doing?"

"Shh," he said, and placed each one of her hands on his bare shoulders. "Keep your hands there and don't move." He used the tone that he used with Christopher when he meant business. Then he returned to wiping her makeup off. He had to refold the washcloth a few times in order to get all of the heavy makeup off. While he wiped, she cried—silent tears. As though he was pulling off her protective mask and he'd finally see how ugly she really was.

After he finished removing all her makeup, he did something that he'd never done to a black woman before: he pulled off her wig. At first she screamed and tried to clutch onto the horrid thing as though it was life support. But he wrenched the wig out of her hands and tossed it behind him on the floor. Then he took off her wig cap and was shocked to see the thick, naturally curly hair that sprang to life. He pulled her to her feet, then made her stand in front of the bathroom mirror. He stood directly behind her, fluffing out her hair with one hand, his other arm securely around her waist.

"Open your eyes, Raleigh." Her eyes were so tightly closed that they looked like stitches. "Please, Raleigh."

Again, she shook her head no.

Chris put his lips against her ear and said in his deep timbre, "I swear to God you are one of the most beautiful women I've ever laid eyes on. I swear it to you. Please open your eyes so you can see what I'm seeing."

He wasn't sure if it was his words or his erection poking into her backside that finally made her open her eyes. But when she did, her eyes widened in surprise, and she stared at the woman in the mirror as though she was looking at a stranger.

Still looking completely dumbfounded, she leaned against the sink, her fingers touching her face as though she was seeing herself for the first time. Again, tears streamed from her eyes. But Chris sensed that these tears were tears of liberation—freedom from the gooey mask that she had been forced to wear for so many years.

While she looked herself over, Chris hurried into the room, then returned to the bathroom with the yellow diamond earrings in hand. He carefully placed a teardrop earring into each one of her ears, and instead of being astounded by the jewelry—like Angelique would've been—she simply smiled and touched each earring. "They're beautiful," she gushed.

"They only complement your natural beauty," he told her, and smiled as she continued to gaze at herself.

Then he touched the scar on her forehead, the one that the makeup had made obsolete. "What happened here?" he asked.

Through sniffles and tears, she said, "The car wreck that killed our mother and father. I was in the backseat. I was the only one who lived. My sisters…they've always blamed me for what happened. They said…they said that my baby died because of karma. I killed our parents, so God killed my baby."

"Come here," Chris said, and pulled her into his arms. "Your baby didn't die because of karma. Your baby died because for whatever reason, it was part of God's ultimate plan. And don't you ever blame yourself for your parents' death. When it's your time, it's your time—and there's nothing anyone can do to stop it."

At that very moment, he wished he was a sponge to soak up all of this woman's pain so she wouldn't have to deal with it anymore. To hide such a beautiful woman behind such an ugly mask; to hide such an ugly past behind such a beautiful smile. Her courage inspired him. With his arms securely around her, he felt like he could protect her from the world. He wanted to hold her forever, so that no one would ever hurt her again.

"Thank you, Chris," she whispered against his chest. "For everything."

"Swear to me that you'll never hide behind all that makeup again."

Instead of swearing it to him, she went in the room and emptied her purse on the floor. Then she took the heel of one of her stilettos and began crushing her cosmetics. As she crushed them, she laughed and giggled, almost giddy with joy. She looked over her shoulder. "Come help me, silly!"

Chris thought it was the craziest thing he ever did, but he took her other stiletto and helped her crush the cosmetics into bits. He knew that housekeeping would have a time trying to get that big pile of mess out of the carpet the next morning.

After washing their hands at the sink, they crawled into bed and Chris slipped his arms around Raleigh. Her eyes twinkled in the dark as she looked at him.

"Chris, I'll never forget you. You are amazing. Tell your wife to hold onto you because she's truly got something special."

Chris kissed her forehead, then let his heavy eyelids fall close. He heard her whisper his name. "Yes, Leigh?"

He felt her hands slip into his boxers. "I know you're married, and I'm trying to respect that. But after tonight, I'll never see you again. And you know what they say…what happens in Vegas stays in Vegas."

Chris's eyes popped open in the darkness and he looked her direction. "You serious?"

"I'm serious."

"No regrets in the morning?"

"None."

Chris hesitated only a second longer. If Stephanie wasn't lying about seeing Angelique shake her ass on the pole, then what else was she doing that Chris didn't know about? Melvin was right; only God Himself knew what Angelique was up to over in Miami. For all he knew, she could be meeting some dude and giving him the panties for a wad of cash.

He hadn't spoken a word to his wife since her plane lifted off the ground. Obviously, she could make time for everyone else, but she couldn't make time for him. So why should he beat up himself when another woman had not only made time for him, but paid big bucks for his time, and made him feel like he was somebody—like he was actually desired and appreciated, despite his faults and flaws. Using these thoughts as gasoline to fuel his fire, Chris rolled atop Raleigh with his arousal digging into her thigh, and slowly slid her red panties down to her ankles.

Twelve

I could've kicked Chris in the teeth for all the anger I had built up toward him. I didn't sleep a wink last night in Miami after that nightmare. I stayed up all night plotting my revenge on that deceitful bastard. My first thought was to poison him, kill him slowly. Then I thought about stabbing him while he slept, or doing a Lorena Bobbitt. I ruled out thoughts of doing him physical harm when logic settled in. I was claustrophobic, so being locked up wouldn't work for me. Plus, no one could raise my son better than me, so I couldn't do anything that would land me in jail and take me away from him.

I had some other ideas for getting even that included sleeping with someone else and letting Chris find out about it. For a brief moment I entertained the notion of having revenge sex with that sleazy, slimy Melvin, but the mere thought of Melvin's grimy hands on me made me want to puke. Not to mention Chris would probably willingly catch a case for killing us both. Something about screwing a man's best friend just sets a man off. The jury would most likely feel sorry for him and let him off claiming heat of passion. I'd be dead, and he'd be free to run off with the bitch he cheated on me with and live happily ever after raising my son. Not going to happen.

The flip side would be if Chris didn't get off and had to spend the rest of his life in prison. Again, my thoughts circled back to Christopher. Where would he be if his father was locked up for killing his mother? No kid deserves that. That's when I made up my mind that if I did sleep with another man, he'd have to be someone my husband didn't know. Did I really just call Chris 'my husband'? There's a whole lot I feel like calling him, and 'husband' isn't one of them.

I hate that I've allowed Chris to get so deep inside of my head. I'm not the type of woman who cries over a man, but Chris broke my heart. He shattered my heart and crushed my dreams. I'm sure that if I listen closely enough, I could still hear my heart breaking. If I didn't love him so much, I'd hate his sorry ass.

To add insult to injury, I couldn't even enjoy my soothing massage in a private oceanfront cabana. All I could think about was Chris giving *my pene* to some other bitch. Every time I think about it I want to punch him in the throat!

I was so glad that Dexter hadn't ridden to the airport with me. We had different flights. The last thing I felt like doing was talking, or worse, pretending as though all was well when it wasn't.

After I got to the airport and checked in, I went to a bar and had a glass of hard liquor so that I could sleep during the entire flight. And sleep I did. The flight attendant had to shake me to wake me up.

The drive home could've been stressful, but I called Tori and told her about my suspicions. At first she tried to convince me that Chris loved me and would never do anything to deliberately cause me pain. When I told her that my female intuition told me otherwise, she changed her tune.

"Sister, you've got to be smart about this," Tori had said. "If you really think he's cheating, you're going to need evidence. Don't confront him without evidence. Men deal in facts, not emotions. You telling him that you had a dream will make him laugh in your face and tell you a bold-faced lie."

I knew she was right. We talked all the way until I pulled up in my driveway. I then got off the phone and mentally prepared myself to deal with Chris.

When I walked in the house, I froze in the foyer area and stared at the dining table. Chris had prepared a romantic dinner with candles lit and rose petals sprinkling the table. He even held a rose in his hand. The guilt must've really been kicking his behind.

If I wasn't so pissed off with him, I might've actually felt sorry for him...not! He should feel guilty. I hope the guilt eats him up to the verge of insanity.

Completely ignoring the amazing presentation, I said, "Where's Christopher?" I needed to see my son, inhale his scent, and hold him close.

Chris frowned. "He's upstairs. In his room."

I left Chris standing in the living room looking stupid so that I could recharge and regain my strength. Being near my son helped me to do that.

Tangled in his bed sheets, Christopher was fast asleep. I didn't care; I pressed the side of my face against his cheek, then kissed him. I craved his energy to help bring me back to life. He didn't move. I sat up and rubbed his back, trying to fight back tears, wondering why Chris would be willing to let go of everything we've shared.

A few minutes later, I found the strength to leave Christopher's room and let him sleep in peace.

From downstairs, Chris called out, "Baby, everything's okay?"

No, everything was not okay. My world was falling apart because my husband was cheating on me again. But I couldn't tell him that. What proof did I have, besides that incriminating dream?

"I'm fine," I yelled down. "About to take a shower."

I heard his footsteps coming up the stairs, but I didn't wait on him. Once in the confines of my bedroom, a few tears escaped from my eyes. As I wiped my face, I went into the master-bathroom. I felt like screaming. What in the world was Chris up to? Was this some sort of a cruel joke? Lit candles surrounded my Jacuzzi tub, which had been filled with bubbles. I closed my eyes, shook my head, and exhaled. Chris hadn't done something as romantic as this in a while, and as much as I wanted to stay mad at him, it was getting harder to keep my anger well lit.

I took off my clothes and relaxed in the tub. The water temperature was perfect—hot. I closed my eyes and thought about the seriousness of the situation. I had so many decisions to make. If and when I found the evidence of Chris's infidelity, what did I plan to do with it? Would I divorce him, or stay with him and make him suffer? How could I ever trust him again? How would a divorce affect our son?

Then my mind drifted in a direction it didn't need to go. I started wondering what the other woman had that I didn't have; what did he see in her; was he still attracted to me? I stopped myself cold and said to no one in particular, "Forget that! Chris is just an ass." I refused to blame myself for Chris's shortcomings. I'm just as fabulous today, if not more so, than the day Chris met me. So, forget him.

I opened my eyes when I heard Chris enter. He had a glass of wine in his hand as well as a small, handheld basket.

"I missed you, baby," he said as he sat the glass on the tub. "I poured this for you."

My jaw clenched. It took everything inside of me not to douse him with that wine and crack the glass over his round head. I had to play it cool, though. I needed proof before I busted him out. So, in a calm voice, I said, "That was sweet of you. I appreciate you running this bath for me and cooking dinner. I'll be down in a bit to eat." I forced a smile and smelled the wine before taking a sip. Not that I thought he'd try to poison me, or even be capable of such a thing, but hey, I didn't think he'd cheat on me either.

To my dismay, Chris started stroking the spot behind my shoulder—one of my erogenous zones. I wanted to tell him to stop, that I didn't want his filthy hands to ever touch me again, but I kept my mouth shut. Then he took the small square-shaped basket and opened it. The room filled with a scent that I hadn't smelled in years. A citrusy honey fragrance. Orange blossoms. The flowers I'd used to decorate my entire wedding, along with creamy white tiger lilies. That fact that Chris had remembered the flowers from our wedding touched me in a profound way. He poured the basket of orange blossoms into the bath water, and the pale orange flowers floated along with the bubbles. Mesh bath sponge in hand, he started bathing me from the neck down. I closed my eyes and sighed. His touch felt good.

"Come on, baby," I heard Chris say as he held a plush towel to wrap me in.

I blew out the candles, stepped into his open arms, and allowed him to wrap me in the warmth of the towel and his arms. He kissed me on the forehead, then looked me in the eye.

"What's wrong?" he asked again and kissed the corner of my lips.

"Nothing. Just tired from the flight. Jetlag." I averted my eyes to a strand of hair on the floor. I refused to lose sight of what Chris had done and make the mistake of allowing him to woo me, win me over.

He dried me off from the crown of my head to the tip of my toes. "Would you put on something sexy tonight?" I sucked in a shaky breath, realizing that my husband's deep baritone aroused me just as much as his touch.

I exhaled slowly. "Sure." The nerve of this guy, I thought.

I put on a short baby doll nightgown with a thong and followed Chris downstairs. One of the long white candles on the table had went out. He relit the candle, then made me a plate of spaghetti with garlic toast. He blessed the food and I picked up the fork, but he took the utensil away from me. Confused, I stared at him and watched him twirl noodles around the fork tines before bringing it to my mouth. I couldn't remember the last time my husband had fed me. And I couldn't understand why he was being so perfect and making my anger melt like a glacier suffering from global warming. Whether I had proof or not, I was sure that he had cheated on me. But the sweeter and more affectionate he was being, the harder it was for me to remember why I was supposed to be mad.

After he had fed me nearly half the plate, I turned the next forkful down.

"Chris, it's delicious," I admitted, "but I can't take another bite. Aren't you going to eat?"

"I plan to. But I don't have a taste for spaghetti."

My lips released a sound, half-moan and half-gasp. I have no idea where this Chris came from, but I'm loving him.

Chris led me to the couch and asked me to hold my hair up. "For what?"

He took out a small box that I knew was jewelry. Chris

hadn't bought me a piece of jewelry since our wedding rings. My mouth half open, I watched him untie the box and remove a pair of silver earrings with hanging diamonds surrounding a beautiful pearl. These things cost him some money, I thought as I hooked them into my ears and admired my reflection in one of the wall mirrors. "Baby, where'd you get the money to afford these?"

"Don't worry about it. Just know that you deserve it. Lay back for me." I willingly fell back against the couch cushions and moaned while he massaged my feet. He always said that I had suckable toes. All the while he kept telling me how much he loved me and how much he had missed me.

"Baby, listen to me," he said, still massaging my feet, "I almost gave up on us this weekend."

Gave up on us? What in the hell was he talking about? Instead of saying anything, I kept quiet and let him finish talking.

"Would you believe that someone had me thinking that you were a stripper at a gentleman's club?" The blood in my veins froze. Chris laughed and kept talking. "And I actually bought into it. I actually believed that you would stoop that low in order to make enough money to keep up this lifestyle. So when my plane touched down, I went down to the club myself, to ask some questions and see what I'd find out."

Fear paralyzed me. I wasn't sure which way he was going with this thing, but I knew that if my heart beat any faster, I would probably die.

"In retrospect, I can't believe that I had such little faith in you. I figured that the person who told me knew what he was talking about."

The word 'he' cued me in. "Melvin told you that, didn't he?" I never recalled seeing Melvin at the strip club, and knew he couldn't afford the elite club that I performed at anyway. But I knew in my heart that Melvin was the one who had ran his mouth. I couldn't stand his nosey fat ass. "Well, it's not true. He's telling you a lie."

"Baby, baby, calm down. Whether Melvin told me or not, that's beside the point," Chris said. "I know it isn't true."

"You do?"

He nodded and sucked my big toe until my hips squirmed restlessly on the couch. "I went down to the 'so-called' club that you strip at and saw the woman who they mistaken for you. She looks just like you, Angie—hair, figure, skin tone, height, everything. Y'all even favor a lot in the face. And as soon as I saw that woman, I started laughing. I knew it was a mistake. And then I felt like a fool. For as long as I've known you, I should've known that you aren't the kind of woman who would disrespect herself like that. You have too much pride and dignity to drop that low."

Relief washed over me and I felt my heartbeat slow its pace. Damn, that was a close one! I mentally thanked God for my lookalike who was in the right place at the right time. Then his words really hit me. *You have too much pride and dignity to drop that low.* But I had dropped that low. *You aren't the kind of woman who would disrespect herself like that.* But I had disrespected myself like that. For the first time since taking on the stripper job, shame burned my cheeks. Here I was pissed at Chris, but if he only knew the truth about me, he would not be on his hands and knees, performing cunnilingus to my pinkie toe.

I tried to pull my foot out of Chris's hand, but instead of letting my foot go, he grabbed both of my feet and spread my legs wide. Then he licked his thick long tongue up my wet core, catching my sensitive love button between his lips. It was difficult to maintain my focus with him working his mouth with such expertise; it was difficult to remain upset at him because of a nightmare. The only thing I could focus on was his tongue working its magic, and the grunting sounds he was making, as though devouring me was turning him on just as much as it was sending me over the edge.

Right when I was on the brink, he pulled away and wiped his mouth.

"Nooo," I breathed out. "Please don't stop."

"I've gotta feel you babe," he said as though he was apologizing. In record time, he came out of his pants and dropped his boxers. His *pene* saluted me. Chris positioned me to the edge of the couch and dove right in. As wet as I was, I knew it felt like he had dived into the Pacific Ocean. I thought he was going to go hard and fast, since we hadn't had sex in months. But instead of rushing through it, he went slow and deep, making sure that I felt his full girth and every inch of his long stroke. About ten minutes was all I could take before I felt the onslaught of an orgasm. I yelled out so loud that Chris had to clamp his hand over my mouth. Seconds later, he growled my name and I knew his release would follow shortly.

We laid on the couch, both of us completely out of breath and unable to lift a finger. "Baby, that was best sex we've had in a while."

"I know," I said between pants. "Where did all that come from?"

"You had me backed up."

"Well maybe you need to be backed up more often."

He chuckled and leaned over, kissing the tip of my breast. "While I was in Vegas, I was reminded of how much I love you. You mean the world to me, Angie."

I couldn't be mad at him anymore. Yes, he might've cheated. Yes, he'd probably gone to Vegas and did something he had no business doing. But I hadn't been an angel myself in Miami. And by the grace of God, I had managed to stay incognito concerning my disgraceful profession. I wasn't perfect, and neither was Chris. But our love for each other was perfect. And love is enough to cover a multitude of sins.

"I love you too, Chris." I leaned over and kissed his forehead, his nose, his lips.

Chris carried me upstairs to the bedroom and before we made it through the door, he was already buried inside me again. That night, I made a decision that I knew I should have made six months ago. But better late than never.

Thirteen

"So you mean to tell me," Melvin said, pausing as he finished cleaning the 28" tires on the white and gold Yukon, "that you got this bitch in the bed—"

"—She's not a bitch."

"A'ight fine then. You got this thick ass chick in bed; you on top, willy out, her panties to her ankles, and your man just… just deflates like a tire with a nail in it? What the hell is wrong with you? You need some ginseng or something? Man, I just saw this infomercial on TV the other day; they got this new stuff out called LS pills—"

"LS?"

"Live Strong pills. They give you an erection so hard you can nail a hammer through the wall with your dick."

Chris winced at the thought. "Sounds painful to me."

"What went wrong, man? You know that ain't even like you."

Chris sat down in the driver seat of the purple Nissan that he was cleaning out. Melvin was right about his joke—a lot of women were nasty as hell when it came to their cars. This Nissan had gotten repossessed three days ago. The woman had came and gotten all her valuables, and left everything else behind. Chris was working on his third 15-gallon bag of trash. The inside of her car looked like the city dump—and smelled almost as bad, too.

"Well, when I was about to, you know, go in…the phone rang. And it was Angelique's ringtone—"

"And you actually answered it?"

"No, I ignored it. But she kept calling, back to back. Then

I started thinking too much. Started thinking about how much I love my wife, how good things were before I lost my job. And then I started thinking about Raleigh, how beautiful she is, inside and out...and I just...I just felt like she deserved better than me..."

Melvin gave him a weird look, then turned on the water hose and sprayed down the tires on the Yukon. "You hear yourself talking, right?"

"What?"

"You talking like you feeling old girl.'"

"What you mean?"

"Don't play dumb. You talking like you got a sweet spot for Ms. Vegas."

Chris shook his head, returned his focus to picking up more trash. "Naw, it ain't nothing like that. But I'll be honest; we really did connect. She went to the wedding all natural, Mel. Not a stitch of makeup. Wore her hair up—her real hair—and those earrings I bought looked so nice hanging from her ears. A guy came up to her after the wedding, asked her if he could take her out to dinner later that day. She said yes."

"Really? And how'd that make you feel?"

"Happy for her, you know? Happy that she's found her inner beauty. She's like a whole new person. I met her with tears in her eyes, and I left her at the airport with a smile covering her face. And her smile, Mel..." Chris smiled just thinking about her smile. "Her smile is contagious."

"You hear yourself talking right?"

"What?"

Melvin twisted his lips sideways as he looked at his friend. "You talking like you in love."

"I am in love. With Angelique. We've been making magic in the bedroom. I've never heard her scream so loud or felt her body shake so hard." Chris caught his bottom lip and squeezed his eyes closed for a second while he remembered. "If our marriage doesn't work out, it's not going to be because of me. Going to that wedding in Vegas just reminded me of how much I love my wife. I'm determined to do everything in my power to make this work... even if it means quitting the escort business."

"Quitting? Fool, you just started! Do you know how many men would kill to be in your shoes?" Melvin shook his head as he sprayed down the Michelin tires. "I can't stand ungrateful dudes like you."

"How am I ungrateful?"

"What's your main source of income?"

"Escorting."

"And how many inches is you slinging?"

Chris pointed a finger at his friend. "You on some real gay shit right now."

"I'm just being real, my dude. You ungrateful. You living the life! I mean, look at it this way: you got the looks and the body. You get paid thousands of dollars to spend a day with some fine ass woman, and you slinging nine inches of—"

"How you know how many inches I got?"

"Really, Chris? How many times we done pissed together?"

"So you be staring at my piece?"

"Naw, bro, but I glanced at it once or twice. Pissed me the hell off. I gotta hold mine with my fingers when I piss; you get to use your whole hand—"

"Make one more homo remark, and we're no longer friends—"

"No homo, I'm just being real. See, that's why I was scared for Stephanie to spend the weekend at my crib. We ain't get it in, but I could tell she wanted to. But on the real..." Melvin paused and looked away for the briefest second. When he started talking again, he couldn't look his friend in the eye. "I'm scared to let her see it."

"See what?"

"*It.*"

"What is 'it'?"

"My dick, man, my *dick.*"

Melvin was talking so loud that his voice woke up Christopher who had been fast asleep in the hammock strung between two willow trees. Christopher instantly popped up, yawning and rubbing one of his eyes. "Daddy," he said, "what's a dick?"

"It's the flap of skin and cartilage between your legs that makes you a man—"

"Melvin, cool it." Chris pointed a warning finger at his friend, then said to his son, "Uncle Melvin has a potty mouth and used the bad word for penis."

"Penis, dick—it's all the same. Hell, if he don't hear it from me, he's gonna hear it from some little knucklehead at school. These kids nowadays ain't cut from the cloth we was cut from, you feel me, Chris? They grown as hell. Little girls walking around with grown women bodies, breasts, booty, and all. And these little school boys walking around with nuts bigger than mine."

Christopher yawned again and said, "Uncle Melvin, is my penis bigger than yours?"

"It might be small, but it ain't that small," Melvin answered with a serious face. "I might got you by an inch or two."

"Junior, go in the house and use the bathroom. I made you a peanut butter sandwich; it's on the kitchen counter. And flip on the TV; it's already turned to cartoons."

"Yes, sir." He obeyed his father and Chris threw a threatening glance at Melvin, telling him with his eyes that he needed to watch his mouth.

Once Christopher had entered the house and was well out of earshot, Chris said, "Don't ever talk like that around my son again. Show some type of respect."

"My bad, Chris. Calm down; take some of that bass out your voice when you talking to me, too. I was just playing."

"That's your problem. You play too much."

Chris returned his attention to cleaning out the car, angrily stuffing trash in the bag. He loved Melvin like a brother, but sometimes, he wished Melvin knew when to joke and when to be serious. Whether Melvin realized it or not, he was just as much a role model to Christopher as Chris was. Chris had struggled long enough himself trying to figure out how to be a "real" man when all the male role models in his life were either inmates, deadbeats, or bums—especially his father. He didn't want his son thinking it was okay to say whatever he wanted, whenever he wanted, however he wanted. But being around Melvin was definitely teaching him that.

"What you over there all swole up in the face for?" Melvin asked as he moved over to the next SUV and hosed it down. "You mad?"

Chris didn't reply.

"A'ight, cool. I'll change the subject." Melvin continued spraying down the SUV and said, "You're a bigger fool than I thought you were if you believe that bull about Steph mistaking Angelique for a lookalike. You just believing what you want to believe, but that don't stop the truth from being the truth—"

"Mel, I really don't want to talk about that right now."

"Sure you don't. But if you think quitting the escorting business is going to save your marriage, then you are deaf, dumb, and blind. Angelique don't give a shit about you; she cares about those Benjamins. Look at what you doing just to keep your wife styling and profiling. Why you investing so much time in the pretense of a marriage? 'Cause that's all it is—a pretense." Melvin pointed one finger at the entrance of the house. "The only reason why you still hanging in there is 'cause of that little dude there, and you and I both know it—"

"Now I done told you once to chill out about my wife, Mel. I'm tired of you disrespecting her like that. You might not like her, but at the end of the day, she's still my wife. And anyway, Stephanie was wrong, okay? It wasn't Angelique; it was a woman who favored her—"

"Bullshit."

"How are you so sure?" Chris turned on his friend and glared at him. "Unless you saw her up there stripping with your own two eyes, how can you be so sure that it was her?"

Melvin worked his jaw for a second, then said in a low voice, "How you know I didn't see her with my own two eyes?"

Trying to decipher the truth of that statement, Chris looked Melvin up and down, but finally decided that he was full of hot air. Melvin didn't like Angelique, had never liked her; and since he sensed the marriage was starting to unravel, he was just trying to pour gasoline on the situation to help it burn faster.

A dark cloud that had been setting off in the far corner of

the sky slowly began to creep forward. "Let's change the subject," Chris said as he looked up at the sky. "We need to knock out these cars before it starts raining."

"The truth ugly, ain't it?"

Chris sucked his teeth, praying to God that his friend shut up before he ended up punching him in the mouth.

"But you wanna know what's even uglier?" Melvin continued to taunt. "Not being true to yourself. Telling yourself a bullshit lie, then eating it up like it's sweet potato pie. Your wife's a gold-digger. A gold-digger and a trifling woman who would go behind her man's back, strip down to her birthday suit, and let every man with cash in his hand get an eyeful. While her pitiful husband gobble up that bullshit lookalike lie."

Unable to control his anger for a second longer, Chris threw down the trash bag and said, "What about the bullshit lie that you've been gobbling up since I've known you?"

Melvin's forehead crinkled into wavy lines as he scrunched up his face in confusion. "And what lie is that?"

Chris didn't waste a second to toss back the insult. "That you're actually funny. That you're actually a comedian. That people actually want to hear your lame ass performing on stage."

Melvin smacked his lips and crossed his arms. "Take that back, Chris, or we ain't cool no more."

"I ain't taking shit back," Chris retorted, realizing that he had crossed a line but unable to stop himself, "because it's the truth. You got so much to say about me and my wife, but what about you? You suck, Melvin. You can't tell a good joke to save your life. All your 'so-called' jokes are staler than left-out bread. The truth is the entertainment business is not for you. But I ain't wanna tell you that 'cause I didn't want to hurt your little feelings. But here's some truth for your ass. Quit getting on stage making a damn fool out of yourself. Stick to your car-detailing business, since that's what you do best."

Melvin sucked in a deep breath and did it in such a way that it sounded like he was choking for air. Chris looked over at his friend who had dropped the water hose on the ground, even though it was still spewing water full stream. The water hose wiggled and whipped around on the ground like a green garden snake.

At first, Chris thought his friend was trying to be funny. But after taking one look at Melvin's face, Chris hurried over and grabbed the head of the hose, then asked his friend what was wrong.

Instead of answering, Melvin crumpled to the pavement like a crushed soda can. His head lolled back, releasing a sickening crack as it hit the concrete. The clouds split open, giving birth to huge raindrops that fell in heaps, decorating the gray pavement with splatters of wet dark spots.

Chris didn't realize he was yelling, practically screaming at the top of his lungs until his son appeared on the porch wearing a worried expression.

"Junior, call 911!" he screamed.

His son remained frozen on the stairs, staring at the unmoving body sprawled across the ground. "Is Uncle Mel...is he dead, Daddy?" Christopher asked.

"Go, Christopher! Go in the house and call 911 right now!"

It took his son a while, but eventually Christopher tore his eyes away from the grisly scene. Chris sat on the pavement beside his friend and pulled his head in his lap, trying to shake life into him by slapping his cheeks. He checked his friend's pulse by placing two fingers against the side of his neck.

Relieved that he felt a heartbeat, Chris let out a rush of pent up air. But the relief was short-lived. Melvin's heartbeat was weak, faint, fading, fluttering.

"Mel, this ain't funny," Chris said as he shook his friend helplessly, knowing that his friend wasn't playing a joke. "Stop playing so much, Mel, 'cause this ain't funny."

Still, his friend remained lifeless, unmoving. A faint heartbeat that was getting weaker with each passing second.

Clutching his friend tight, as though his grip could keep Death at bay, Chris whispered, "Hang in there, Melly Mel. It's going to be all right. Help is coming; I know it is. Help is coming soon."

He just hoped soon wouldn't be too late.

Fourteen

I went to work and danced, but my heart wasn't in it. My heart ached thinking about the possibility of losing Chris, if I hadn't already. I hoped that my performance hadn't suffered because of my internal turmoil, but judging by how the DJ was staring at me with that perplexed expression, I figured it had sucked after all.

"What's going on with you, Butterscotch?" he asked as I walked past him. "You usually come harder than that. If you need some inspiration, just let me know. I got something that'll inspire you," he said, eyeing my body and licking his lips.

Not in the mood for sexual harassment or jokes, I just shook my head. "Is Dexter still here?"

"Why you so worried about him?" The DJ leaned forward on the stereo system, propping himself up on his elbows. "Y'all two are mighty close. If I didn't know any better, I'd swear y'all was getting it in. I thought you told me you married?"

"Is Dexter still here?" I asked with steel lining my voice.

"Okay, okay," he said, finally falling back. "Yeah, he's up there in his office." As I walked off, he added, "Go'n in there and give him a kiss."

Ignoring his jab, I changed into a long shirt with leggings and heels and headed to Dexter's office. Instead of taking the steps, I took the private elevator to the second floor where his office was located. His door was wide open and he sat in front of his computer, staring at the monitor.

I hesitated before knocking.

Looking up from the screen, he smiled like he was surprised but pleased to see me. "Come on in and close the door behind you."

I did as he requested and took a seat on a red accent chair in front of his contemporary glossy desk. So many colorful, expensive paintings covered the walls that I thought I was in an art gallery.

Dexter rested his hands on his desk, revealing a platinum and diamond encrusted bracelet. "What's up, baby girl?" He motioned toward the huge flat screen TV mounted on the wall that showed security surveillance of the entire club. "I just watched you perform on the monitor, and I could tell that something's bothering you. Talk to me."

Still, I hesitated. I had wrestled with this decision all night long, and I knew it was the right thing to do—even though I didn't want to do it. Since I'd gotten back from Miami and Chris returned from Las Vegas, our relationship had changed so much. I still didn't know exactly what had happened in Vegas, but whatever had happened had changed my husband into a better man. He catered to me; he treated me like a precious, rare jewel. As much as I wanted to stay mad at him for cheating on me—because even though I didn't have tangible truth, I still believed he cheated on me—I felt like the pot calling the kettle black. How could I be mad at my husband for hiding something from me when I was hiding something from him?

I couldn't do this anymore. If my house and car were truly blessings from God, then He would make a way for me to keep my blessings, and I wouldn't have to lie and demean myself any longer to maintain my lifestyle. For that reason, I had to break the news to Dexter. If he didn't like it, oh well.

"Dexter," I said and kept my eyes glued to the top of his desk, "I quit. I'm not stripping anymore."

A long silence stretched between us. He scratched his forehead. "Is this, uh…because of Miami?"

I shrugged. "Not really. I'm just tired of living a lie. I need to make some changes in my life, and I'm going to start by not dancing at your club anymore."

Clasping his hands together, he nodded his head. "I knew this was coming." He sat back in his seat and his eyes looked pained. "Angelique, listen to me. I knew I was taking a big risk by tricking you into spending that weekend with me. I was completely out of line and I shouldn't have overstepped my boundaries as your boss—"

"Dexter—"

He held up a hand to stop me.

I swallowed my words.

"Baby girl, I'm not going to lie to you or myself and say I don't want you. Because I do. I burn for you, Angelique. I swear I do." He scratched his forehead again. "But I care for you enough to set my feelings aside for your best interest. If you don't want to strip anymore, I can respect that. But I don't want you scrapping to find another job, just to make ends meet."

I didn't want that either, which was why I had already updated my resume and cover letter and had sent them out to at least a dozen potential jobs.

He got up and walked around his desk, leaning against the edge with his right foot planted firmly on the ground and his left propped up. "Listen. I'm ready to take my businesses to another level." He pressed his hands together. "The only way I can do that is to put the right people in place. That's where you come in, if you're interested."

I gave him a questioning look.

"Didn't you tell me before that you have a degree in International Business?"

"Yes." I sighed, wondering where he was going with all this.

He shifted his body. "And I already know that you speak Spanish." He smiled at me. "Baby girl, I want you to be my Director of Marketing."

"What?" My body felt numb. Director of anything usually meant a fat paycheck.

"I'm not gonna lie to you; you're in for some hard work. We're about to go international, baby girl. You and I," he gestured with his right hand to emphasize his point, "are about to be spending a whole lot of time together. I hope you have a passport."

Was he kidding? I kept a passport. I believe that as long as I stay ready, I won't have to get ready. I cleared my throat. "Tell me more."

He jumped off the desk and clapped his hands one time. "That's what I was hoping you'd say." He came up behind me and massaged my shoulders for a quick second, then returned to his computer. Within minutes, he had printed off a stack of papers, stapled them, then handed them to me.

I skimmed the documents. "What's all this?" I held the papers in the air.

"The documents on the top are your new job description and a contract," he explained. "I think you'll find the salary satisfactory." He sounded confident. The smirk on his face let me know he felt just as confident as he sounded. "Of course, you don't have to take the job. But the way the job market is in this economy, if someone is handing you a prestigious position, you'd be a fool to let it slip by."

Giving the contract a quick scan, my eyes became fixated on the salary. Six figures. I thought my heart was about to explode, or at least beat out of my chest. Not wanting to seem too anxious, I said, "Give me a day to look this over with my attorney."

"Fair enough," he agreed and sat back down. "The rest of the documents are an overview of my operations." He paused then continued. "You already know about my strip clubs."

I nodded.

"I also own adult novelty stores in," he counted on his fingers, "Dallas, Atlanta, Miami, San Diego, Los Angeles, Las Vegas, and New York City."

That was news to me. I wiped the corners of my mouth.

"Plus, I have a production company and distribution company. We produce adult movies and distribute them on a national level."

I had caught wind of that, but this was the first time Dexter had confirmed it. "Really?" He had his hand in every area of the adult entertainment industry, I thought. "How did you get in this industry?" My curiosity had gotten the best of me.

"You ask too many questions," he cautioned me. "Just know that I worked my way up, from the bottom to the top. And *every* dollar that I make or spend, I *earned* it."

"You're not into anything illegal, are you?"

He laughed and leaned back in his chair. "Not at all, baby girl. There's only one thing I like more than money, and that's my freedom. I've never been to jail and," he pretended to knock on his head, "knock on wood, I never will. See, the escort business flourishes mainly in Vegas. You know prostitution is legal in Vegas."

"So I hear."

"Can't get into trouble in Vegas if an escort sleeps with a client. The laws are trickier here, but hey…" His thoughts seemed to drift for a moment. "Anyway, you can trust that I'm a legitimate business man." He looked me in the eyes. "You know how that guy Carlos Slim built a telecommunications empire after he bought out Mexico's state-run phone monopoly?"

"I remember hearing about that." I crossed my feet at the ankles. "He became richer than Bill Gates and Warren Buffett."

"That's right." He grinned. "Over the next five years I plan to become an international conglomerate. I want you to be right there with me." He stroked his chin.

I stared at him, wondering why he wasn't married. Any man with dreams that big—especially a *black* man—needed a strong woman supporting him. "Why aren't you married?" I blurted out.

"Because no woman in her right mind would have me," he joked. "I work all the time. I care more about money than romance. What woman would want that?" he challenged me.

"One who puts security and stability above all else," I shot back.

Judging by the smug look on his face, I could tell that my answer impressed him. "Why are you married?"

I felt like he had sucker punched me in the gut. He had taken a pin and burst my bubble. Why did he have to go there? His gaze made me so uncomfortable that I shifted in my seat. I searched my heart and gave the most truthful answer I could find. "I married the love of my life."

He shook his head. "That was your first mistake."

Confused, I frowned. "Excuse me?"

"Baby girl, a woman should never marry for love alone. Feelings change, then what?" He didn't wait for me to respond. "I haven't been married, but I know that marriage is a partnership. I wouldn't go into business with anybody who couldn't help me get more than I can get for myself."

I allowed his words to marinate in my brain. Then I said, "I don't regret marrying my husband. He's a good father, and he's not afraid to work."

"That's good. We should live a life void of regrets, and full of learning experiences." He cracked his knuckles and glanced at his big-faced watch. "You should get going. It's time for you to pick up your son."

"You remembered that?"

He said in an endearing tone, "I remember everything that's important to me."

His words pierced my heart. I gathered the papers from my lap. "Thanks for the opportunity. I'll get back with you on this."

He pretended to salute me and I left.

En route to get Christopher, I remembered that he'd had a dentist appointment today and Chris had already picked him up. I hooked a U-turn in the road and was almost home when Tori called and asked me if she could come over and talk. By the time I arrived home, Tori was already parked in front of the house waiting for me. Surprisingly, my son was with her.

When Christopher saw me, he jumped out her car and wrapped his thin arms around my waist. I returned his hug, ruffled his hair, and gave him a big wet kiss.

"How'd it go at the dentist office?" I asked.

"He cleaned my teeth and gave me a new toothbrush. See!" He held up a bright orange and blue toothbrush. Then he said the words that made the muscles in my heart cease to beat. "Mommy, Daddy's in the hospital."

"Daddy's in the what?" I basically screamed.

Easily six feet tall with heels, Tori stood beside me and rubbed my back in soothing circles. "He's *at* the hospital not *in* the hospital. Melvin is the one who's sick. He had a stroke or something."

My knees felt weak and I envisioned myself hitting the pavement. Christopher's words had caused so many nightmarish thoughts to catapult through my head. Chris mangled from a car accident; Chris impaled with a pole from a freak accident; Chris shot in a convenience store robbery. Thankfully, in all the years of our marriage, one thing we never had to deal with was sickness— me or him. As bad as it sounds, I was so relieved that it was Melvin who'd been admitted to the hospital, not my husband.

With her hand still behind my back steadying me, Tori escorted me to the house. As soon as we got inside, Christopher raced upstairs to his room while Tori and I took a seat in the front room. My hands had stopped trembling, but I still felt a little shaky on the inside. I asked Tori for details about Melvin and the stroke, but she didn't know anymore than she'd already told me.

I called the hospital and asked for Melvin's room, but when they transferred me, no one answered.

Tori took the phone from me and put it away. "Angie, Chris is fine, and Melvin will be fine too. Let's just change the subject. Did you quit today like you said you would, or did you have a change of heart?"

Thankful to have something different to think about, I filled her in on my job offer and showed her the contract. She put on her paralegal glasses and reviewed the agreement.

"He hooked you up," she said, handing the agreement back to me. "I wouldn't normally advise you to sign a contract as-is, but he looked out for you." I smiled, thankful that I hadn't been swindled. She continued, "Now you can actually tell Chris the truth about your job. You can be honest about your promotion."

I sat back on the couch cushions and crossed my legs. "I'll admit; it's a relief to tell him the truth. That night when he brought up stripping, girl I just knew I was caught up. I don't know where my 'lookalike' came from, but I thank God for her. Maybe she was an angel sent from heaven."

"Yeah, well, at least you *almost* got caught up. Your old man wasn't so lucky."

A sour feeling expanded in the pit of my stomach. "What

do you mean?"

Rubbing her hands on her denim covered thighs, Tori said, "Did you see in the newspaper yesterday where Womack's IGA got robbed?"

I didn't recall hearing about that, so I shook my head.

"Well, I read it. And the store manager was complaining about how this is their third robbery this year, and it's only May. So instead of just having a day-shift security guard, they're going to start hiring night-shift security guards as well."

"So...?" Unsure of where she was going with this, I tapped my foot on the carpet and waited for her to continue.

"So," she said, dragging the word out so long that it had five syllables, "since they're just about to *start* hiring night-shift security guards, how was your husband already working as a night-shift security guard there?"

Her words struck home. Yet and still, it didn't make sense to me. Why would Chris lie about working as a security guard at the IGA store?

Confused, I struggled to find words, but Tori held up a finger to halt me. "And," she continued, making me hold my breath even more, "because his blatant lie made me curious, I googled Diamond-Elite Business Solutions, and no such company exists. Couldn't find it in the phone book either."

My only response was a wide-eyed blink. Once I finally came to, I nearly gnawed my bottom lip to bits. I jumped off the couch and began pacing my spacious front room, barely able to control my anger. "So he's been lying to me all this time! When he was 'so-called' going to work at night at the store, and when he flew over there to Vegas, he was probably laid up with some scank—I *told* you I got that feeling that he was cheating on me. Didn't I tell you, Tori?"

"Angelique, don't take this the wrong way, but you aren't Little Miss Innocent here." I glared at her, angry that she wasn't taking my side. "I mean, look how long you've been lying to him about stripping. And when you went over to Miami, you weren't on your best behavior either—"

"Yeah, but at the end of the day, I'm doing what I have to

do to pay the bills. I'm not laying up and giving away my goods and lying to my spouse about having sex with someone else."

While I paced and cursed, Tori stood to her full height and shouldered her purse. "This is all I have to say about the situation. You and Chris have a lot invested in your marriage and in each other. He's been good to you. You've never had to wonder about his love for you or his son. Plus, you love him. He's human. Everybody makes mistakes. If he did cheat, that doesn't have to be a deal breaker."

"You can't be serious." I sounded disgusted. Who was this imposter and what had she done with my best friend?

She halted her hand. "Hear me out."

I sulked.

"Nobody is perfect, but Chris is perfect for you." She paused. "For argument's sake, let's say he did have a weak moment and tipped out on you. It's just sex. His heart belongs to you. He comes home to you. Ever since he's known you he has given you everything he has." She patted my hand. "Take it from me, if you get rid of a man every time he messes up, you'll keep going through men. I dropped two ex-husbands for cheating." She seemed reflective. "I wonder what would've happened if I had tried to work it out with at least one of them."

I took a deep breath and exhaled. "I have to know that I can trust my man."

"You already know that you can trust Chris. You've worked hard to get him where he is now. He cleans up behind himself, cooks, and helps with Christopher. Plus, he's romantic. The man adores you. It's obvious every time he looks at you."

"How can I trust him if he's lying to me? He keeps lying to me about everything!" I started crying, something I had been doing a lot of over the past couple days.

Tori hugged me. "It'll be okay," she comforted me. "Fight for your love and hold on to your marriage. Don't let another woman come between you and your man. You aren't the first person who's had to deal with this, and you surely won't be the last."

As if on cue, I heard the garage door and knew that Chris

had arrived. I hurried up and wiped my face; I didn't want him to see me crying.

Easily changing the subject, Tori acknowledged Chris with a smile and asked how Melvin was doing. With a grim expression, Chris explained that Melvin had had an isthmetic stroke and that the hospital had admitted him. Lines of worry creased his forehead as he explained that his friend had went into cardiac arrest and flatlined while in the emergency room. They were able to get his heart working again, and now he was in ICU in stable condition.

"It's all my fault," Chris said, shaking his head. "I was arguing with him, and I just got carried away. I overdid it."

"Baby, it is not your fault," I said, going to him and touching his face. "Don't you dare blame yourself for this."

"I'll give you two some privacy," Tori said, looking at both of us. "Don't you worry about Melvin. He's always been a fighter; he's going to pull through this and he'll be fine. He'll be laughing about it by tomorrow." She kissed me on the cheek and gave my arm a squeeze before making a speedy exit.

We stood in the kitchen, me leaning against the counter and Chris leaning against the island. I could feel Chris's eyes on me, but I wouldn't look up from the floor. I knew that now probably wasn't the best time to have this talk, being that Chris had already been through enough today. However, his lies were lying heavy on my heart. And I felt like if I didn't get this off my chest, I might go into cardiac arrest myself.

Finally, after much hesitation, I said the words I knew would set the tone and get his attention. "Chris...we need to talk."

Fifteen

As Chris sat in the cushioned chair in the waiting room, he ran his sweaty hands over his creased khakis and stared at the water fountain, counting down the time when the blue-tinted water would gurgle again. Every two minutes or so, he would look at the entrance door, reposition himself in the seat, get up and use the bathroom, flip through a magazine. He felt much more comfortable at the Diamond-Elite center located in Vegas than this one which was only twenty-six miles from his house. He'd walked in with his tweed cap pulled low and large Docker shades covering the top portion of his face. He had hoped that they'd quickly call him to the back. There was only one other person in the waiting room besides him, a chick of possibly Indian descent with endlessly long legs and dark eyes. But they'd both been sitting in the waiting room for nearly twenty minutes now.

He retook his seat and flipped through another magazine, but he wasn't paying attention to the articles or the pictures. Instead, he was thinking about the discussion him and his wife had had last night. She'd given him the golden opportunity to come clean, and yet and still, he hadn't had the courage to tell her the truth. He knew how Angelique was; she was the kind of woman who would forgive, but would never forget. To this day, she still threw moments of his pre-marriage infidelity in his face every chance she got. If he told her about this escorting gig, he'd never hear the end of it. So rather than tell her the truth, he decided to tiptoe around it instead. He admitted that he lied about being a security guard when he was really a night-shift stocker at Womack's. But when it came to explaining the trip to Vegas, he used Melvin as a scapegoat. He admitted that he created the Diamond-Elite Business Solutions Company just to make her proud of where her man worked rather than ashamed. However, he claimed that he went to Vegas with Melvin to support him performing as a comedian at a casino.

In all honesty, he felt ashamed to have to lie on his friend— his sick friend who was hospitalized and facing the possibility of never being able to speak or walk normally again—in order to save his own ass. But Angelique had bought it, hook, line, and sinker, and they ended up sharing passionate, mind-blowing sex all night long. He'd given it to her so good that by the time they finished, her walls were swollen, his gonads were sore, and the covers were soaked with sweat and human bonding fluid.

But what bothered him the most was that while he was making love to his wife, images of Raleigh and those yellow teardrop diamonds kept coming to mind. While making love to his wife, he was imagining that he was finishing what Raleigh and he had started weeks ago. And that made him feel uncomfortable to say the least.

It bothered him. Tremendously so. Guilt gnawed at him like a worm gnawing at a dead man's coffin. It wasn't only guilt about fantasizing about another woman who wasn't his wife, but it was also the guilt of causing his friend's stroke and heart attack. He didn't care what Angelique said. He knew that if he hadn't come off on Melvin so hard, he'd probably be at home right now, detailing some car, or working on jokes for his next standup comedy session. What had happened to Melvin helped him realize that life is entirely too short to live a lie. He couldn't continue this escorting charade anymore than he could continue constantly lying to Angelique. Melvin didn't deserve him exploding on him like that, and Angelique didn't deserve him spoon-feeding her one ridiculous lie after another. For that reason, he had asked to meet with Mrs. Whitmeyer, but her schedule hadn't allowed an impromptu meeting. Instead, he was meeting with Dexter King to let him know that he was resigning from the position.

"Chris Hines."

A bit surprised that they'd called his name before the Indian woman's, Chris stood to his feet and followed the secretary down the long corridor. She led him to the fifth door on the right, which bared the name Dexter King, and informed Mr. King of their arrival. He beckoned for Chris to come in.

Unlike Mrs. Whitmeyer's office, Mr. King's office was cluttered, full of filing cabinets, manila envelopes, and stacks of paperwork on his desk. Mr. King was a dark-skinned brother, average height, medium build with a well-edged low cut. Even though he looked like he was well acquainted with the gym, he still had an air about him that declared that he wasn't the kind of man to get his hands dirty working on a car or working out in the yard. Maybe it was his manicured nails or his arched eyebrows, or the shiny gold cuff links on his collared shirt. He looked like he could be an escort himself.

"Mr. Hines," he said, holding out his hand and giving him a firm handshake. "A pleasure to finally meet you. Sorry about missing our first meeting. I had to fly to Miami for some…serious business."

"I understand," Chris said, taking a seat in the offered chair. "My wife had to fly out there for the same thing. That's life; things happen. Pleasure to finally meet you as well, Mr. King."

"Please call me, Dexter." He retook his seat, then placed his elbows on the desk, laced his fingers together, and rested his chin on the back of his hands. "So are you enjoying your job so far? Good money, beautiful ladies, luxurious places. Unbeatable, huh?"

"It's, uh…" Chris repositioned himself in the chair and became transfixed with a hangnail protruding from his pointer finger. "That's actually what I wanted to talk to you about."

"I'm sure you do want to talk about it. You are a hot commodity every since we've put you on the website. You have requests lined up back to back. If you'd like, you could do four or five outings a month for the next six months. That's over twenty thousand a month. Sounds good, huh?"

Chris didn't answer. But his silence was answer enough.

"Is there a problem, Mr. Hines?"

Again, Chris hesitated before answering. He'd be a fool to turn down that type of money. Just like Melvin had said, most men would kill to be in his position. It was the kind of job that most men could only dream and fantasize about. And this fantastic opportunity had practically fallen into his lap, and he was about to give it all up…all in the name of love.

He cleared his throat then said, "Mr. King, this is it for me. I'm done with escorting. I quit."

As though it was a joke, Dexter looked at him and smiled, showing off stunningly white teeth in his dark brown face. He started laughing excessively hard, even banging his fist on the desk. But then his boisterous laugh turned into chuckles, then into a grin, and finally into a completely perplexed expression when he realized that he was the only one laughing.

"You can't possibly be serious about this." He waited for a response, but Chris gave none. Then the man began sounding a bit offensive. "So what's the problem? We're not paying you enough? Because if it's the money, I'm sure Mrs. Whitmeyer wouldn't mind going up on your fee. Fifty-five hundred? Six thousand per client? We can take eight percent instead of ten. Just let me know what works for you."

In an even, calm voice, Chris said, "Nothing works for me. You don't get it, do you? I'm not quitting because of the money. I'm quitting because of my wife and my marriage. It's not worth it."

"What the hell do you mean? You only went out once with a single client. You haven't even given this thing a chance."

"Once was enough."

"Why?" Dexter raised his eyebrows. "Did your wife find out about it?" His eyes searched Chris's for the answer. "No, that's not it, is it? Could it be that you started catching feelings for the client? It usually doesn't happen during one outing, but every now and then, you come across this special woman and one encounter is all it takes for her to get beneath your skin. Is that what happened, Mr. Hines?"

"What does it matter what happened?" Chris exploded on the man. "The only thing that matters is that I'm not feeling this anymore and I quit."

Feeling that his mission was complete, Chris stood to his

feet only for Dexter to swivel around in his chair and begin tapping at the keyboard keys. "You might want to take a seat for a second," Dexter said without casting him a glance. "Obviously you didn't read the handbook thoroughly."

Again with this damn handbook, Chris thought as he rolled his eyes. Reluctantly, he retook his seat and tapped his foot impatiently.

Dexter printed out a single sheet of paper, then passed the printed sheet to Chris. Again, he rested his chin on his laced fingers as he watched Chris's eyes scan the paper. While Chris looked over the excerpt quickly, he read aloud certain parts of the handbook. When he got to one particular line, it dawned on him why Dexter had asked him to read this portion. The paper read: "All escorts are bound by contract to complete four outings with either the same client or a variety of clients before the employee is permitted to cancel his or her contracted position with Diamond-Elite Escorting."

"Do you understand what that stipulation entails?"

Chris's eyes darted to Dexter's smug face. In response to his question, Chris balled up the paper and flicked it at Dexter. It hit his forehead with a *plop* before tumbling across the desk and falling to the floor.

Smoothing the creases out of his shirt, Chris stood to his feet and walked over to Dexter's desk. He leaned across the desk until their faces were only inches apart. As though he was speaking to someone who was mentally challenged, Chris spoke slowly and overly pronounced each syllable. "Fuck you; fuck that contract; fuck Diamond-Elite. I quit. Do you understand what *that* stipulation entails?"

Dexter didn't flinch as he leaned away from Chris and crossed his arms before crossing his ankle over his knee. While Chris walked away, Dexter said, "One down, three to go. Your second client is Fiona Anderson. She's a widow, lonely. Your final two outings will be with the same client. She's already paid in full and given you a gracious tip that is equivalent to your fee—that's double the money, ten thousand per day. And that client, Mr. Hines, is Mrs. Whitmeyer."

Those words brought him to a stop. He turned at the door. "Mrs. Whitmeyer? *The* Mrs. Whitmeyer? The owner of Diamond-Elite?" Chris shook his head. "That's preposterous. I'm her employee. She can't sleep with her employee."

"And who's going to fire her? She's the one who's ultimately in charge. She makes the rules, she breaks the rules."

"This is bullshit."

"Call it how you see it. All the information you need will be sent to your e-mail account, including plane tickets. If you fail to keep your end of the bargain, Diamond-Elite will press charges for breach of contract—a criminal offense. So I'd think twice about ignoring our e-mails, Mr. Hines. Mr. Hines? Mr. Hines, do you hear me talking to you?"

Ignoring him completely, Chris kept walking down the hallway with stiff shoulders and his head held high. Once he was in the safety of his car, he slammed his fists into the steering wheel as though the wheel was Dexter's face. This was some bullshit, a trap, a setup. They had him backed against the wall, and he knew whether he wanted to or not, he would have to finish what he started. Like a female spider closing in on her prey, he knew it was just a matter of time before this job sucked the life out of him and left him empty, hollow, nothing more than a mere shell of the man he used to be.

Shaking him out of his reverie, his cell phone rang, and he had half the mind to ignore the call. Just before it could ring for the final time, Chris glanced at the caller ID and his eyes widened in surprise when he recognized the unexpected number scrolling across the screen.

Sixteen

Early Sunday morning, I awoke with an overwhelming desire to go to church. I'm Catholic, but I hadn't been practicing since I started dancing. Chris is Baptist, and he has no desire to convert to Catholicism. So, whenever we go to church as a family, we go to a Baptist church. I used to be so dedicated that I'd get up extra early just to go to Sunday Mass and then go to a different church with my family.

I looked at the digital clock next to the bed and the time read 8:00 a.m. I shifted my body and faced Chris. Just watching him as he slept stirred up emotions within me. My eyes filled with tears as I thought about how much I loved him. I used to consider Chris to be my best friend, but now I realized that was a lie. With all the secrets I had been keeping from him and he had been keeping from me, there was no way he could be my best friend. I missed being able to talk to him about just about anything, everything, nothing. I missed him.

His chest heaved as he breathed. I placed my hand on his smooth chest before resting my ear over his heart. His heart beat to its own rhythm, calming my spirit.

I felt Chris wrap his arm around my shoulder and smack his lips. "Mornin'," he said.

I lifted my head. "I want to go to church this morning."

He squinted his eyes at me and rubbed his hand along my arm. A moment later he said, "Okay."

"All of us…as a family," I clarified.

"Okay," he repeated.

I pressed my eyes shut trying to force the tears that threatened to spill back into my eyes. I felt as though we needed to get our spiritual life back on track. We hadn't gone to church in at least six months, and we had stopped praying together just as long, if not longer. Our physical life reflected our struggling spiritual life.

For the past couple of days my conscious had been bothering me. I wanted to tell Chris about my new job, but how could I do that without telling him the whole story? I still hadn't figured that part out yet. I hoped that going to church would help me get some clarity on the situation and my marriage. If we had a snowball's chance in hell of keeping our marriage together, we needed to rearrange our priorities and put God first like we vowed to do on our wedding day.

Plus, I could tell that something had been bothering Chris. I caught him looking at me a few times like he wanted to say something but didn't know how. His eyes seemed...apologetic. He's even started talking in his sleep. Not complete sentences or full confessions, but stuff like, "Stop!" "Don't!" "No!" "I don't want to..."

Determined to make the best of our situation, I kissed Chris on the side of his neck and got out of bed. I went into the bathroom and showered while Chris shaved with his electric razor. When I finished, I slathered baby oil all over my body and pat dried with a plush towel as Chris splashed aftershave on his face and neck. In perfect sync, we flossed our teeth, brushed, and gargled. My teeth felt smooth as I ran my tongue over them, and my mouth had a minty taste.

After putting on some light makeup, I blow dried my dyed strawberry blonde hair and noticed that my walnut brown roots were showing. Time for a touch up. I made a mental note to make a hair appointment for the upcoming week.

Chris glanced at me through the mirror as he brushed his wavy hair. "You want me to fix you something to eat?"

I shook my head. "No thanks. I'll get some fruit." I paused. "But, if you could feed little man while I get dressed—that would be greatly appreciated." I smiled at him.

He nodded. I heard him deactivate the alarm before going downstairs. In my walk-in closet, I surveyed my options before selecting a coral-colored wrap dress and nude high heeled sandals. I put on the dress but kept on my fluffy house shoes. Chris had complained that my heels scuffed up the glossy wood floors downstairs, so I usually waited until time for us to go and put my shoes on at the door.

Chris came back into the room and handed me a ceramic mug filled with green tea. I thanked him and peck kissed him on the lips.

"You look nice," he complimented and touched the small of my back.

A smile graced my face. Before I could say anything, he headed down the hall to wake up little man.

I stood in the middle of the bedroom and sipped my hot drink. The tea had a calming effect as the liquid eased its way down my throat. Just the right blend of lemon, honey, and sweetener I thought as I took another sip. The phone rang, and I wondered who could be calling so early in the morning.

I made my way over to the phone resting on the night table next to the bed and answered.

"Good morning, baby girl," the male voice said.

I nearly dropped my tea. Surely, Dexter hadn't grown an extra set of balls and called my house. I cleared my throat as I looked over my shoulder, hoping that Chris had gone back downstairs, or at least down the hall out of earshot.

"You know better than this," I breathed into the phone.

"I know better?" He sounded perturbed. "Calm down, girl; it's your brother, Elonzo. I know we haven't spoken in a minute, but dang. You forgot my voice already?"

Elonzo is the youngest of my brothers, and we're two years apart. He lives in Puerto Rico with his wife and their three kids.

I giggled, trying to play it off. "Sorry, El. I didn't catch your voice. My bad. How's everything?"

"I just wanted to give you a heads up."

I sighed as I waited for the bad news.

"I spoke to Mario, and he told me that Mom has gotten

remarried."

Mario is the oldest, and he has always had a close relationship with our mother. I wondered why Elonzo was calling me with this. He knew that I hadn't seen or spoken to our mother since she turned down the invite to my wedding. After our papi died my junior year in high school, our mom changed. She became consumed with politics and being a social climber. With me being a daddy's girl, I didn't like the way my mom disrespected my father's memory. Our relationship became even more strained, and she didn't seem to care—neither did I. When I went off to college on a full academic scholarship, my mom and I only interacted when we had to...holidays. She didn't even attend my college graduation, because she was on a ski trip with one of her boyfriends. That's why I shouldn't have been surprised when she didn't show up for my wedding or the birth of my child—but I had to admit, her nonchalant attitude cut deep.

"Good for her," I said without any enthusiasm. "What's this got to do with me?"

"Look, Miss What's This Got To Do With Me, she's in politics and married some rich oil tycoon, and they're living in San Antonio, Texas."

My jaw dropped. "Oh." I sipped some more tea and leaned against the mattress.

"Don't be surprised if she tries to contact you," he continued.

I took a deep breath and looked up to the heavens. Was this a test? I wondered. Logic kicked in, and I said, "Why would she contact me? She doesn't have my number."

He laughed into the phone. "You act like she can't get it, baby girl." His tone turned serious. "Don't you think it's about time you forgive Mom? I mean, she made a lot of mistakes and she's not perfect, but she's the only mom we've got. Life is too short to hold grudges."

"*I'm* not the one holding any grudges," I corrected him. "I am toxic to Mom, and you know that. She's hated me since the day I was born. Out of all of her kids, I was the only one who gave her postpartum depression. She didn't want anything to do with me."

The reality caused my voice to crack. "Daddy practically raised me as a single parent. She was in the house raising her sons, but she didn't do anything for me. Tori's mom taught me how to be a girl. When I got my period at twelve years old, she's the one who bought my pads and explained to me what was happening to my body. Yvonne taught me everything I know about how not to be a sorry parent," I spat. "Won't you tell me why our mother has never met her son-in-law? Won't you tell me why our mother has never laid eyes on her grandson? Christopher doesn't even know Yvonne exists. So, you need not talk to me about *our* mother."

I heard him breathe into the phone. "I know you have good reason to feel the way you feel. I was just hoping you two could make amends. You're her only daughter."

"I love you El, but you can't possibly understand how I feel. You have a mother. You have her love. I don't." I sat my cup down. "I forgave Mom a long time ago, because that's the right thing to do. I'm not bitter or angry. However, I choose not to deal with her because that's what's best for me and her. Now if you'll excuse me," I said, blinking back tears, "I need to finish getting ready for church."

"All right, baby girl. Tell Chris I said hello and give my nephew a hug for me."

"I will."

"Love you too."

"I know," I said and hung up the phone.

I was too outdone with my mother. She didn't even deserve the title. That selfish wench! According to my brothers, she boycotted my wedding because she didn't think Chris had enough money. How would she know? She had never met him.

"Babe, are you okay?" Chris asked, peeking his head into the bedroom.

"Yeah, I'm fine," I lied. "Me and El just shared a few words. That's all."

Chris didn't look like he believed my lie, but he tapped the doorframe and said, "I'll go start up the car."

We arrived at Praise International at ten o'clock on the dot.

Chris looked like a number one stunner in his tan linen suit, breezy coral shirt, and tan newsboy cap—which he removed the instant we reached the church doors. Christopher looked like a miniature version of his father from shoes to hat. We could've easily been ready for an *Essence* magazine photo shoot.

We first stopped at children's church and signed Christopher in. The kindergarten room already had about ten children there. Two female teachers, both with pleasant demeanors, greeted us with smiles. We kneeled down and gave Christopher hugs and kisses and waited until one of the teachers grabbed him by the hand and helped him get settled in.

As we made our way to the sanctuary, I laced my fingers through Chris's. I could feel his positive vibes and appreciated them. The usher directed us to the third pew from the front where we stood and sang along with the rest of the congregation. Chris sang low, doing some amazing runs with his strong, sultry voice. I had often tried to persuade him to join the choir or the praise team. They could definitely benefit from his talented pipes, but he was adamant about singing from the pews.

Two songs later, an associate minister led us in responsive reading followed by church announcements and more worship. We spent most of service on our feet until the pastor came in and delivered the sermon titled, "How Sin Separates One From God."

He read 1 John 3:4 New King James Version: *Whoever commits sin also commits lawlessness, and sin is lawlessness.*

He then said, "The word 'lawlessness' is translated into the Greek word anomia, meaning without law or against law. What's conveyed here is that sin is an active violation of God's laws and basic moral principles." He walked across the altar. "It's not just referring to actions that are outside the bounds of God's law, but actions that are in deliberate rebellion against those laws—deliberately trampling on and rejecting that boundary."

I felt my heartbeat speed up. With a convicted heart, I realized that my household wasn't going to be peaceful again until I stopped being so deceptive. I closed my eyes and silently repented, asking God to forgive me for working as a stripper, disrespecting my husband, and lusting after Dexter. I even prayed for God to soften my heart enough to forgive Chris in the event he had gone astray.

I opened my eyes, and Chris reached over and squeezed my hand. The minister asked us to stand as he opened the doors of the church then performed the benediction.

After service, we made our way through the crowd and picked up little man.

"Let's go out to eat," Chris suggested on our way to the car. "My treat."

I bit my lower lip. "How can we refuse that?"

Chris took us to the child-friendly Golden Corral Buffet and Grill. I was okay with his selection. I started out with a salad. Chris fixed his and little man's plates. I looked at Chris's plate, and he had half of the buffet. He could eat whatever he wanted and stay in shape. Lucky dog.

I finished munching on lettuce and put my fork down. "Chris, I have some good news."

He gave me an incredulous look.

"I have a new job," I announced with a wide grin.

"Really?" He stopped cutting into his steak. "Doing what?"

"I'm the new Marketing Director for Lumpkin Enterprises International." I popped a small red oval grape tomato in my mouth.

A reluctant smile appeared on Chris's face. "That's great, baby. How'd you land this job?"

That's Chris—always full of questions. I sighed. "Believe it or not, my boss recommended me for the position."

He furrowed a brow. "You went from a sales rep to a director in what…less than a year?"

My throat suddenly felt dry, so I sipped on some ice water. "My boss knew my background when he hired me. My entry job was just to get me into the organization. It was never meant to be permanent."

"Good deal. Congratulations, baby. I'm proud of you." He resumed eating his steak, then said between chews, "I've got good news as well."

Surprised, I lifted both eyebrows. "Really? What's your

good news?"

"A few days ago, TCP called and offered me my job back."

"Get outta here!" I exclaimed. My excitement was too much to contain, and I couldn't stop smiling. "Baby, that's great! Why'd you wait so long to tell me?"

He stopped chewing for a moment and tilted his head to the side as if he were trying to process some information. He straightened back up and said, "Because I've been going through a lot, baby."

I understood completely. They'd moved Melvin from the hospital to a rehabilitation center; he needed around-the-clock care, and every chance Chris got, he was right by his friend's side. As much as I disliked Melvin, I felt bad for him. He was the same age my husband, only thirty-two years old; he shouldn't be living in a nursing home.

According to Chris, the therapists were teaching Melvin how to walk, talk, and write again. He could still speak, but his language was garbled; he could write what he wanted to say, but his handwriting looked like that of a preschooler. As of now, he was confined to a wheelchair, but they were working diligently toward him using a walker or a cane. To me, it was just a sad situation, and I could feel Chris's pain. They were more like brothers than best friends.

I swallowed the lump in my throat and ran my hand over the back of Chris's head. "I know it's hard, baby."

"It is," he agreed without hesitation, nodding his head repeatedly as he looked off into the distance. "I kind of feel like Peter from the Bible."

"Peter?" That wasn't the biblical name I was expecting to hear. Maybe Job, but Peter? "I don't get it," I said, shaking my head. "Why him?"

"Peter denied God three times," Chris continued, still looking at a place that no other eyes could see but his. "People have the misunderstanding that he denied God because he was a coward, afraid of being arrested. But really, he denied God out of necessity. He wanted to try to save Jesus, but he knew that the only way he could save Jesus from being arrested was if he kept his own identity a secret. That's why he claimed he didn't know Jesus; that's why he lied; that's why he sinned. He did it because he was desperate, and he couldn't come up with any other plan to save the man he cared so much about."

Still confused, I touched Chris's hand and squeezed until he looked at me. "But baby, what does that have to do with you?"

Chris looked at me and blinked as though he was seeing me for the first time. He leaned forward and kissed my lips, gently; then, he reached over and ruffled Christopher's hair before giving both of us a hint of a smile. "I'm doing what I have to do because I have no other choice. My back is against the wall, and I'm doing what I think is the right thing to do—even though I don't want to do it."

He might as well have been speaking a foreign language to me. The more he talked, the more confused I became. "So…you don't want to take your job back at TCP Robotics?"

Chris sighed. "Angie, there's a lot of things I don't want to do, but I gotta do it." Unwilling to explain anymore, he delved his fork into his broccoli covered with cheese, then swallowed it down with a sip of sweet tea.

They say that women are complicated, but I beg to differ. Chris is one of the most complicated men I've ever been with. But he loved me and our son dearly, and that was all that mattered. It didn't hurt, either, that he was in the process of getting his job back and would soon be bringing home those hefty paychecks. It was only up from here. With my man back on his feet and God at the forefront steering our marriage, I knew that things could only get better.

"My two men," I said as I put my arm around Christopher and covered Chris's hand with my own. "I love you guys."

I meant that from the bottom of my heart. I didn't know what I'd ever do without them. I prayed I'd never have to find out.

When I looked at Chris, I saw *my* Chris. His eyes were filled with love for me. I had gotten the nerve to tell him about the new job, but I didn't have the heart to tell him about my stint as a stripper. That would hurt him deeply, and I didn't want to do that. He was right; just like Peter sometimes you had to lie to save the things that meant the most to you. Unless the good Lord himself ordered me to confess the truth, I think I'll take that tidbit of information to my grave.

Seventeen

"That was the first time I've ever seen someone lowered into a grave," Fiona said as she worked her way through yet another rack of dresses that displayed price tags equivalent to double his mortgage payment. "Now I didn't cry when he died," she continued, talking excessively with her hands, "because he had a tendency to be a bit rude to me." She dropped her voice to a whisper. "Don't tell anyone this, Solomon, but I was almost relieved when he croaked over. When he fell down the steps, I stood there and stared at him for about ten minutes before I called the EMTs. I wanted to make sure he was dead; I would've hated if the EMTs came and were actually able to revive him. But *shhh*," she whispered, placing a finger against Chris's lips. "Don't tell anyone. His family already thinks I killed him. They don't think he fell down the steps; they actually think I pushed him."

Before he could stop himself, Chris asked, "Well, did you?"

Fiona gave him a grin that made his skin crawl. Then she said in a sing-song voice, "I'll never te-ll."

What have I gotten myself into, Chris wondered as he followed the petite redhead to the next rack of dresses.

This woman was a lunatic. When Dexter had told him that he'd be escorting a "lonely widow" of a man who had passed at age 89, he was expecting some old dried-up coon, late-fifties, early-sixties; a woman covered from head to toe with varicose veins and age spots, maybe even toting around a breathing machine. One thing he was *not* expecting to find was a size 1 redhead, age twenty-three, who had modeled on the covers of

Vogue and *Elle* magazines, and who was now a three-time widow.

Her first husband was seventy-eight when he passed of colon cancer. She was only eighteen when they married, and he left everything to her. Her second husband was eighty when he passed in his sleep. She was twenty when they married, and he too left her everything. And she was married to her last husband for two years when he died from an unfortunate "fall" down the steps which broke his neck. He wondered how many years she'd wait before she remarried again. He also wondered if she wasn't somehow the catalyst behind all three of her husbands' deaths. Chris wished that Melvin was here so that he could formally introduce him to a legit gold-digger.

Finally, Fiona settled on a hunter green, asymmetric and pleated Christian Lacroix dress. She then found a pair of two-thousand dollar nude pumps to match, and paid for her ten thousand dollar purchase with a swipe of her Black Card.

Their limousine awaited them outside, and the chauffeur drove them to the MGM Grand, the five-star luxurious hotel that not only was Fiona staying at, but scheduled to attend a political campaign party for Justin Lewitt, a wealthy man and politician who was trying to win over rich white folks so he could become Nevada's next governor. He was sixty years old, a bit young for Fiona, but she had her eye on him and was determined to make him her next husband. She'd already explained the entire situation to Chris. He would play like he was her beau for one reason only: to make Justin Lewitt jealous. She hoped to make him so jealous in fact that he would come to her hotel room, and Fiona would "kick Chris out" in order for Lewitt to spend the night—which would definitely round up some brownie points in her favor.

As they traveled down the busy freeway, Chris leaned his head against the window and stared up at the many skyscrapers. He felt bad about lying to Angelique once again about his whereabouts. But she wouldn't understand that he had to come to Vegas to escort these women in order to conclude a contract. So instead, he had lied and told her that Melvin had requested to be sent to northern Texas to his mother's house—who was a RN— because he was tired of living in the nursing facility. Now, this wasn't a complete lie. Melvin's mother, Ms. Eloise, had already signed the paperwork to have her son released to her…but that wasn't taking place until next week. However, Chris had lied to his wife and told her that he'd be staying up there for a while with Melvin because his best friend needed him by his side. Thankfully, Angelique had bought the lie with no questions asked. And thankfully, Chris's mom had offered to act as a live-in babysitter for Christopher until he returned.

His mother knew the truth. He had tried to tell her the same lie, but his mother hadn't bought it for a second. She knew her son was lying before he could finish his sentence good.

"Christopher Quinton Hines, don't you sit up here and tell that bold-faced lie to your momma," she had reprimanded him with a frown. "What you going up to Las Vegas for? To be with some woman? And tell me the truth because I'll beat you backwards if you tell me another lie."

Knowing his mother wasn't joking Chris had given in and told her the whole truth, starting from the very beginning.

His mother's response had been one of compassion but tough love. "Chris, you know I didn't raise you like that."

"I know, Mama, but—"

"I raised you to be a man of integrity and honesty." He had dropped his head as he listened to his mother correct him with love. "When you met that girl and said you wanted to marry her, I told you that you needed to wait. I told you that good things come to those who wait. But you were hardheaded, have always been hardheaded and stubborn. And proud! Just like your daddy. So proud and stubborn—"

"Mama, don't compare me to that man. I'm nothing like my father."

"Hmm. That's what you think."

Before he could say anything, his mother held up a weathered hand to stop him. "Your father made a lot of mistakes in his life. But his biggest mistake was trying to change himself for other people. He tried to change himself for me, but it didn't work out. He tried to change himself for all those other women he was messing around with, but none of that ever worked out for him either. He spent his whole life trying to conform to others instead of being true to what was right here…" She placed her hand over her son's heart and looked him square in the eyes. "And in the end, he went crazy trying to please people. There are dire consequences to pay when you aren't true to yourself…"

Her words carried weight.

She looked at Chris and shook her head. "Life is too short to allow people and situations to turn you into something you aren't. You've never been money hungry; that's not how I raised you or your sisters. And look what you 'bout to go to Vegas to do, all in the name of the mighty dollar."

Chris tried to speak, but again his mother held up her hand.

"People got it all wrong, son. Money isn't the root to all evil. It's the love of money that's sending people to hell by the dozens. Don't be in that number, son. Be true to yourself. Follow your heart. 'Cause when you do, you ain't always gonna get it right, but you won't never get it wrong."

"Are you asleep?" Fiona's nasal voice asked before her blood red nails wrapped around his bicep and gave it a shake. "Ooh!" she commented. "Your arms are so big and solid and hard. You make sure you wrap those arms around me a lot at the party, okay? Wrap them right around my waist, and look at Justin Lewitt when you do it. Kind of tease him with your eyes a little bit. You remember the picture I showed you of him, right?"

Chris nodded and fought back a yawn as they pulled into the hotel parking lot and drove to the valet section.

"Good. And just in case you don't remember, as soon as we get into the banquet hall, I'll point him out. You can't miss him. He's got a face as big as a pie and a great big parrot nose." She shuddered and shook her head, then sighed. "Golly, Solomon. If only these older men could be as sexy as you are. Or, on the other hand, if only you younger men could be as rich as these older men. That would make my job *so* much easier."

The limousine came to a stop and the chauffeur hurried out to open Fiona's door. She stuffed the two shopping bags into Chris's lap, then stepped out the vehicle as though she was a celebrity giving the paparazzi time enough to snap a whole photo album of pictures.

Chris exited the backseat, then followed her to the room. She showered first, and he helped her into the Christian Lacroix dress, zipping the back for her. He showered next and put on the white Armani tailored suit that she'd purchased for him.

With his arm circled through hers, they made their way to the elevator and pressed the button that would take them to the first floor where the banquet hall was located. The elevator came to a stop on the third floor, and when the doors opened, Chris literally stopped breathing. His eyes bounced from Raleigh to Raja, from Raja to Raleigh. All three of them wore similarly stunned expressions. Try as he might, Chris couldn't pull his eyes away from Raleigh, even as the elevator attempted to close at least three times.

Raja was the first to recover and grabbed her sister's arm as she pulled Raleigh into the elevator. Sensing that something was amidst, Fiona dug her claws into Chris's arm and said under her breath without moving her lips, "What in hell's fire is going on?"

Never the one to miss a thing, Raja kept her eyes on Chris as she said smugly, "I'm wondering the same exact thing. Raleigh, you told us that Chris moved to Texas. So what is he doing right here in Vegas in the same elevator with us?" Raja rolled her eyes and then added, "I get it now. He left you for a white woman."

Raleigh's mouth opened and closed, gaping like a fish out of water.

"Who is Chris?" Fiona snapped. "Is she talking about you? 'Cause if you're talking about him, his name isn't Chris; it's Solomon." She frowned. "Or is that your escort name?"

"Escort name?" Raja exclaimed.

Suddenly, it had gotten hellishly hot in the enclosed elevator, and he wondered what was taking the stupid machine so long to drop from one floor to the next.

"So you mean to tell me," Raja continued without missing a beat, "that my baby sister was so desperate not to attend Rashida's wedding alone that she hired an escort? How much did she pay you, Solomon? Or Chris? Or whatever the hell your name is? And did her package deal include a night of crazy sex, or did she have to pay extra for that?"

"It's none of your damn business what she paid for him," Fiona tartly replied. "What does it have to do with you anyway?"

"Woman, I wasn't talking to you," Raja snapped with plenty of attitude.

"Well, dammit to hell, I'm talking to you! And my name is not 'woman,' it's Fiona."

"I don't care if your name is Fajita. I wasn't talking to your ass, so why are you all up in my con—"

Much to Chris's relief, the elevator dinged and finally opened. Chris had to literally tug Fiona out of the elevator. He was upset to see Raja step off the elevator as well. "I *know* y'all ain't going to Justin Lewitt's party. That's where *I'm* headed."

"Oh Lord, grant me serenity," Chris whispered as his eyes darted up to the ceiling.

While Raja and Fiona walked and fussed, distracted by each other, Chris stuck his foot in the elevator before the doors could close. He slipped Raleigh one of his escorting business cards. "Call me. Please."

"Hello? Excuse me? Date? Where are you? You're gonna make us late for the party."

Chris stared at Raleigh until the elevator doors came together, then he hurried over to Fiona. As she grabbed his arm and pulled him toward the banquet hall, Chris couldn't stop thinking about how gorgeous Raleigh looked. He had barely recognized her on first glance without a stitch of makeup and her all-natural hair, thick and kinky, pushed back from her face, showing off her high cheekbones, full lips, and chinky eyes. But what had touched him the most was the fact that the yellow earrings he bought her were hanging from her ears, accentuating the delicate curve of her neck. Never in his life had he prayed so hard that a woman would actually use the number he'd given her.

He tucked his cell phone in his waistband and waited for the phone to ring and vibrate with her voice on the other end.

Eighteen

When I heard the three light knocks at the door, I sent Christopher upstairs to his room and took the four partially frozen margaritas out the freezer. Tori had told me she wouldn't be able to come over until seven for girl talk, but it was only a few minutes past six.

"I know, I'm early," Tori said as I opened the door for her. "I got bored sitting at the house. So, what's the latest on the marriage horizon?" She flung her oversized purse on the love seat and settled onto the couch.

I set our strawberry drinks on coasters and took a seat next to her. "After some serious prayer and soul searching, I made a decision." I sighed. "I made a list of the pros and cons of being married to Chris. Our financial struggles was the biggest con, but we're coming out of that," I said with confidence as I thought about the TCP job that I was certain Chris would accept. I leaned forward and sipped my drink then I straightened back up. "There's so much that I love about Chris." I reflected for a moment. "I love the way he rubs my feet whenever we watch TV together, or the way he plans romantic evenings for us, or the way he makes me feel like his girl and his woman at the same time."

Tori smiled at me. "You love his dirty drawers," she joked.

"Something like that," I admitted, taking another sip.

"I think you're doing the right thing." She grabbed her glass and took a large gulp. "Like I said before, nobody's perfect. You don't have any solid evidence that he cheated, but even if you did, sometimes sex is just sex. Chris's heart and soul belongs to you. He comes home to you every night, and he shows you the utmost respect. Plus, he's an exceptional father. He's the complete package, and as close to perfect as you're going to get."

Although I didn't necessarily need her assurances, hearing her say such glowing things about Chris affirmed what I already knew. He's The One, and the love we share only comes along once in a lifetime. Getting rid of Chris would be like discarding a Bentley just because it had a scratch.

I smoothed a strand of hair behind my ear. "You're never going to believe what El told me."

"Your brother?" She sounded surprised.

I licked some salt around the rim of my glass and took another sip. "Yes. He told me that my mother, of all people, has moved to San Antonio, Texas."

Her jaw dropped. "Shut the front door!"

"*Sí, yo sé, pero hay más.*" My Spanish sometimes slipped out when I was talking to Tori. "Peep this…she's into politics and married to some big wig oil tycoon."

"Well, dayum." She smirked. "Has she tried to contact you?"

I gave her a look like, "Are you kidding me?"

"Dumb question." She licked the remnants of her empty glass before setting it down. Then she looked me in the eyes. "Do you think you and Ms. Yvonne will ever have a normal mother-daughter relationship?"

I had to think about that for a moment. What was normal? Most of the women I knew had decent relationships with their mothers, but all of them complained about their mothers. Either their mothers were too controlling, too overbearing, too needy, or just plain got on their nerves.

Even though Tori and her mom have a close knit relationship, Tori doesn't confide in her mom about everything, and if her mom hangs around too long, she gets on Tori's nerves. So, I have concluded that just like beauty, normalcy is in the eye of the beholder. Normal is whatever works for the people involved. Dysfunction can be normal, if that's all someone knows.

But I had to admit, Chris's relationship with his mother made me jealous; not because she treated him like a "mama's boy"—which, thankfully, she did not. But it made me jealous because they were so tight. He could talk to his mom about anything. And she respected me. Every time I came home to get Christopher, she politely asked about my day before making her departure. It was bittersweet. Sweet because even though she didn't like me, she still treated me kind. And bitter because I wish my biological mother could do the same. If she'd only treat me like I actually exist, at least that would be a start.

"I wouldn't mind having a relationship with her," I finally said. "Maybe she'd be a good grandmother since Christopher is a boy instead of a girl." I paused, feeling a tinge of hurt.

"What does Chris have to say about the situation?"

"He knows about it, but he isn't aware of the severity of it." Chris had never met my mother, or so much as talked to her on the phone. This first time he was going to meet her would've been at our wedding, but Yvonne didn't feel the need to show up. I had told him how things were when I was coming up and why my mother and I didn't have a relationship. He respected my decision and didn't press the issue.

"I'm about to give you my honest opinion, but don't snap on me." Tori held up her hand. "I think if you truly want a relationship with your mother, then you need to be the bigger person and make the first step. Reach out to her."

"Be the bigger person? Reach out to her?" I shook my head. "I already have. Plenty of times. And every time, she turned me down."

"She's *your* mom. The only one you've got, and the only one you'll ever have." She reached for my hand and held it. "There's no harm in trying again."

I started crying and that angered me. Not because I was crying, but because I cared so much about a woman who didn't give a flyin' fruit cake about me.

"Your mom has issues," Tori said. "All moms do. But there's got to be a reason why she's treating you like this. Have you ever thought that maybe it's because you're younger and prettier than she is?"

I turned my face away from her. I felt embarrassed and

ashamed. The fact that my mother could be so superficial and shallow was an embarrassment to me. Yet, a small part of me blamed myself. She loved her boys, but despised me. I often wondered why my mom couldn't accept me for who I was. I had no more control over my gender than I did my genetics. Growing up, I often overheard neighbors down-talking my mother for how she treated me. The thought that the woman who helped create me could ever be jealous of her own flesh and blood, seemed asinine to me.

"Maybe being in a house full of men made your mom feel like a queen. Then you came along and took some of her shine. Not to mention your daddy's heart." She paused. "Didn't you once tell me that your parents hadn't planned on having any more kids after your brother El?"

I wiped my wet face with my hand and nodded in agreement.

"I'm sure that was hard on her." She patted my hand. "You never know what insecurities she may have felt. You know your mom has always been a head-turning, beauty pageant winning type of woman."

I sniffed and looked at her. I hadn't realized it before, but I had hardened my heart toward my mother. Perhaps as a defense mechanism, like self-preservation. For the first time, though, I felt the ice melting. I wanted, no, I needed to talk to my mother. I had to find out why she was the way she was. Why had she emotionally abandoned me? I needed answers, and only one person could answer my questions.

After Tori left, Christopher and I went for an evening walk around the neighborhood. There was a beautiful nature trail that meandered around the expanse of the lake; streetlights and solar-powered lights lined the trail, so no matter the time of day or night, we could walk the entire trail without fear of falling into the water or having a water snake slither past our feet.

I remembered when we first moved out here. Chris and I used to walk this trail all the time, hand in hand, talking about nothing and everything. I remember once, we'd even had sex on the nature trail up against a tree with low hanging branches that shielded us from any possible onlookers. If I wasn't mistaken, that was the night I conceived Christopher Jr.—and wow, was it an explosive conception.

"Mama, I'm getting sleepy," my son said as he stumbled over his feet, nearly losing his balance.

"Well, let's go inside. It is starting to get dark," I said, and held Christopher's hand tightly as we made our way back to the house.

Instead of making him take a bath, I let him take a two-minute shower, put him in his jammies, and read him a night story that I'd read so many times, I could've recited it by heart. Before I got half way through the book, he was already fast asleep.

Gently closing his door, I went over to my bedroom and called Chris to ask him how everything was going. There was some weird music playing in the background; classical, symphony music.

"Melvin's mom got a thing about classical music," he explained, sounding almost like he was whispering. "She says it helps soothe Mel's nerves."

"Why are you whispering?" I asked, whispering myself.

"I'm not whispering I'm just...okay, I am whispering," he said with a laugh. "Mel's right beside me sleep, and I don't want to wake him up. How's little man doing?"

"He's fine. I just put him in bed."

"How're you doing?"

I sighed and looked at my journal as well as the fountain pen setting atop my journal. "I'm about to do something that I think I should've done a long time ago."

"What's that?"

"Write my mother a letter."

"Oh."

It wasn't a nonchalant "oh," but one of those kinds of "ohs" that sounds like someone knocked it out your chest. Chris didn't know the whole situation with my mother and me, but he knew enough about it to know that I despised her and the feeling was mutual. So for me to actually reach out to my mother, it was a serious quantum leap for me.

"Let me know how it goes for you, okay? And if you need me, call me."

"Thanks, Chris. Love you."

I noticed that he didn't say "I love you" back, but I didn't trip. Sometimes whenever he rushed off the phone, he'd hang up before I even got the words out good. So I didn't take it to heart. Instead, I lay across the bed and opened my journal to a blank page. After much deliberation, I finally decided to send my mother a one-line letter. It read:

Dear Mama,
What did I ever do to you to make you hate me so much?
Your daughter,
Angie

Nineteen

For Raja, the political campaign party was a flop. She had obviously come to the hotel to vie for Lewitt's attention as well, but Lewitt hadn't spared two glances her way. For Fiona, the political campaign party was a complete success. Like a puppet being pulled by imaginary strings, Chris did everything she asked of him. He either kept his arms around her waist or his hand pressed into the small of her back. It didn't take a genius to notice that her plan was working flawlessly. The politician, Justin Lewitt, couldn't keep his eyes off the stunning redhead. But even as Chris played his role and pretended to be engrossed in the dull conversation, he could not keep his mind off of Raleigh and could not stop checking his cell phone every few minutes or so to see if she'd called.

The night ended just as Fiona had hoped. Around two o'clock that morning, parrot-nosed Lewitt came knocking at her hotel door. She had stayed up all night waiting on that knock, and when she finally heard it she had nearly pinched Chris to bits while she whispered in his ear, "It worked! My plan worked!"

Dressed in a translucent night gown, she had stepped outside to speak with Lewitt, and minutes later, she returned to the room and said in a very firm voice, "Solomon, it's been great, but I can't do this anymore. My heart belongs to another. You have to go."

They had rehearsed this scene to the point that it was a memorized script in Chris's mind. He pretended to be crushed by the breakup and begged Fiona not to do this to him. Of course, she remained resolute in her decision, and looking like a sad puppy,

Chris gathered his things from the floor and walked out the hotel room with his head held low.

Lewitt wasted no time rushing into the room and quickly closing the door behind him. Chris couldn't help but wonder how long it'd take until wedding bells were ringing, and how long Lewitt would last before Fiona became a four-time widow and beneficiary.

Relieved that he'd completed his second escort assignment, Chris dressed himself in the men's bathroom, then checked out of the hotel. As tired as he was, there was no way that he'd spend the night in that expensive hotel. He left the hotel walking and caught a taxi to the three-star hotel he'd spotted earlier during the limousine ride.

Chris wanted to go home, but he knew it was pointless. His two-day escort meeting with Mrs. Whitmeyer was only seventy-two hours away, so there was no point in traveling home, then having to come up with another excuse to leave again. Angelique might have bought his lie the first time, but she wasn't a fool. Women's intuition would eventually rat him out.

By the time he slid his card to open his room door, his eyes were so tired they felt as though someone had filled each eyelid with sand. Fully clothed, he fell into bed and slept until late the next afternoon.

When he finally did awake, he called his mom to check on Christopher. She assured him that his son was doing fine. He talked to Junior for a little while, then ended the call. In the bathroom, he undressed down to his avocado-green boxers—a color that Angelique absolutely abhorred—and turned the shower on full blast, then waited for the water to heat up. The shower was so loud that he didn't hear his phone ring, but he saw the red light flashing. The word 'Restricted' flashed across the screen. Chris didn't usually answer restricted calls, but part of him hoped that it was her voice on the other end. Tentatively, he answered the call with a curious, "Hello?"

"So I hear you're quitting on me."

The mellow-smooth voice was all too familiar. Chris had been expecting this call eventually, but he'd made up his mind that no matter how much Mrs. Whitmeyer tried to talk him out of it, his decision was non-negotiable.

"Good morning, Mrs. Whitmeyer. How have you been?"

"It's not morning, baby. It's afternoon."

He glanced at his watch and noted that she was right. It was a few minutes past three. He wondered how he had managed to sleep for so long. "Guess I had a long night," he explained.

"Mmm, Chris. You have a very provocative, very seductive over-the-phone voice. Have you ever considered being a phone sex operator? Because I can make it happen for you; just say the word."

"Thank you, but no thank you. After our..." he tried to find a better word, then finally said, "...after our *date*, I'm finished with the sex industry. This is not my forté."

"Oh, but it could be. You get such rave reviews and—"

"Mrs. Whitmeyer," Chris said, standing to his feet and stretching his hands above his head as he let out a loud yawn, "I'd rather not have this discussion with you. My decision is final, and there's nothing you can say or do to change my mind."

She pouted into the phone. "Too bad." Then on a different note, she added, "Make sure you rest up for Friday. I promise you'll need every ounce of your strength to maintain endurance and stamina. I have the energy of a twenty-year-old."

Chris frowned at the phone. "What do you have planned? An aerobics class? A cardio workout?"

A smoker's laugh filled his ears. "You can call it that, sweetheart."

Catching her gist, he said, "You have the wrong idea about me, Mrs. Whitmeyer. Like I told you from day one, I'm a married man and I don't intend to sleep with any of my clients. I haven't slept with one yet, and I don't plan to start with you."

Again, she purred into the phone. "I like a man who *thinks* he's in control. But know this, Mr. Hines." Her voice changed, took on an edge that held a bit of a threat. "I'm the head bitch in charge, and I'm the one who's steering this ship. You're nothing more to me than a pawn on my chessboard."

"Must be a mighty expensive pawn piece, being that you

dropped twenty-thou to spend two days with me."

"Believe me, baby, I'm getting every penny's worth."

"Great. That means that after Saturday, it'll be checkmate for me."

She chuckled, unperturbed by his smart-alecky remark. "You don't realize the truth of those words. I have you in check, Mr. Hines. Move your king around to your heart's desire, but eventually you'll find out that no matter what square you move to, I got you trapped. I'm cornering you, sweetheart. And I always win. Always. Cliché as it may sound, I have eyes in the back of my head, baby, and you never know exactly who is on my side of the chessboard."

Something about the tone of her voice, the way her words slithered from her mouth like drips of venom, made Chris feel as though he was on the phone conversing with the devil. His skin tingled and a cold feeling settled in the bottom of his stomach.

"You enjoy the rest of your day, Mrs. Whitmeyer. I'll see you Friday at 12 at the Trump Hotel."

"I look forward to it," she said, sounding like she genuinely meant every word. "And Mr. Hines, for the record, I'm a 'briefs' kind of woman, not boxers. But if you do choose to wear boxers, please don't wear such a hideous shade of green. It's very unbecoming on you." She smacked a kiss into the phone before ending the call.

As though the phone was a heated coal, Chris dropped it and shook his hand like it had burnt him. Immediately, his eyes looked down at his avocado-green boxers, then flicked over to the half-parted drapes. He hurried across the room and glared out at all the skyscraper buildings, as though he'd actually be able to see Mrs. Whitmeyer's face pressed against a glass window somewhere in the distance. With his skin still crawling, he yanked the drapes closed, then returned to the bathroom.

The rushing stream of the hot shower massaged some of the tension out of his shoulders, but it didn't help with the tension that had built up within him. She was watching him, spying on him. The thought creeped him out, made him feel itchy all over. And her word choice on the phone—the entire chess analogy. Checkmate, cornering him, trapping him. For the umpteenth time, he hit himself in the forehead and wondered what kind of a mess had he gotten himself into. Mrs. Whitmeyer wasn't the kind of woman one crossed for any reason. She possessed the deadly trio combo: she was spoiled, she was rich, and she was ugly—not on the outside. She'd paid enough money to make her outside look impeccable. But her insides? Rotten, decaying, putrid, corrupt. The offensive odors should have been enough of a warning sign to make Chris lace his running shoes and haul ass. But just like she'd said, he was trapped. Bound by contract.

The only plan Chris could come up with was to meet with her Friday and Saturday, be the perfect gentleman, then walk out of the Trump Hotel and shred his contract to bits, throwing the pieces to the wind. Comforted by this sound disposition, Chris lathered his body with soap and washed every bit of worry and stress down the drain. He stepped out of the shower feeling renewed and refreshed and ready for whatever life had to throw at him.

Twenty

Chris had no idea what he was going to do to kill time for today and tomorrow. It was times like these that he wished Melvin hadn't had his stroke. Melvin wouldn't hesitate to jump on a plane—only if Chris was paying—and fly straight to Vegas to kick it with him.

As he dressed himself in a black tee and a pair of fitted jeans, he couldn't help reflecting on his friend. It broke his heart to see Melvin so emaciated. God, what he'd give to hear his friend tell one more stale joke or let out one more of those belly-wrenching laughs. He thanked God for Stephanie. She was the definition of a real woman. Ever since Melvin's incident, Stephanie had been there every step of the way. She was at the emergency room, had slept in his hospital room every night, and had visited him in the rehabilitation center every day for hours at a time. Chris could literally see a light turn on in Melvin's eyes every time Stephanie came into the room. He didn't care if Stephanie and Melvin had been talking for a few weeks or a few years—he knew true love when he saw it, and what they had was legit.

With Melvin weighing heavy on his heart, Chris called his room to check on him and smiled when he heard his friend's voice. It was difficult to understand Melvin's speech, but he caught the gist of what his friend was saying.

"Stephanie said," Melvin breathed into the phone, "that yo' ass still out there being a ho."

Chris laughed, glad to hear Melvin in such high spirits in spite of. "I'm finishing up some unfinished business, that's all."

"You be careful out there," Melvin said on a more serious note.

"Nah, don't worry about me. I'ma be fine. You just take care of yourself. How're they treating you at the center?"

"Keep stuffing me with that hard ass orange Jell-o. Man, I thought Jell-o was supposed to be soft. Then they got this new nurse. He a dude. You ever seen a dude-nurse before? This some ol' homo shit right there."

Chris rolled his eyes. "Melvin, it's nothing gay about a man being a nurse."

"At least they should call them something else. Maybe they should call women nurses, and call men helpers. Real talk, Chris, would you rather be a nurse or a helper?"

"Melvin, eat your Jell-o and take your ass back to sleep."

Melvin laughed in the phone, then stopped because his throat filled with mucus. Once he cleared his throat, he said, "Chris, I love you. It might sound homo, but I don't give a damn. If you wouldn't have been out there that day, I would've died, man. You know that, right?"

Choked up, Chris couldn't say a word. Melvin had it all wrong. If he wouldn't have been out there that day, jumping down his friend's throat to start with, it would have never happened.

"Stephanie told me that you blaming yourself. Stop that bullshit, my dude. I did this to myself. You ain't stuff food down my throat and shovel plaque around my heart. You ain't do that to me. I did. With my sorry eating habits. So don't beat yourself up, man. You my angel. Don't worry, angels are unisex, okay? Ain't nothing homo about being an angel."

Chris blinked repeatedly to keep the tears in his eyes.

"A'ight, man. I'm 'bout to get off this phone, get me some rest before my booboo come. You be easy, bro. Take care of yourself. Remember what I said."

"All right, Mel. Talk to you later."

Once he ended the call, Chris lifted his eyes toward the ceiling and mouthed the words "Thank you" to God. He needed that conversation. Knowing that Melvin didn't harbor any ill-will toward him gave him a measure of peace and he felt as though an elephant had stepped off his shoulders.

He reclined on the bed and flipped through the channels,

but nothing interested him. Actually, the only thing the TV succeeded in doing was putting him back to sleep. With a much lighter conscience, he slept without tossing or turning.

***

The next day was another boring day that he spent primarily in his room. The first thing he did when he awoke was check his phone to see if Raleigh had called. No missed calls, no text messages. He spent the whole day in bed, flipping through the channels or surfing the complimentary Internet. Every half hour or so, he'd check his phone to see if Raleigh had called. Nothing. Still no missed calls or texts from her. His wife had called quite a few times and he called her back. She was in bed, but found enough energy to wake up for a few minutes and tell him about her day. They ended the call by telling each other, "I love you," but Chris felt like a hypocrite because he was still wondering why Raleigh hadn't called. Had she lost the card? Misplaced it?

Before he knew it, night had fallen again. He hadn't eaten or drunken a thing, so he finally decided to order room service—a Mexican burrito and black beans and rice. While he ate, he sulked. To be honest, he thought she would've called by now. But obviously, seeing him in the elevator with another woman had been enough to dissuade her from reaching out to him. A thousand times he had replayed that incident in the elevator, wishing it could have played out differently. What he would've given to have been in that elevator *alone*; and to have had those doors open with the stunning and all-natural Raleigh walking in *alone*.

But then he realized that everything happens for a reason. Because God knows that the way he was feeling, if Raleigh and he would've found themselves in that elevator alone, the gentleman within him would've melted away and he would've had Raleigh all up against that elevator wall. Kissing her luscious lips, sucking on her tongue, relearning the curves of her hips, her butt, her thighs, feeling himself completely implanted deep within her, hearing her soft voice crooning his name…

Groaning, Chris took a pillow and jammed it against his rock hard penis. What was wrong with him? Here he was, trying to quit the sex industry so that he could make things right with his wife. But another part of him wanted to—no, not wanted to. *Yearned to.* Another part of him yearned to explore the possibilities with this one individual who had intrigued him so much that he couldn't get her out of his mind. His nose remembered her scent; his hands had recorded the soft, silky texture of her skin. Like a strong, penetrable fragrance, her presence had washed over him and he felt like he was drowning in it. He had never felt this way about a woman before. Never. Not with his first love, not with any of the women he'd had sex with in his prime, not with his wife. He didn't understand why he was feeling so intensely about Raleigh.

"I know what it is," Chris said to no one in particular. "It's sex. It's a sex thing. I'm feening for her because I never got to finish what we started that night. But if I have sex with her, finish what we started, then I can get her out of my system."

Convinced that that was the solution to his problem, Chris walked out onto the balcony and sat in the metal lawn chair, breathing in the dry and warm night air. Night blanketed itself around him, making him feel better protected from spying eyes, or binoculars, or whatever Mrs. Whitmeyer was using to look at him.

On the balcony, cocooned in darkness, he stared down at the cars whizzing by below in whorls of color. Off in the distance, he heard music, laughter, horns honking. From where he sat on the fifth floor, the night was calm, serene. But five floors below, the night was alive and moving, even for a Wednesday night.

Chris thought about the business trips he'd taken to New York City when he was working for TCP Robotics. They called New York City the "city that never sleeps," but that wasn't true. Once night fell, businesses started closing down in New York City. But here in Vegas, it didn't matter the day nor the time, the night was always alive, the streets always breathing.

This was a place that he could see himself moving to. But if he took the job offer at TCP Robotics, if he went back to doing the same old engineering of advanced computer sensor software, integrating systems and inventing new patent-pending chips…then he could kiss Vegas goodbye. Working at TCP was a fifty-hour-a-week job. When he'd worked there, he had hardly slept, hardly spent time with Angelique except when they were getting sweaty under the sheets, and hardly even seen his son but to cook him breakfast and say "Good morning" and tuck him in and say "Good night."

That was one thing he didn't miss about his old job. Being able to spend so much time with his son was priceless. But Chris had to be realistic. The world revolved around money. What was he going to do in Vegas? Move out here and escort some more? Or maybe he should take Mrs. Whitmeyer up on her phone-sex operator job. It was expensive to live in Vegas, and he knew Angelique would not be willing to uproot from her job and relocate on a whim.

Chris sat on the balcony and watched the streets for about two hours, then he returned to his room. Try as he might, he couldn't sleep. He'd seen a vending machine at the end of the hallway that sold a variety of different medications—pain medication, headache pills, fever reducer, laxatives, antacids. He wasn't sure if they sold sleeping pills or not, but he was about to find out.

Slipping into his bedroom shoes, Chris shuffled down the red carpeted hallway, passing a closed door where somebody was definitely getting it in. The man was grunting like he was riding a bull, and the woman was faking, making tiny noises while she assured him that, "His was the best," and that he was "tearing her punany up." Chris twisted his lips to the side and rolled his eyes. He'd watched enough porn to know what counterfeit sex sounded like. But hey, at least someone was getting some loving on the hallway. More power to them.

The vending machine sold every kind of medicine under the sun...except for sleep medication. Unwilling to return to his room empty handed, Chris settled on nighttime Nyquil capsules. He bought two packs, which equaled four pills, and took all four at once. Then he shuffled back to his room.

He was almost to his door when he heard a man behind him aggressively say, "...waste of my damn time. To hell with you and your drawings too. I'm not buying a damn thing from you, you washed-up tease!"

Curious, Chris turned his head slightly and noticed that

the man had on nothing but his boxers and socks. The rest of his clothes were jumbled in his hands, and he had fresh scratch marks—more like gouges—across his face and chest. Again, Chris shrugged and kept walking. Some people were in to kinky sex; Chris didn't knock them. Whatever floated their boat.

That's what he was thinking until he heard Raleigh's voice say, "I'm sorry you got the wrong impression. I never intended to sleep with you—"

Chris's neck nearly broke from whipping his head around so fast. There was Raleigh, dressed in business attire—a navy blue pant suit. But her black blouse was badly ripped, her breasts hanging out of the shirt, and her feet were bare. Chris didn't think, simply reacted.

"I think it's time for you to go," he said, stepping to the half-dressed man's face. The guy was much shorter than him, but very stout and muscular. He had a tarnished gold tooth that looked more green than gold right at the front of his mouth, and a nasty scar beside his right eye, like someone had tried unsuccessfully to gouge it from its socket. Even though the man was stocky and a bit intimidating, Chris knew that if it came to blows, the man would put up a good fight—but he'd still get that ass beat.

"And who the hell are you?" the man growled, his tarnished gold tooth gleaming dully.

Chris's fist had a mind of its own. It pulled back and gave an uppercut to the man's jaw with such force that it literally lifted him off the floor. He soared for only a brief second before falling to the floor like a bowling pin that had been knocked over. Raleigh stared up at Chris, wide eyed and speechless, her hand covering her mouth.

"Did you kill him?" she finally whispered.

"Did he hurt you?" Chris asked, looking at the blood lining a scratch across her chest.

Her shaky fingers pulled her hair behind her ear as she tried to fix her blouse to look even moderately presentable. "He tried, but I…you didn't kill him did you? He's not moving, Chris."

"That bastard ain't dead. He might be sleep for a while, but he ain't dead. You want me to call the cops? You want to press charges?"

"No," she said, shaking her head and hugging herself gently. "I just want to wake up and this all be a horrible dream."

"Come on," Chris said, motioning for her to follow him. "I'm not letting you spend the night by yourself."

She seemed hesitant. "Chris..."

"I'm not going to touch you." He held up his hands. "I swear it to you. You sleep in the bed; I'll sleep in the chair. I just want to make sure you're okay. That man looks like a criminal; a dressed up thug. And I don't trust him at all."

She looked down at the man whose only movement was a slight rise and fall of his chest cavity. "We're just going to leave him there like that?"

"Absolutely."

Raleigh only hesitated for another second, then she said, "Okay, give me a sec. Let me grab something." She went in the room, then returned with a leather-bound case that was about the length and width of an average-sized window. Then she followed Chris into his hotel room and wasted no time crawling beneath the covers.

A smile lifted the corner of her lips as soon as her head touched the pillows. With her eyes closed, she said sleepily, "These covers smell just like you."

Working his knuckles, Chris pulled the chair near the bed and turned it to face the door. He was still heated about the encounter with the mystery man and actually hoped that the man would awake and come to even the playing field so he could knock his ass out again. It felt good feeling his fist crack against that man's jaw.

"It's so crazy how we keep running into each other," she said through a yawn.

"So who was he?" Chris asked as he watched Raleigh pull the covers up to her chin.

Her voice was heavy as she talked around the sleep threatening to take her over. "Who was she?"

"She?"

"The redheaded woman in the elevator."

So that's why she hadn't called. Because of Fiona. He wondered if he detected a hint of jealousy in her voice. "She's nobody to me. Just a woman that I escorted."

She turned in the bed so that he was facing her back. "You sleep with her?"

Yeah, he knew jealousy when he heard it. For some reason, he found her jealousy endearing. "Look at me, Leigh."

She turned around and her chinky brown eyes sleepily trailed over to him.

"No, I didn't sleep with Fiona. Had no desire whatsoever to sleep with her." From the look in her eyes, he could tell that she believed him. Then he asked, "What about old dude out there sleeping. Why was he in your room at midnight?"

Her eyes fell closed and a sad expression weighed down the delicate features of her face. "A business transaction gone wrong."

"A business transaction?" Chris frowned, immediately thinking of drugs.

"That's why I was at the hotel that night. Meeting him. He acted like he was interested in buying my work—my collage of graphite sketches. Said he wanted to come over, look at a few more pieces. But the only 'piece' he wanted to look at was a 'piece' of ass."

Again, Chris's fists balled at his sides and he had to mentally command himself to remain in the chair. Every fiber in his body wanted to put on a pair of shoes, go out in the hallway, and kick the shit out of that perverted, would-be rapist. A million *what-ifs* bombarded his mind. What if he had stayed on the balcony for another hour? What if he hadn't went to get that Nyquil? What if he hadn't shuffled his feet, but had walked briskly instead? Raleigh could've been in her room getting raped right this very second. The thought sickened him, made him feel lightheaded, made him feel thankful that he was in the right place at the right time.

"I promise you," he said softly, "that man will never lay his hands on you again."

Before he'd finished making that declaration, her soft snores filled the quiet room. He watched her breasts rise and fall beneath the cover in an even rhythm. For hours, he sat with his feet firmly planted, his eyes riveted on the door, hoping—no, fervently wishing—that the man would get up, come to Chris's room, and try to lay one brown finger on Raleigh. The way he was feeling, by the time Chris finished with him, he'd need a body cast and full facial reconstruction. When he had hit the man, there was a dangerous look in the man's eyes. One Chris didn't fully trust. The man's eyes were like that of a cobra's. He knew that this was the kind of man that you didn't cross. Yet and still, Chris wasn't scared. He was ready for a fight; it had been years since he'd had the opportunity to whoop somebody's ass.

Just as the Nyquil was about to overcome him, he finally heard moaning and groaning from the hallway. Every muscle in Chris's body tensed as he waited to see what the man was going to do. His ears became acute as he listened to every groan and curse that escaped the man's lips. Footsteps approached the door and Chris poised himself in the chair, ready for the worse. The bronze door knob twisted from side to side, the metal latch clicking as the fragile lock struggled to stay in place.

Twenty-One

Thursday morning I woke up feeling excited about my first day as Marketing Director. Chris's mom came by to babysit Christopher, and she helped me pick out a powder blue blouse and gray fitted pant suit. She wanted me to wear a pair of slide-ins, arguing that they looked more professional than my Jimmy Choo pumps—but that was one argument that she was not going to win. I thanked her for watching Christopher, kissed his cheek as he swallowed down a spoonful of the cinnamon raisin oatmeal his grandmother had cooked, and bid them both farewell.

Far from being a morning person, I made the huge sacrifice of selecting 7:00 a.m.-4:00 p.m. as my work schedule. I wanted to make sure that I could still spend some quality time with Christopher every day. Once Chris started his job at TCP again, I knew that I'd need the morning shift. The hours he worked at that place were crazy—but I wouldn't complain. It was a paycheck, and a weighty one at that.

Dexter had instructed me to report to the company headquarters in downtown Dallas instead of the club. When I arrived at ten minutes to seven, feeling antsy with butterflies fully alive in my belly, the water sluicing over the ledges of the expansive Cascadia fountain décor piece situated directly in front of the building immediately put me at ease. The fountain had a calming effect, which was probably what they were going for when they purchased it.

As though it had been extracted from an exquisite painting, the travertine and dark bronze glass building screamed high quality sophistication and a bank-load of money.

I parked my car in the employee parking deck and took the elevator to the main floor. Once inside, I saw a security guard standing in front of the receptionist's desk exchanging playful banter with the middle age receptionist. I greeted them both with a smile and introduced myself as I signed in the visitor's log, since I didn't have my badge yet. Then I took the elevator.

As the conveyor ascended to the twelfth floor, I inhaled deeply and exhaled through parted lips. I didn't know what to expect, but I prayed that it was all good. My nerves were getting the best of me, so when I noticed that I actually had a signal in the elevator, I immediately speed-dialed my husband. He answered the phone sounding like a frog; his voice was heavy, sluggish, and laced with sleep.

"Chris, is everything okay?"

"I'm fine," he croaked into the phone. "Had a long night."

"Really?" My eyebrow lifted. "What happened?"

He mumbled something into the phone that I couldn't decipher, then yawned so hard that it made me want to yawn.

"Baby, today is my first day on my new job, and I can't shake my nerves. I really want to make a lasting first impression."

"You'll do fine. Just be yourself."

His lack of enthusiasm made me grimace. I knew it was early in the morning and that he'd had a long night, but still, it wouldn't have killed him to pretend like he actually cared about what concerned me.

Annoyed and ready to end the call, I said, "I love you, Chris."

"Yeah."

"Yeah?"

"Me too."

Me too? What the hell did he mean by 'me too'?

Before I could say anything else, he ended the call. Hung up in my face. He might as well have slapped me. I was more than perturbed—I was pissed the hell off. He couldn't say "I love you" back? Now, the first time he did that, I let it slide. But twice in a row? This was getting ridiculous and redundant, and my woman's intuition was telling me that I needed to keep my eyes wide open.

The doors opened, and I stepped out the elevator with half the mind to call Chris back and cuss him out. But I was already pressed for time; there was no need for me to be late my first day on account of his stupidity. I stood there for a moment gathering my composure; then I looked to my right and left. A sign that read "Lumpkin Enterprises International" caught my attention, so I headed in that direction.

Refusing to allow my suspicions about Chris to dampen my mood, I pasted a confident smile on my face and entered the varnished hardwood double doors; my heels clanked on the granite floor with each step. Gigantic potted plants, contemporary leather furniture, and expensive art covering the walls decorated the room; this was easily one of the most lavish office suites I'd ever seen.

An Asian lady who looked like a porcelain doll looked up at me from her computer screen. Since she was sitting behind a fancy desk in the reception area, I figured she must've been the receptionist, so I told her who I was. Her face lit up.

"Mr. King told me you'd be coming in today." She pushed her chair back and stood up. Extending her slender hand to me, she said, "I'm Brenda Lee."

I shook her hand and said, "Nice to meet you." I noticed that she sounded Americanized. No distinct accent that would link her to any particular state or country, but she definitely had a strong grasp of the English language. No hesitation in her speech whatsoever.

She released my hand and came from around her desk. She wore a fitted mini-skirt that showed off her toned legs. "Let me show you to your office."

My office. I liked the sound of that. I hadn't realized just how much I missed being in corporate America until she said those words. I trailed her as she led me down a hallway that led to a nice sized office with an impressive view of the city.

"I hope you like the décor," Brenda said. "Mr. King had an interior decorator working all weekend to make it perfect for you."

Warm and fuzzy, that's how I felt. Dexter never ceased to amaze me. The office exceeded my expectations. He remembered that my favorite colors were beige and gold. The combination looked classy and elegant. I felt as though I had arrived yet again.

"Yes, I like it…a lot," I said coolly as I touched the back of the butter soft leather couch.

She smiled her pleasure. "If you want, you can lock your purse in your desk drawer while I give you a tour. The keys are in the middle drawer. You'll get to meet the full staff during the Monday morning meeting."

I removed my cell phone from my purse and did as she requested. She showed me the formal conference room which was used for meetings with clients and making group presentations. The mini conference room was typically reserved for smaller gatherings, including staff meetings. She told me that a full gym was on the first floor. We went into the break room, which had a refrigerator, microwave, vending machines, small tables and chairs, and a pot of coffee brewing. The aroma of the coffee lured me into pouring myself a cup. If I was going to be doing early mornings, caffeine was about to become my new best friend. Brenda fixed herself a cup too.

An attractive blond haired white guy with eyes the color of deep turquoise walked in and introduced himself to me as Jorge Jonsin, the IT Specialist. His eyes seemed hypnotic. I had never dated a white guy before, but if I ever did, I was certain he'd be my type.

Brenda checked her watch and said, "It's 8:00. Time for our meeting."

Jorge and I cut our casual conversation short, and we all went into the mini conference room where ten people were already seated and a handful more scurried in with us. The faces in that room exemplified diversity. I felt like we were a bunch of Skittles—every color of the rainbow. Even still, one thing that stood out to me was that there wasn't a single aesthetically challenged, or in layman's terms, unfortunate looking person in the room. Was Dexter practicing a form of discrimination? He seemed to only have two types of people working for him: attractive and more attractive.

I took a seat around the oval table, and Brenda handed me a blank legal pad and ink pen. I appreciated her efficiency and thanked her. She asked if I needed anything else, and when I replied, "No," she excused herself back to her work station.

Assorted muffins, Danish, and mixed fruit were in the middle of the table, along with two pitchers of ice water, and a pitcher of orange juice. An apple Danish was calling my name, but I had been depriving myself of sweets for so long that it was easy to ignore the calling.

People chatted amongst themselves for a couple of minutes as they prepared their plates and poured drinks. The meeting then officially began. The VP of Operations, Veronica Herrell, introduced me to the group. I gave a brief spiel about my professional background and education. Introductions were made, but there was no way I'd remember nearly twenty names. Times like this, I wish people wore name tags. It would help a lot.

However, I did pay careful attention to the names of the people who would be working directly for me. In fact, I wrote down the names of the fiery redhead Dana Scott, the Nigerian Ibahima Oni, and Canadian Pamela Cooper. Pamela boasted of her Canadian heritage proudly. She wore an imaginary Canadian flag on her chest.

The meeting lasted two hours, and each department head gave a brief overview of what they were currently working on. I took copious notes. Although the meeting flowed well, and the people seemed well prepared, I noticed that they interjected humor whenever possible to keep the mood light. I liked that…not too stuffy. I could tell that I'd fit right in.

At the end of the meeting, everyone welcomed me once more. I engaged in some small talk before retreating to my office. I smiled to myself and thanked God for giving me a way of escape from being an exotic dancer. Just a week ago, I was bouncing my ass for cash in front of rich, stuffy white men. Now, I had my own office and was working among an elite group of professionals. It felt good to put that chapter behind me and focus on my professional aspirations again. I felt good about myself.

A box filled with office supplies sat on my chair, and a laptop sat in the middle of my desk. Since neither were there before I went to the meeting, I figured that Brenda must've placed them there.

After unpacking the box, I started up my computer and waited for it to boot. While waiting, I pulled a few things out of my oversized purse—things of sentimental value that brought a little feeling of "home" into the office. First, I pulled out a family picture that Chris, Christopher, and I took at Disney World two years ago—we all looked crazy eating Mickey Mouse cream-sicles and wearing Mickey Mouse ears. I propped it up on my desk. Then I pulled out Christopher's school picture he took last year when he'd lost one of his front teeth. The huge gap in his mouth really stood out, but it fully captured the essence of childhood and innocence. Lastly, I pulled out a clay teacup that Christopher had made for me in art class for Mother's Day when he was in pre-school. I figured the cup would make an excellent pencil and pen holder.

Just as I sat the cup on my desk, there was a light knock at the door. Straightening my back and squaring my shoulders, I pasted a friendly smile on my face and called out, "Come in."

The last person I expected to saunter through my office door was Dexter. But there he was in the flesh, looking even more handsome than I remembered. His teeth looked sparkly white in his dark face; his tapered mustache sat above that catching smile of his, making him look sexy and hip at the same time. He wore gray dress pants and a light blue collared shirt with a matching tie. It almost looked as though we had purposefully chosen matching outfits for the day.

He stood in the doorway; his arms crossed as he leaned back against the doorframe and just stared at me.

Feeling a bit self-conscious, I nervously ran my fingers through my hair. "What? Do I have something on my face? In my hair?"

"No, no," he said with a chuckle. "You're perfect."

His words made me even more self-conscious, especially since this morning while getting dressed I'd noticed a pimple taking form near my temple. I had tried to cover it by sweeping my hair over the reddening bump, but I still knew it was there. I was far from perfect.

"You just look so beautiful sitting behind your desk like that. As many times as I've seen you nude on stage, I've never seen you look as striking as you look now."

His words made my face glow. "Thank you, Dexter."

He came into the room and took a seat in the metal chair, as though he was my client instead of my boss. Scooting the chair closer to my desk, he leaned his elbows atop the desk and stared into my eyes. His cologne was strong. I smelt it as soon as he had walked through the door, but with him this close, it was even stronger—but not in an overpowering way; it was intoxicating. Like he was using that citrusy sandalwood fragrance to cast a spell on me.

"How's your first day going?" Dexter asked.

Mentally chastising myself to remain professional, I leaned back in the chair. "Fantastic," I beamed. "The people seem cool and my office…" I held up my hands in a sweeping gesture. "It is lovely. Thank you so much."

He smiled his gratitude. "And Brenda's taking care of you, right?"

"She's an angel. She's been on point from the minute I met her." I crossed my legs and noticed Dexter peeking over the desk to watch the movement. A part of me wished I'd worn a skirt suit instead of pants. That way I could have teased him with a flash of thigh. In my book, there was nothing wrong with a little harmless flirting.

"So…what are you having for lunch today?" I asked, figuring that since he'd done so much for me, the least I could do is treat him to a nice lunch and foot the bill.

He looked pleased with my question. "I was thinking dinner."

Normally, this would have posed a problem. Having lunch with your boss was one thing, but having dinner with him would be a bit more difficult to explain. However, Chris had made it easy for me with his trip to Amarillo, Texas. I wouldn't have to come up with a lie or explain a thing. Add that to the fact that his peculiar behavior was really starting to make me wonder about his integrity, I felt no hesitation or reluctance in agreeing to dine with Dexter.

"I'm in," I said, typing a reminder alarm into my phone. "Just tell me the time and the place."

"Tonight at 7:30 at Three Forks Restaurant."

A two-story restaurant, Three Forks Restaurant looked a lot like a late-Medieval castle with its pointed arches, stone pillars, and wide windows. Spanning 25,000 square feet, the place was spacious and exuded pure elegance from the gold embroidered heavy drapes to the French table linens to the handmade Riedel Sommeliers wineglasses. I didn't know what to say—such an upscale place for a business meeting. Then again, I shouldn't have been surprised. Dexter was a big baller, shot caller, through and through. Of course he'd dine only at the finest eating establishments.

He quickly typed something into his iPad, then his eyes dropped down to the teacup that Christopher had made me. "Your son made that for you?"

"Yes," I said, smiling as I held up the cup as though it was a trophy instead of fired clay. I went on to explain to him how and why Christopher had made it.

Then Dexter's eyes moved to the family picture that we'd taken at Disney World. "So this is your family, huh? And this is your lucky husband, or is it one of your brothers?"

"No, that's my husband." Still smiling, but feeling a little uncomfortable talking about my spouse with him, I explained the story behind the picture. The more I talked, the more Dexter scrutinized the picture until he was practically holding the portrait up to his face.

"You're sure that's your husband?" he asked, his eyes still glued to the picture.

"Uhm…yes," I said, dragging out those two words as if I wasn't completely sure.

"Chris Hines?"

Immediately, both my eyebrows shot up on my forehead. I was pretty certain that I had never mentioned my husband's name around Dexter. I had always referred to him as 'my husband.' So it struck me rather odd that he knew Chris's name.

"How do you know my husband's name?" I asked him as

an unsettling feeling washed over me.

Instead of answering my question, he asked questions of his own. "Do you know Giovanni Mercer?"

Even more confused, I shook my head. "Mercer? No, I don't know anybody by that..." I paused a minute, thinking, then said, "I've never heard of Giovanni. But I know a Stephanie Mercer. She's what you could call a mutual friend of my husband and me. Why do you ask?"

His eyebrows pinched together until they nearly formed a line across his forehead. "I don't understand what's going on..."

"Neither do I," I quickly responded. "How do you know my husband?"

He pulled at his chin hair and his frown deepened even more. "And what about...what about Yvonne Whitmeyer? Do you know her?"

When he said my mother's name, my heart skipped a beat. "How do you know my mother?"

The way Dexter reacted one would've thought I had just chanted a death curse on him. His face lost all of its color, looking ashen and gray, and he pushed up out his chair so fast, he made me jump out of my chair as well. His reaction frightened me, and I felt like I was caught in a twilight zone. Nothing made sense. He knew my husband's name, my mother's name—San Antonio, Texas was not one of those tiny country bumpkin towns where everybody knew everybody. I knew this was a small world, but it wasn't *that* small.

"But that doesn't make sense," Dexter whispered under his breath.

"Nothing's making sense right now," I yelled at him, needing him to explain this thing to me because I felt like I was spiraling out of control. "What is going on?"

"I can't..." Dexter shook his head, looking as though he was trying his hardest to figure out the solution to Rubik's cube. "But I can't understand why she'd do something like that."

"Something like what?"

Completely ignoring my question, he pulled at his chin hair and asked, "Does your mother know your husband?"

"Yes—I mean, no. I mean…I don't know." I scratched my head and looked at Dexter with wild eyes. "I mean, she's never met him in person. She didn't come to our wedding. But I'm sure she's seen a picture of him or something."

"Has he ever seen a picture of her?"

I was embarrassed to answer that question. But finally, I admitted, "No. He's never seen her or met her."

Lost in thought, Dexter paced around in circles, then headed for the door. "I'll see you tonight at seven thirty sharp—"

"No, wait!" I exclaimed. "I need some answers."

"So do I."

As much as I begged him to stay, he kept walking, leaving me sitting in my beautiful office with a million ugly thoughts swimming in my head. Something was not right. I kept my personal life personal. Dexter knew more about me than he should have known. Had he been spying on me? Had he sent out a private investigator to probe through my life? But no, that wouldn't make sense. Truth be told, Dexter seemed just as confused as me by the whole situation.

Brenda appeared in the doorway and asked me if everything was okay. I lied and assured her that everything was peachy.

"Well great," she said, shuffling some papers in her hands. "I hope you've had time enough to settle in, because there's more of the building I want to show you and more staff members to meet."

"Oh, okay," I said, trying my best to don a professional demeanor, even though my thoughts were still spiraling in a murky vortex.

While we walked through the building, I noticed that Dexter was still in the vicinity, conversing with some of his employees. When our eyes caught, I noticed that his eyes seemed just as troubled as mine. But we were both good actors and played our professional roles immaculately. Dexter impressed me with the way he treated his executives. He ran a professional organization. Had I not come in on the adult entertainment side, I never would've believed his enterprise had been built on the sex industry.

Brenda walked and talked, telling me that after this walk-through, I'd have to fill out a stack of paperwork for my access badge, gym membership, company credit card, tax elections, and benefits enrollment. She also told me that beginning next week I would begin the hiring process for my personal assistant.

She added, "I would've taken the liberty of hiring one for you, but people can be picky when it comes to someone being so close to them. That type of relationship is based on chemistry even more than skill, so I'll leave that up to you."

I laughed. "Okay, thanks."

I had a full day interacting with the various departments and getting better acquainted with my team. We meshed well together, and they were full of creative ideas. But at the back of my mind, those unanswered questions were still swirling. I was less anxious about dining with Dexter in the luxurious restaurant and more anxious about dining with him to see if he had found the answers to some of my questions.

When I got home, the smell of onions, meatloaf and green beans met me at the door. Chris's mom asked me how my day was, but she took one look at my face and already knew the answer. Thankfully, instead of leaving like she usually did once I came through the door, she took Christopher to the nearby park so that I could have a moment to myself.

Once they returned, she went in the kitchen to make Christopher's plate, and I went upstairs to shower for my date with Dexter.

I didn't want to go too overdressed or too casual, so I chose the attire that I couldn't go wrong with: my little black dress. Form-fitting and cinched on one side with one sleeve off the shoulder, it made me feel sexy and chic at the same time. I pulled on a pair of black heels that strapped around my ankle.

"Angelique, I put your plate in the…" Ms. Hines's words trailed off. She stared me up and down as I descended the stairwell. With one hand on her hip and her head tilted to the side, she said, "And where are you going?"

I almost said I had a date but caught myself in the nick of time. "It's a business meeting."

She didn't seem reassured by my response. "And who's going to stay here with Christopher?"

Sighing, I cursed myself for not asking her to babysit first before assuming that she'd stay. "Please, Ms. Hines. I really need to go to this meeting. There's some very pertinent information that I need to know."

Ms. Hines's only response was to purse her lips and walk away. I felt bad for using her, especially after all she'd done for Christopher and me. But today had caught me off guard; I wasn't expecting a last minute invitation to a five-star restaurant. And I certainly wasn't expecting to find out that not only did my boss know my husband by name, but he knew my mother too.

I kissed Christopher good night and jumped in my convertible, cruising over to Three Forks Restaurant. It wasn't until I was literally two minutes from my destination that Dexter texted me an apology and a solemn vow to reschedule our 'date.' I called him repeatedly, but every call went unanswered.

Twenty-Two

Chris awoke Thursday morning with a hellish headache and a painful crink in his neck from sleeping the whole night in that uncompromising position. Groaning, he pushed out of the chair and shuffled his feet to the bathroom to relieve his bursting bladder. As he pissed, he mentally relived the incident that had occurred only hours ago. When that man had came back to the room, trying to force his way through the door, for the briefest second, Chris had regretted hitting the man. People didn't fight fair anymore these days. As far as he knew, the man could've had a loaded revolver or an automatic on him. Chris knew he could fight a fist, but no one could fight off a bullet. But thank God, the man had given up on trying to barge into the room and had left without any further complications.

Raleigh is lying in my hotel bed.

The thought came to him as though someone had literally whispered it in his ear. He had never been the kind of man who believed in coincidences. Not only had he ran into her at the Trump Hotel, but he ended up as her savior, and was unknowingly staying just five doors down from her hotel room. What were the odds? Confirmation comes in threes, so to him, this was nothing more than confirmation. But confirmation of what?

"Raleigh?" he called her name, but there was no answer. He didn't find that too surprising, being that she'd had a rather trying night. He was certain that she was worn out and would probably sleep until twelve or one.

An idea came to him. He could order room service and serve her breakfast in bed. But he had no idea what she liked to eat. For all he knew, she could be lactose intolerant or a die-hard vegan. To be on the safe side, he decided to order a continental breakfast—muffins, donuts, fresh fruit, milk, and orange juice. Couldn't go wrong with that.

"Raleigh," he called her name again as he exited the bathroom. It was only then that he noticed the bed was empty except for tousled sheets and a folded letter resting atop the pillow.

Chris took a seat on the edge of the bed and opened the letter. It read:

Woke up, decided to go see sharks for artistic inspiration. You should come join me. I'm at the Shark Reef Aquarium in Mandalay Bay. Won't be there long, so if you're coming, put a move on it.
Leigh

He could have made the Guinness Book of World Records for how fast he got dressed. Within minutes, he was in a taxi headed toward the aquarium. He spent the next hour walking through the underwater tunnels with a 360 degree panoramic view of the ocean. He had no idea that so many different species of sharks even existed. There was something exhilarating and frightening about being surrounded by so many tons of water and dangerous predators of the sea, knowing that nothing more than a sheet of glass separated him from these fierce creatures. He wanted to take pictures to show Christopher but knew he would have a time trying to explain how he got these pictures in his phone while he was supposedly in Amarillo, Texas. So instead of snapping photos with his phone, he made a mental promise to return to the aquarium with his son in tow. He figured Christopher would appreciate the real thing more than still-life images anyway.

Pausing in front of an alligator pool, Chris watched in amazement as the professionals, adorned in steel mesh gloves that nearly reached their elbows, fed the gators slabs of raw fish. There was no amount of money that anyone could offer that would motivate him to crawl into an alligator pool with no form of protection but mesh gloves.

"I didn't know albino alligators existed until I came here."

She stood behind him and spoke near his ear. He could feel the warmth of her body against his back, could feel her breath on the nape of his neck. "They remind me a lot of myself."

Turning slightly, he looked at her and said, "Really? How so?"

She'd changed from the torn pantsuit into a pale yellow blouse, white shorts, and flip-flops. Her hair was up atop her head in a curly bush, and yellow teardrop earrings hung from her ears, swinging back and forth with her every step. She walked up to the glass, put her fingers against the thick sheet, and her breath formed a circle of condensation. "They stand out so much that they're unable to camouflage in their natural environment. That's why it's so rare to find a white alligator that's lived for a long time in his natural habitat."

"How does that remind you of yourself?"

She turned to face him and hugged her waist. "Because they're fragile. And they stick out like a sore thumb."

"You think you stick out like a sore thumb?" She nodded, but Chris shook his head. "If you stuck out like a sore thumb, it wouldn't have taken me so long to find you in this aquarium."

"You didn't find me," she said, laughing. "I found you!"

"Which comes to show you that you might not stick out as much as you think you do." Chris cuffed her chin. "I don't think you stick out period. I think you stand out. In a great way."

She blushed and dropped her head, then walked off. She paused and gestured for him to follow her. "Come on, I'm starving."

They left the aquarium and climbed into a taxi together. Raleigh shocked him when she decided to stop and eat at a hotdog joint. There were only two occasions when he got to eat hotdogs: on the Fourth of July and during Junior's birthday parties. Other than that, hotdogs were out of the question. Raleigh ordered two foot-long hotdogs with the works and ate every bit of it. Not one to be outdone, Chris ordered three loaded foot-long hotdogs and downed each one.

While they waited for their food to digest, Chris said, "Tell me about yourself, Raleigh. I want to know more about you."

She patted her full belly and sipped on a glass of ice water. "I mean, what exactly do you want to know about me?"

"Everything. Like why someone as beautiful as you is not married."

"I haven't found 'The One' yet."

"Besides the child you lost with Darryl, do you have any kids?"

"No."

"Where do you live? Where are you from?" He watched her shift around in her seat, looking slightly uncomfortable. "My questions aren't bothering you, are they?"

"No." She spoke to her glass instead of him. "I just don't like to feel like I'm being interrogated. I don't like a lot of questions."

Interrogated? Her word choice intrigued him. He didn't think he was 'interrogating' her, but simply asking common questions to get to know her better. "My father once said," Chris continued, "that people who don't like questions have something to hide."

"That's not true. I ain't got nothing to hide." She sounded offended. Sitting straighter in her seat, she faced Chris dead-on and asked, "What's your next question?"

His lips lifted in a smile. She looked cute when she got upset. "You still didn't answer my previous question."

Raleigh frowned, trying to recall his question, then said, "We grew up here in Las Vegas, then moved to Villanelle when I was in middle school. Villanelle's a small town on the outskirts of Vegas, so small that we have like two stoplights and one McDonald's in the whole town."

"Where did you graduate from?"

"If you're talking about college, I didn't go to college. It's not for everyone."

"Oh." Chris shifted in his seat; not because he was uncomfortable, but because he had unbearable gas. "What do you do for a living?"

"I draw."

"And that's it?"

She shrugged. "I'm getting by. My house and car are paid for. I used the money we got from our parents' death to pay off everything, so I don't have any major bills."

"Then how did you...how did you afford my services?"

Once again, her eyes returned to her sweating water glass. "I, uh...took out a loan."

"Ah, Raleigh, you didn't have to do that—"

"No," she said, shaking her head, "don't feel sorry for me. My money isn't where I want it to be, but one day soon— very soon—a door is going to open for me. I'm going to get my drawings in a museum, people will know my name. I'll be able to walk into doctor's offices and expensive restaurants and see my work framed on the wall. It's going to happen for me, Chris. I guarantee it. I've got big dreams."

Chris admired her passion and optimism. As much as he wanted to feel sorry for her, he couldn't. He was proud of her; proud that she was determined to do whatever it took to climb her way to the top. By the time they left the restaurant, they both were gassy, full, and that "-itis" was starting to settle upon them.

"I'm leaving in the morning," Raleigh told him as they slipped into the back seat of another taxi. "And I'll probably never see you again. So I have a favor to ask."

"Anything," Chris whispered, giving her the most serious, intense stare. "Just say the words." He held his breath while he waited for her to ask him to make passionate, crazy love to her once they got back to the hotel.

"Chris," she said, her voice whisper-soft. "I want you to..."

"Yes?"

"...to let me draw you."

It took his mind a moment to register the words. "You did say make love to you, right?"

She laughed. "That is not what I said."

He grew quiet and focused on the road as the driver weaved in and out of traffic. Their legs touched as Raleigh shifted across the back seat, moving closer to him. He didn't realize he'd been frowning until she rubbed the wrinkles out of his forehead.

Looking at her with earnest eyes, Chris said, "Raleigh, I've got to be honest here. I want you. I mean, really really *want* you."

"Chris, I'd be lying if I told you that I don't want you just as much as you want me." She placed a hand on his knee. "But you're married."

"I can't stop thinking about you."

"Chris…"

He covered her hands with his, then laced his fingers through hers. "Give me one night."

Raleigh turned her head and looked out her passenger window. She whispered, "Chris, if I gave you one night, then I'd want forever."

For the time being, they grew quiet, the air heavy with everything that had and hadn't been said. A few minutes later, they pulled up in front of their hotel. Chris paid the taxi driver and held on tight to Raleigh's hand as they walked into the lobby, afraid that if he let her go, she'd disappear like heated breath against the cold night air. They went up to Chris's room, making small talk about the aquarium, as well as the fast-paced life of Vegas.

Raleigh sat Indian-style on his bed and asked, "So you're certain about letting me draw you? It usually takes a few hours."

Chris took a seat in the chair that he'd slept in all night, afraid that if he sat on the bed beside her, he wouldn't be able to keep his hands to himself. He shrugged his shoulders as he sat with his legs spread. "I have nothing but time to kill anyway, so hey, why not?"

"Okay, then." Raleigh pulled out the large leather-bound album that she'd brought to the room with her last night. From a pencil holder within the leather case, she removed a sturdy graphite pencil and sharpened the edge. From her purse, she removed a pair of thin framed glasses and pushed them up the bridge of her nose. With glasses on, she looked even sexier; she reminded Chris of a seventh-grade teacher who he'd constantly fantasized about having sex with on her desk during recess time.

"Take your clothes off."

He knew he had heard wrong this time. "Take my clothes off?" Chris asked.

She nodded and said with a serious expression, "I draw

people in the nude."

Chris gave her a naughty smile as his hand went down to his belt. "So you like to draw freaky stuff?"

"No, nothing freaky. Everything's strictly professional and artistic. Come here," she said and patted the bed. "I'll show you."

Curious, Chris walked over and sunk down on the mattress beside her. The leather-bound case was so large that when she opened it, it filled both his lap and hers. Inside were unbelievably realistic drawings of naked individuals who looked sad, somber, depressed. One picture was of a woman, lying in bed naked, the sheets twisted around her body as she reached over beside her and touched the empty spot where a man should've been. At the top of that picture was the cursive word *Widow*. The next picture was of a naked man standing near an open closet, which had a three-piece suit and tie hanging on a hanger. In his hand, he held a piece of paper, and a profound anger and sadness twisted his face. At the top of that picture, it read *Unemployed*. The leather bound case was filled with similar portraits, both men and women. With her pencil, shadings, and hatch marks, Raleigh had captured the very essence of everyone's pain.

"Naked," she said as she flipped to the last page that read 'Suicidal' at the top, but had no picture beneath. "That's the title of my collection. People whose pain is exposed for all the world to see. They are literally and physically, naked. I started this project during my therapy sessions, after my sister and Darryl...you know. It really helped me get through the loss of my child too." She flipped to a picture of a woman whose belly looked about four months pregnant. The woman was kneeling beside the toilet, her hands covering her face. At the top of the picture was the cursive word *Miscarriage.*

"Wow." The word came out more like a breath of air. Chris flipped through each picture again, amazed at her talent. "And that's why the guy came over last night. To buy your collection."

"No," Raleigh corrected him. "He came over with the pretense of buying my collection. But I'm not worried about it. When one door shuts, God opens a window."

"So you want me to do a suicidal pose?"

Raleigh nodded. "If you don't mind. I already have an idea for the pose."

"My father committed suicide."

"Oh."

The room became deathly quiet. Chris felt her eyes on him, but he couldn't look at her face. He didn't realize how much hatred he still harbored toward his father until he became aware that he was too choked up to speak. Raleigh circled her arms around his waist and rested her forehead on his shoulder. Her touch comforted him, calmed him.

"I was fifteen," he continued once he could speak again. "He had been missing for a few months. He did that often, you know? Would come home to Ma for a few months, then disappear for a few months, just back and forth like that all the time. This time he came home, no one was there. He laid on the couch, put the gun to his jaw, and blew his face off. I came home first. My school always let out fifteen minutes earlier than my sisters'. Usually I walked over to my boy Melvin's house, but I came straight home that day. And I found him…just like that…"

"I'm so sorry," Raleigh whispered and pressed her lips to his shoulder. "If I would've known, I never would've asked—"

"He came to me."

Raleigh lifted her head, but remained quiet.

"His ghost came to me, about a month ago. He sat on my porch steps and we actually had a conversation. I never told anyone because I knew they'd think I was crazy. Do you think I'm crazy?"

"A total nut," she responded. Her words hurt until he looked up and saw the lazy smile that she was giving him. No, she didn't think he was crazy. She was just being sarcastic.

"Chris, you don't have to do the pose—"

Despite how close the picture hit to home, Chris was more than impressed by her work and willing to do whatever he could to help. Without hesitation, he swept his shirt over his head and undid his pants. Wearing nothing but his boxers, he asked, "Where do you want me to stand?"

The corner of her mouth lifted in a smile. "On the balcony."

"You want me to stand naked on the balcony?"

She had to be out of her mind. It was broad daylight. All someone had to do was look up, zoom in on their digital camera, and snap a picture of him. He'd be arrested before he could pull his boxers up. He wanted to help Raleigh, but she was pushing the limits here.

"What's wrong?" Raleigh asked with a teasing smile. "You aren't scared are you?"

"No, but it's called common sense. I'm just being logical here."

"Why do we always have to be so logical? Why can't we just go with the wind?"

Her question truly resonated with him. Why did we always have to be so logical? Why couldn't we take chances sometimes, change up the rules, take risks? Why did we always have to play it so safe?

"Okay," Chris said, dropping his boxers to the floor and stepping out of them before kicking them aside. His penis hung limply to the side, brushing against his inner thigh. With his shoulders squared and his back straight, Chris marched to the balcony and waited for Raleigh to give him direction.

She had him rest his hands on the metal railing, elbows bent, legs poised as though he was about to leap over the side. She then asked him to look over the balcony at the cars zooming below while wearing an expression of utter despair. It wasn't until he was standing in the position, looking at the pavement hundreds of feet below that he began to truly feel what a man at his wit's end might possibly feel. Someone who would make such a finite move like this was beyond desperate. For the first time in his life, he had stepped in his father's shoes.

For the briefest second, Chris flicked his eyes across the thousands of windows looming from the skyscraper buildings around him. He wasn't sure if it was his overactive nerves or what…but he felt this overwhelming feeling that he was being watched. Not from a random passerby who just happened to look up, but from someone who had their eyes trained on him for one specific purpose. For what, he wasn't sure. But he felt like a kindred spirit with those posed in Raleigh's graphite sketches. Naked and exposed; physically and figuratively.

***

Raleigh was right. It did take a few hours to complete the sketch—three seemingly endless hours. By the time she put the finishing touches on the portrait, the sun had already tucked itself behind the clouds and faint stars and the moon were visible in the darkening sky. Chris ached all over from a combination of sleeping in the chair the night before, standing in one position unmoving for so long, and finally feeling the effects of being thirty-two. Once she said, "All done," Chris nearly collapsed with relief. As he stared at the portrait, he knew it had been worth every agonizing second. Raleigh was truly gifted with the pencil.

"Do you use any other mediums?" he asked.

"I tried acrylic and water color, but my favorite is my pencil." She sprayed the portrait with an aerosol can and explained that the protector would keep the pencil marks from smearing. Then she thanked him for posing for her.

"I really appreciate you doing that for me. Once I get someone to buy the collection, I'll pay you something for—"

"No, ma'am," he said, shaking his head as he stepped into his boxers. "I don't want another dime of your money. I did that because you asked me to, not because I expected payment."

"Thanks, Chris." She put away all her utensils, shouldered her purse, and grabbed the leather-bound case. "I'm going to get some shut eye. I leave in the morning. I'll stop by to say bye before I go. I swear I'm going to miss you."

Before she could exit the room, Chris caught her wrist and squeezed, not hard enough to hurt her, but hard enough to get her full attention. He didn't say a word, but he didn't need to. His eyes said it all.

As though he had asked her a question, she whispered, "I'll think about it." Then worked her arm loose and left.

Frustrated, Chris collapsed back on the bed and stared up at the golden ceiling fan that spun in lazy circles overhead. He was burning for Raleigh. He knew how he felt about her was wrong, but he couldn't stop his heart or his body from feeling the way that it felt. Part of him wanted to go to her room and beg for her to allow him to make love to her. But he wouldn't do it. Not that he had too much pride. But because he respected her decision to leave things unfinished.

Instead of driving himself insane with desire that would never be fulfilled—at least not by Raleigh—Chris thought about the fact that after Saturday, he could put this entire escorting gig behind him and focus solely on his future. He called his mom to check on Christopher and tell him goodnight. Then he called Stephanie to speak with Melvin who was surprisingly awake and able to talk to Chris for a few minutes before becoming overwhelmed with fatigue.

Chris didn't realize he had fallen asleep until he heard a light tap at the door. He opened the door to find Raleigh standing there barefoot, covered in a shawl. She opened the shawl to show him that she was naked beneath. Chris didn't ask any questions. He pulled her in the room before she could change her mind, pushed her against the door, fused his mouth to hers, and slid inside of her, opening her inch by inch, until her teeth chowed down on his earlobe and her nails dug into his shoulders, and she chanted his name like it was a song: "Chris, Chris…Chrisssss."

His name leaving her lips was the most beautiful melody he'd ever heard.

Twenty-Three

Chris was not answering his phone, Dexter wasn't answering his phone, and I was five seconds from losing my mind. I still wanted answers and I was determined to figure out what was going on. As much as I knew it was a bad look, I left my new job at lunchtime with absolutely no intentions of returning until Monday. If Chris wouldn't answer my calls, then there was no way he could avoid me face to face.

I called Tori and asked her if she could pick up Christopher from school.

"Pick him up from school?" she asked frowning. "He doesn't get out until three, and it's only twelve. Why can't you get him?"

"Because I'm going to Amarillo."

"Amarillo? For what?"

"To get some answers out of Chris."

Tori had a thousand more questions, but I didn't feel like talking right now. I'd had another dream last night—one of Chris banging this woman against a door, and in my dream, the woman looked just like my mother. I didn't know what was going on, but I knew that something was going on and I wanted answers.

The drive to Amarillo took four hours, and I drove straight there, stopping only once to put some gas in my tank. I'd only been to Melvin's mother's house once, and that was when she'd invited everyone over for Thanksgiving dinner. I hadn't been back since then. I'm not the one to talk about people, but her house was a mess. His mother is a hoarder, spending at least one hundred dollars per week at yard sales and thrift shops, buying a whole lot of unnecessary items that she will never use and that only serve one purpose—to clutter her house. I hated being there, thinking that a rat or a snake would crawl out the piles of junk and bite me or my son. After that Thanksgiving, she had invited us over many more times. Chris went back, but I never did. And that was three years ago.

By the time her little two-bedroom brick home came into view, a whooshing breath of air escaped me. Her dookie-brown station wagon was parked in the front yard, which meant that she was home. I had been afraid that I would drive all the way out here only to find that nobody was home. I would've definitely thrown a fit then.

Ms. Eloise lived on the "ghetto" side of town, so when I stepped out of my car, I made sure to lock the doors and check three times to make sure my car alarm was set. Then I made my way up her concrete steps, warily eyeing a brown cat with a missing eye that was nestled on the windowsill. Keeping one eye on the cat to make sure it stayed in its place, I rung the doorbell.

"Hold on. I'm coming!"

Ms. Eloise hurried to the door, sounding like she was undoing about fifteen locks before she finally opened the door. She was wearing bedroom shoes and a housecoat, and her hair was wrapped in a hairnet.

"Hey, Ms. Eloise, I didn't wake you, did I?"

"No, child!" she exclaimed, pulling me into a hug and nearly taking my breath away with the stench of moth balls and peppermints. "It's so good to see you! I tell you, it's been years. You done wasted away to nearly nothing. Last time I seen you, you had more meat on your bones than that." She grabbed my hand and pulled me into the house. "Come on in, come on in. I have some leftover fried chicken and potato salad in the kitchen. Let me fix you a plate."

"No, thank you. I'm really not that hungry," I said, trying my best to pull my hand free, but the woman's grip was amazingly strong.

"You don't have to eat the whole thing. Just take a bite or

two. I'm sure it'll do you some good."

With no other choice, I followed the lady into the kitchen, which was so cluttered with odds and ends—three kerosene heaters, an ottoman, two mini-fridges stacked on top of each other, something that looked a lot like a shelf that's supposed to be in a grocery store, and a mountain of clothing that touched the ceiling—that there was barely space to move.

"Ms. Eloise, I swear I'm fine," I said, feeling itchy all over. I was so ready to get out of that house. "I ate on my way over here and I'm about to burst," I lied. Quickly changing the subject, I added, "I'm sorry to hear about your son. Melvin's a really nice guy."

"Yes he is," she said, sighing as she moved China dishes out the chair so she could sit at the kitchen table. "I told him to take better care of his self. Strokes and heart problems run real bad in our family. His daddy died of a heart attack when Melvin was only three years old."

"Oh, man, I'm sorry to hear that," I said, shaking my head. "I know it's a relief having Chris here to help you care for your son."

"Yes," the woman said, nodding her head repeatedly. "That boy loves your husband like it's his own brother. He don't get along too well with his real brothers. They're ashamed of him. Say he don't do nothing with his life. But I say leave him alone. He work on cars, he tells jokes, he got a nice house, and he pay his own bills. Long as he happy, what does it matter what folks think about him?"

"Amen to that," I said, still scratching away at my arms and the side of my leg. I had to get out of that house. I felt like something invisible was scurrying across my skin. "Is Chris here?" I asked. "Do you mind if I talk to him for a second?"

She looked at me confused. "Why would Chris be here?"

Now it was my turn to look confused. As though she was mentally challenged, I said very slowly, "Because he's here helping you take care of your son, Ms. Eloise."

"Nah, child," she said, looking even more confused. "I don't know what you talking about. I ain't seen your husband

186

since December when him and Melvin came by and brought me a lemon pound cake and that foot massager tub. Ooh, child, that foot massager thingamajig works so good!"

Her words slapped me in the face. "Well…who's here helping you take care of Melvin?"

"Child, what's wrong with you?" Ms. Eloise asked, pushing up out of the chair and heading over to the stove. "Maybe you need something more to eat 'cause you're talking crazy talk. Melvin ain't here. He's at the rehabilitation center in San Antonio. They ain't releasing him until this upcoming week. Then he's coming up here. Child, what's wrong with you? You look like you done seen a ghost."

I couldn't breathe. I felt like I was having a panic attack, something I hadn't had since I was twelve years old and heard the news that my daddy had died.

"Sit down, baby, sit down!" Ms. Eloise said, moving the fastest I'd ever seen her move. She sat me down at the table and fixed me a cup of water and put two fried chicken wings on a saucer. I didn't touch the chicken but gladly downed the water and tried to tell myself to remember to breathe.

He was lying to me *again*. He was cheating on me *again*. I couldn't understand what was going on or why, but I kept feeling like karma had come back with a vengeance. It was as though karma was making me pay for all those months I went lying to Chris about being in sales when I was really an exotic dancer. But couldn't karma give me a break? I mean, I was doing it for an honorable cause! At least me shaking my behind was paying the bills. What benefit was Chris getting out of constantly lying to me besides sex with other women? Ooh, I hated him!

Finally, when I was trying to do the right thing—quit the stripping job, take on a legit position, put boundaries on Dexter and my relationship…and now this no-good, sorry ass excuse for a *man* was out slinging his *pene* again? He had told me yet another bold-faced lie.

Baby, I'm going to Amarillo for a week to help Melvin's mom take care of him.

Bullshit! I had already forgiven him for his womanizing

187

ways when we were engaged, had even forgiven him for his lies just weeks ago…and now this?

"Ms. Eloise, do you need any money?" I asked a little too calmly.

She looked at me curiously. "I mean…I ain't never gonna turn down no money, baby. But I'm doing okay for now. It is a little hard on me not having no man around. But my check stretches just enough to pay the bills."

I undid the earrings Chris had brought me from Vegas. Then I twisted off my wedding ring and tossed all the jewelry on her kitchen table. "Pawn it," I said. "You should get at least a couple hundred off of it. Take care, Ms. Eloise."

"God bless you!" she called out after me. "Take a plate with you! At least take a plate for your boy."

"No, we're good," I called over my shoulder as I unlocked the car and slid behind the wheel.

As expected, Chris's phone went directly to voicemail every time I called him. But that was okay. Two could play his game. And furthermore, I'd have something waiting on his ass when he got home.

When I was almost home, I did something I had never done before. I stopped by Womack's IGA and bought two huge boxes of their sturdiest trash bags. Then I went home and completely ignored Tori's questions as I cleaned out the closet and every dresser drawer of Chris's things. Then I went in the bathroom. Into the trash bag went his battery-powered toothbrush, his electric razor, his clippers, his shaving cream, his robe with his initials on it—a matching robe set his mother had bought us as a wedding gift. Then I walked through the house, throwing family pictures of us into a trash bag as well.

Nothing stopped my rampage until my son pulled at my shirt and said with big eyes, "Mommy, what you doing to Daddy's stuff?"

It was only then did all the fight go out of me and I dropped to the floor, pulling Christopher into my lap as I repeatedly kissed his forehead. "I'm sorry, baby," I said, and I meant it. Sorry that I had married such an immature, uncommitted liar. But even sorrier that I'd borne a child to him.

A million questions brimmed in her eyes as Tori pulled Christopher away from me. "Go, Angie. You need a moment."

"I do," I said with a nod. "I really do."

I got in the car again with every intention of driving around until I cooled down. But then Dexter called. He asked me to meet him at Three Forks, but I wasn't in the mood for it. From the sound of my voice, he could tell that something was wrong.

"Where are you?" he asked.

At that time, I was still in the neighborhood. He told me to park my car and that he was on the way to get me. He didn't want me to drive in my current condition. So I parked once again in my front yard and sat outside until his Bentley pulled up beside me.

For the whole ride, we didn't talk, and no music played in the background. I guess he was thinking as much as I was. I looked out the window, watching cars go by. I felt numb, so I pinched my forearm, and it hurt, just like my aching heart.

We arrived at Dexter's exclusive neighborhood. Even at dusk the houses looked nice and big. A wrought-iron gate kept strangers out of Dexter's estate. He pressed some buttons and the gate opened.

Any other time I would've marveled at his home, but I wasn't feeling that way tonight. Nothing seemed to matter now that my marriage was falling apart. Thinking about Chris kissing some other woman—touching her…sucking her…probably getting sucked by her…fucking her…was more than I could bear. I felt like throwing up.

Dexter opened the passenger door for me and helped me out of the car. We went inside his massive home, and I decided right then that before I left his house, I would even the playing field with my sorry ass husband.

***

"I'm sure you're not up for a tour tonight," Dexter said, and he was correct. "You look drained."

"I am. I could use a drink." And I definitely wasn't talking about a glass of water.

He led me to the den area, which consisted of two lounge

chairs, an L-shaped sofa, a mounted TV that nearly took up the whole wall, a pool table, and a miniature dance floor with a hanging disco ball overhead and a polished wooden floor. To the back of the den area was a fully loaded bar with five stools circling the marble top counter.

"Damn!" I exclaimed. "Your den is the size of my living room, kitchen, and bathroom all put together."

"This little old thing," he said, waving my comment away. "I throw parties in here every now and then. Nothing special. Haven't done it in a while though. What will you have to drink?"

"A margarita, and spike it like you're getting paid to do it," I said falling back onto the cushiony L-shaped sofa. It felt like I was sinking into a bed of clouds.

He made my drink, brought it to me, then turned the stereo system on low. A jazzy instrumental played; the saxophone and snare drum filling the room with a saucy sound. I twitched my foot to the beat as Dexter took a seat beside me.

"What's going on, baby girl?"

I sipped the lime margarita, wincing at its tartness. "My husband is cheating on me again."

"How can you be so sure?"

I told him about my trip to Amarillo and Chris's blatant lie. He didn't say anything at first, just popped a piece of gum and chewed thoughtfully. After a few seconds of jazzy calmness, Dexter said in a low voice, "Chris is in Vegas."

"In Vegas?" My drink sloshed over the rim as I straightened up on the couch. "What do you mean he's in Vegas? How do you...know?"

"He's one of my employees. He works under me for an escorting service. Diamond-Elite Escorting."

I couldn't have looked any crazier if I tried. I waited for Ashton Kutcher to pop out from behind the couch and tell me I'd just been "punk'd." I waited for the cameraman to jump out from behind the synthetic house plants and tell me to smile because I'm on Candid Camera. But no cameras and smiling camera crew emerged. Just me, Dexter, my margarita, and the ugly truth.

Dexter explained everything from the beginning, from the

time his boss gave him Chris's employment paperwork to process, until the time Chris waltzed into his office and told him that he quit.

"He's in Vegas," Dexter went on to explain, "concluding his contract with his final client."

"And he's sleeping with these women?"

"Now that, I don't know," Dexter admitted. "However, the truth is that he wanted to end his contract because he said he was tired of lying to you."

What should have brought some kind of reprieve only caused more anger. Obviously, his plan had backfired because it seemed that he was lying now more than ever. I didn't feel the least bit of remorse for Chris; only anger and extreme disappointment. Even though I now understood how Dexter knew my husband, it still didn't explain how he knew my mother.

"So what does my mother have to do with all of this? How do you even know her?"

He answered my question with one of his own. "What's your relationship like with your mother?"

I finished my margarita and though I wanted to request another, I asked for a glass of tea instead.

"Long Island Iced Tea?"

"No." I shook my head. "Just regular tea, if you have any."

This time, I followed him to the bar and straddled a stool. "What does it matter what my relationship with my mother is like?" I asked, watching him drop ice cubes into a fresh wine glass.

"Because I'm trying to understand why she…why she's doing what she's doing."

"And what is she doing?"

He purposefully avoided my question and filled the glass with store bought tea from a large jug. He passed the glass to me. For himself, he poured straight vodka, no chaser.

"So how do you know her? How did you meet her?" When he still didn't answer my questions, I felt my anger begin to rise at him ignoring me. "Did y'all used to have something going on?" I was intentionally trying to hit him below the belt. "Did you have sex with her? She's known to be the type to marry for money, and you've got plenty of it."

Dexter ignored me.

Realizing I wasn't going to get an answer out of him about my mother, I switched back to the topic of my husband. "So who is Chris hooking up with in Vegas? If he's your employee, then I'm sure you know who his 'client' is."

"That's confidential information, baby girl." Nursing his drink, Dexter said, "I'm going to bed. The guest room is upstairs, the first door on the left. Feel free to make yourself at home." He kissed my forehead and walked away, ignoring the questions that I tossed at his back.

Although some unanswered questions still swam in my head, things were starting to make sense. His lies were to cover his behind for escorting. And how could I be so upset at him when I lied for so long to cover my own ass for stripping? But I didn't sleep with my clients. He was slinging his stick to them and only God knew what else he was doing.

I chugged down the rest of my tea and carefully placed the glass in the sink. Then I stumbled up the stairwell and fumbled with the doorknob before I was able to open the guest room door. The room was huge, twice the size of my bedroom, with a California King bed in the center of the room. Beige, gold, and chocolate hues gave the room a warm, inviting feel.

In the colossal bathroom, I turned on the shower and jumped when Dexter's voice said, "Here's a night shirt to sleep in."

"Please leave it on the bed," I requested without turning to look at him.

I listened to his footsteps retreat, then I stepped into the shower, washing myself clean with the brand new bar of Dove soap. I washed my body and hair and brushed my teeth, hoping to remove all traces of the evening. It didn't work. I found myself thinking about Chris all over again. I tried hard to forget him. If he could do his thing, so could I.

I removed two towels from the towel warmer. I wrapped my body with one and my hair with the other. Dexter had placed the night shirt on the bed just as I requested. Staring at the shirt, I wondered why I was trying to be decent and do the right thing.

Chris hadn't cared about my decency. I had never stepped out on him, but he didn't seem to have any problem tipping around on me.

Angry all over again, I snatched the towel off my damp head and teased my naturally curly hair with my fingers. I hesitated for a moment before dropping the other towel to the floor and walking over to Dexter's room, naked as the day I was born.

"Dexter?" I knocked on the door but didn't wait for his permission before I let myself in. He was in the shower with the bathroom door open. Just as I stepped into the room, the shower shut off and he stepped out onto a thick white towel that was folded on the floor.

My body getting warm all over, I watched the water running down his dark chocolate, flawless skin. The shiny drips followed the contours of his taut body and the crevices of his muscles. He wasn't hard, but even still, his manhood looked thick and hard. Just staring at it made my mouth water.

Tiptoeing across the carpet, I stepped into the bathroom and watched him jump when he noticed my presence. His eyes skimmed over my body, lingering on my hard nipples and the triangle between my legs. He'd seen me naked plenty of times on the stage, but he was staring in awe of my body as though he was seeing it for the first time.

"Baby girl, I don't think..."

"Shh," I said and stepped forward, flattening my breasts against his chest. He didn't lean in for the kiss, didn't move or budge. Didn't even kiss me back. But I kept kissing his sexy lips, licking my tongue across his mouth until I could feel the ridges of his sparkling teeth. He groaned and closed his eyes, but still didn't kiss me back.

"What's wrong?" I asked, pulling my lips away, but keeping my body close. "I know you like me like that, so what's the problem?"

"I like you a lot, Angelique," he finally said. "Way more than I should. But I don't want you to come to me in anger. This would be revenge sex on Chris."

While he talked, I dropped to my knees until I was eye-level with his *pene*. Once limp, it now stood out straight and long, pointing at me with a perfectly rounded head. I brushed my cheek against his erection and he groaned, lost his train of thought for a moment.

"Angie, baby, I want you to come to me because you want me as much as I want you. Not like this." He stepped away from me and secured the towel around his waist.

I felt dumb, on my knees, trying to give pleasure to a man who refused and rejected my come on. I didn't realize I was crying until Dexter squatted beside me and wiped away my tears with a flick of his thumb. He kissed my forehead then said in a low, soft voice, "Can I hold you tonight?"

"That's all you want to do? Hold me?"

His brown eyes were simultaneously dreamy and intense. "No. What I want to do is make passionate love to you." The rawness of his voice and words sent trembles down my spine. "But I want all of you, baby girl. And until you can give me all of you…then I'm okay with just holding you. No rush. I ain't going nowhere."

When he put his arms around me, I melted. There weren't many men I knew that would turn down some freely offered sex—especially oral sex. I had no choice but to respect Dexter's request; his integrity made me see him in a whole new light. But he was honest enough to admit that there was no way that he could sleep holding me if I slept without a stitch of clothing on. So I pulled on the oversized shirt he had laid out for me and stepped into a pair of gym shorts that he said were too tight for him. We slept in his bed with his arms around me, his chin resting on the back of my shoulder, and my body perfectly cradled in his. Despite all I had been through that day, I slept soundly throughout the whole night.

Twenty-Four

Chris had never boned so much in his life. His twig and berries were swollen and if he did one more round, he knew he'd have to go to the hospital and possibly get surgery on his johnson.

"I can't, Mrs. Whitmeyer," he said as she tried to climb atop him yet again. "I'm sore. I'm hurting."

"So am I," she said, still trying her best to straddle him. "But I paid twenty thousand dollars, so I'm going to get my money's worth."

Chris had no idea how he was able to get the woman off of him. He felt weak, lightheaded, and his entire body was hurting—from the follicles of his hair down to his toenails. Never in his life had he been worked so much in bed as Mrs. Whitmeyer was working him. But somehow he found the strength to push her off him and race to the bathroom where he locked the door.

In the bathroom, Chris looked down at his swollen manhood and held it in his hand. He felt like crying; his member felt like one great big pulsating blister and Mrs. Whitmeyer still hadn't had enough. Her sexual thirst was unquenchable.

Sex with Raleigh had been beautiful; it was soft, slow, passionate. He'd done her missionary, looking into her eyes the entire time while he pushed in and pulled out. Then he'd done her from behind against the bed, leaning over her body so that he could hold her by the waist and suck on the curve of her shoulder while he had moved inside of her. And finally, she had gotten on top of him and rode him like she was riding a gentle tide. Chris's toes had never curled so hard, his eyes had never rolled back so far; his

climax had never been so…explosive. He'd literally seen fireworks
with Raleigh.

And when she had left that morning, just two hours before
it was time for him to meet with Mrs. Whitmeyer, he had followed
her to the parking lot and had hugged her for a long time without
letting her go. He knew it would be the last time he'd ever see
her again in the flesh. But he was certain that her memory, her
delicious scent, and chinky brown eyes would haunt him for years
to come.

But Mrs. Whitmeyer. Chris shook his head as he thought
about her. From the moment they'd entered her hotel room, every
stitch of her clothing had come off and she had demanded for him
to screw her. She had used those very words: "I want you to screw
me, and I want you to screw me now."

He had tried to talk her out of it, reminding her that he
was a man of integrity, that he didn't sleep with his escorts. That's
when she had thrown Raleigh in his face.

"What about that bitch you were screwing last night? She
was your first escort, right or wrong? Or what, she doesn't count?"

Chris's jaw had nearly hit the floor. All that time he'd
felt like someone was spying on him, and he'd been right. Mrs.
Whitmeyer was stalking him, like some crazy cougar psychopath.
It scared him because if she would go this far to keep an eye on
him, what would she do after he no longer worked for her? How
far would she go? Would she stalk him all the way back to San
Antonio? She had the money and she definitely had the means if
she decided to do so.

To shut her up, he'd given in to her requests. Unlike the
sweet, intimate sex that Raleigh and he had shared, sex with Mrs.
Whitmeyer was rough, hard, almost animalistic. The harder and
rougher he was with her, the wetter she got. It was almost as
though she got off on being rough-handled, punished.

Chris had numbed himself to the entire ordeal, pretending
as though he was having an out-of-body experience. It wasn't him
banging Mrs. Whitmeyer, but it was his alter-ego, escort Solomon.
He gave it to her all day long Friday, and then again all day
Saturday. The only time they left the bed was to relieve themselves

in the bathroom and to order room service. Other than that, they stayed in bed, getting it on like two wild animals in heat.

Sunday morning couldn't come fast enough for Chris. He bid Mrs. Whitmeyer farewell and she assured him that he'd given her the time of her life. He could really care less. He had fulfilled his end of the bargain, and now he was free—of everything except Raleigh's hold on him. But he knew that with time, Raleigh would begin to fade away and would become a bittersweet memory.

Chris slept during the plane ride home and arrived in San Antonio, Texas by one that afternoon. He stopped by a nearby florist and bought Angelique a bouquet of fresh flowers and reserved dinner at Three Forks Restaurant. He knew she'd be surprised when he told her that they would be eating at that luxurious establishment tonight.

Whistling, he pulled into his yard beside Angelique's car and let himself into the house. Christopher saw him first and took off running with arms open wide.

"Daddy, Daddy, Daddy!" he exclaimed, hugging Chris tightly. "I missed you this much, Daddy! Aunt Tori, Daddy's home!"

Tori came around the corner, looking slightly disoriented.

"You okay?" Chris asked her.

"Yeah, I'm…" Her eyes darted to Christopher and then she said, "When you finish with your son, we need to talk."

"Where's Angie?"

"We'll talk."

"And what's in all these trash bags?"

"Daddy, Mommy put all your stuff in trash bags. She put everything in there last night!"

"Christopher!"

Chris looked from Tori to his son and back to Tori, completely speechless.

"Junior, go upstairs for a moment."

"But Dad—"

"I said *go!*"

Christopher muttered "yes, sir" and took the steps two at a time. Once he was out of earshot, Tori said, "She found out you lied again, Chris. She drove up to Amarillo."

Chris's heart sank. "Are you serious?"

Tori pointed at her face. "Do you see me laughing?"

"Angie!" Chris called out as he untied the trash bags and looked inside at his things thrown together like it was garbage. "Angelique! Let me explain."

Tori grabbed his arm. "She's not here, Chris."

"Her car's outside. If she's not here, then where is she?"

Just then, they both heard the sound of a car pulling up. Chris sprinted out the door with Tori at his heels. When he noticed that his wife was getting out the car, smiling at some black man seated in the driver seat, he felt his temperature rise. With balled fists, he marched off the porch and headed toward the Bentley with every intention of bashing the man's face in. When the man saw him headed in his direction, he threw the car into drive and skidded out the yard. Chasing after the car, Chris flung rocks at the back window, but the man was driving too fast. He was unable to cause any real damage like he longed to.

"What's this about, Angie?" he asked, spinning on his heel before stomping into the yard.

"Christopher, come on. Let's go inside," Tori said, taking his hand and quickly leading him into the house.

Chris had no idea what was going on, but he demanded answers—the first being, why had his wife just gotten out the car with some man? With his fists balled and his jaw tightly clenched, Chris tried to close the distance between them, but Angelique kept backing away, reaching out to steady herself every few seconds.

"What were you doing out with him, Angie?" Chris spat through his teeth. "Don't you dare lie to me either. I want the truth."

"The truth?" She finally stopped backing away from him, only because he'd backed her up until she was pressed firmly against the side paneling of their house. He could see her heartbeat fluttering madly at the base of her throat. "Chris, you should be the last person asking for the truth. You're the biggest liar I've ever met in my life. You lied to me. You weren't in Amarillo with Melvin."

"Did you have sex with him?"

"Did you have sex with her?"

"Who is her?"

"I don't know. Why don't you tell me? Whoever the chick was that you went up to Las Vegas to *escort.*"

Those words took some of the fight out of him. Chris didn't have to ask how she knew the truth. He was certain that his boss had disclosed all that confidential information to his wife, just so he could get inside her panties. Unsure of how to cover his ass this time, Chris weakly said, "Don't believe a thing that man told you—"

"Then what am I supposed to do?" Angelique asked with a laugh that held no humor. "I'm supposed to believe you?" She jabbed her finger into his chest, hard enough to make him wince. "You, my *husband*, who has constantly lied to me time and time again? How can I believe a word that comes out your mouth?"

In shame, Chris dropped his head. He said in a low voice, "I lied for a good cause."

"Well I hope the cause was worth it. Because I'm done with you, Chris. I want a divorce." She held up her ringless hand and wiggled her fingers. "I didn't throw my ring away, I *gave* it away."

Stunned, Chris stared at the light band where her bridal set should've been. His head snapped up and he looked deeply into Angelique's light brown eyes. His pain-filled eyes searched hers for the truth, hoping that what she just said was nothing more than untruthful words meant to hurt. But he saw deep within her watery brown eyes that she was not playing. The pain that tore through his chest nearly brought him to his knees. Somehow, the thought never crossed his mind that he might lose his wife. He knew he hadn't been an honest man. Even when they had first started dating, he knew he often stepped out on her and betrayed her trust. But he had traded in his Black Book for a wedding band, and he had meant his vows when he'd said them. Sex with Mrs. Whitmeyer had meant nothing to him. Sex with Raleigh had been special, but he knew there was no future in that. His future—and his present—was standing right in front of him and he couldn't quite believe that she would so easily throw in the towel on what they had worked so hard to build together.

The fight left his body as he crumpled to the ground and spread his legs, dropping his head as he focused on the bent blades of grass. His voice was a notch below a whisper. "So you leaving me? Just like that?"

Angelique remained standing, and he could hear her unsteady, labored breathing. "Chris, don't make me out to be the bad guy here. This is not what I want to do, but right now, I can't see myself spending the rest of my life with you. I can't trust you any further than I can see you."

"You don't think...that there's a chance that we can rebuild our trust?"

She sat down on the ground beside him and hugged her knees. "If there's any chance of this marriage working, baby, we've got to start by telling the truth. That's why there's something I need to tell you."

Chris's head whipped up as he looked over at her. "You slept with him, didn't you?"

"I'm not going to lie, Chris. I have nothing to hide. I wanted to sleep with Dexter; I actually tried to sleep with him. But it didn't happen. He pushed me away."

"Why would you want to do something like that?"

"Because I wanted to hurt you as badly as you have hurt me." She licked her lips and hesitated before continuing. "At the back of my mind, Chris, I always knew that karma would catch up with me." Again, she licked her lips and hesitated. "I lied to you. I never worked for a life insurance company. I made that all up. Before I got this marketing job, I was, uh...I was a dancer."

"A dancer?" Chris paused for a moment as he fully took in everything she'd just said. As the realization settled over him, he felt his blood come to a boil all over again. "You mean to tell me that all that time I thought you were a sales rep, you were really stripping on a stage? Getting...getting naked in front of all those men? For half a year? You used your body to pay the bills?"

"What else was I supposed to do? Time was of the essence, and it didn't seem like you were coming up with any ideas to keep our home. I did what I had to do—"

"And that was your only option? To be a whore?"

"I wasn't a ho, I was a—" Angelique sighed and smacked her lips. "I didn't have to tell you the truth, Chris. I could've kept quiet and went along with the lookalike explanation that you came up with. But I'm being woman enough to tell you the truth."

His head swam with anger, but Chris kept his cool. She was right; she didn't have to tell him the truth, and he respected her for having enough courage to do so. He knew that his anger at her was displaced—probably anger at himself for allowing the situation to get so out of hand. Now it was his turn for the moment of truth.

"Hold my hand, Angelique."

"For what?"

"Please?" It took her a few seconds to finally place her delicate hand inside his much larger one, but when she did, he held on tightly, afraid to let her go. Her warm hand was his support system, the crutch he needed to lean on in order to say what he knew needed to be said. "Baby, I'm not even going to stay angry at you about the stripping job. I understand. You took that job for the same reason that I took this escorting job—because it seemed like a quick and easy fix and the best temporary solution to our problem. But once I got in the door, I realized that I had made a big mistake."

Angelique's voice cracked when she spoke. "Did you sleep with any of the women? And don't lie to me. Please, no more lies."

Reluctant to speak, Chris squeezed her hand even more, wishing she hadn't asked him that particular question.

"Did you, Chris?"

He inhaled deeply, then slowly blew out on an exhale. He cleared his throat, then nodded. "Yeah. I did."

Angelique dropped her head and tried to pull her hand free, but he wouldn't let go. "How many times?"

"How many times or how many women?"

Without warning, Chris felt something thwack him upside his head repeatedly. It was Angelique's balled up left fist. He tried to shield the back of his head and the side of his face, but Angelique kept hitting and mushing him. With each hit, she yelled out in anger, "You lying dog! You cheating bastard! You sleazy, no-good, asshole! I hate you! I hope your *pene* falls off! I hope you catch AIDS! Ooh, I hate you!"

"What is going on out here?" Tori yelled, racing outside to the front porch. She looked at her friend with inquisitive eyes.

Angelique pointed a shaking finger at her husband. "I might could have forgiven you for being an escort, but I cannot forgive you for being a gigolo. Because ultimately, you were not just escorting them; you were prostituting yourself. And I refuse to remain married to a prostitute. God, Chris, I really hope it was worth it."

"Baby, please, just listen to me—"

"No! Get away from me. Don't touch me, don't call my name, don't even look at me. Better yet, I need you to leave. Get your things and go, Chris. Now. I've already packed your bags, just take them out my house."

"*Your* house?"

"Have I not been paying the bills for the past six months? Yes, this is *my* house."

"Can I at least say good-bye to my son?"

"I will never keep your son from you, Chris. But not now. I need you to go. I can't stand to even look at you. I'll always love you—" Her voice broke and huge crocodile tears escaped her blood red eyes. "I'll always love you, Chris. But I'm not going through this again. I put up with your whorish ways enough in the beginning of our relationship. I'm not going to suffer through this while being your wife. I love myself more than this. I deserve—" She pounded her hand against her chest. "I deserve better than this, and you know it."

Chris couldn't stomach seeing her in so much pain. "Baby..." He went to her, but she held her hands up high and backed away from him.

Tori scorched him with a condescending stare, then ran after her friend.

"I never meant to hurt her like this," Chris whispered to the sky. With his hands on his narrow hips, he walked around in circles, wearing the grass down until it looked like a matted mess. He wanted to go in the house, but shame kept him rooted to the spot. He wanted to shake some sense into her, make her realize that this thing could still work if she allowed it to. Yeah, he had messed up, but they could mend their relationship. If he could forgive her for lying to him, why couldn't she forgive him for doing the same? Why was he the one getting so much heat because of it?

Chris sprinted toward the house, but Tori stopped him at the door. "Chris, please leave. She needs a moment to herself. Give her some time to think this thing through. Both of you are very emotional right now, and it's hard to be rational when you're being controlled by your emotions. Give her a day or two to calm down, and then I'm sure you two can sit down and have a levelheaded conversation."

Reluctantly, Chris nodded. Whether he wanted to admit it or not, Tori was right. If he remained and tried to talk things out with Angelique, he was certain they'd end up in a heated battle and exchange hurtful words that they'd never be able to take back, only managing to make the already ugly situation even worse. What had he been thinking, to take on this escorting job to start with? It was a bad judgment call on his part, and now, his very marriage was tinkering on the brink of destruction. Nothing was worth it—not the money, not the sex, not even Raleigh.

Head bowed, he trekked to his car. He felt just as sorry and worthless as his dad must've felt from all the times he stepped out on his mother and made her cry. All those vows he'd made to never be like his father, and yet he was blindly walking down the same path. Chris backed out of the yard and made it to the second stoplight before he had to pull over. His vision was so blurred by unshed tears that he could no longer focus on the endless stretch of paved road.

Twenty-Five

A month had passed since that episode in their front yard. Since then, Chris had moved in with Melvin's mother to help her care for him. They had discharged Melvin the first of June from the rehabilitation center and a personal speech therapist and physical therapist came by twice a week to work with him on making a full recovery. Not only had Melvin learned how to speak fluently again, but he could even walk without any assistance—though he did walk with a slight limp. Being his nurse—or helper, like Melvin liked to call it—was a great distraction for Chris. Between serving Melvin on beck and call, helping Ms. Eloise with household chores, and spending the weekends with Christopher, Chris kept himself occupied so he wouldn't have to think about Angelique. She wasn't just giving him the cold shoulder—she was giving him "tip of Mt. Everest" treatment.

Unless his phone calls were about Junior, she didn't have anything to say and would hang up on him if he tried to get her to talk about their relationship. Chris couldn't understand how she could act like six years of marriage did not affect her in anyway. And then there was the issue with Dexter, who he saw as the real reason why Angelique wasn't responding to his attempts of reconciliation. It wasn't that he was trying to squeeze information out of his son, but Christopher liked to talk, and Chris did encourage him every now and then: "Did you, Mommy, and Mr. Dexter hang out today? Where did y'all go? Does he touch Mommy the way I used to touch Mommy? Does Mr. Dexter make Mommy laugh a lot?"

From his son, he had learned a wealth of information that didn't set nicely with him. Dexter and Angelique spent a lot of time together—entirely too much. Dexter, Christopher, and she would go out to eat together, to the movies, and to the park. Christopher had been to Dexter's house on numerous occasions and described it as a mansion. He assured Chris that Mommy and Mr. Dexter did not kiss, they did not hold hands, they did not sleep in the same room. According to Christopher, the only thing that Angelique and Dexter did was hug—but he wondered if it was a platonic hug or a "I can't wait to get your clothes off" type hug. He tried to talk to Angelique about it, but she tartly told him that it was none of his business. Chris had gotten so desperate that he'd resorted to driving down to San Antonio in the middle of the night and parked blocks away, just to make sure that Dexter's Bentley wasn't pulling an all-nighter at his wife's house. That was when Chris realized that what he was doing was pathetic and something had to give.

Usually, Chris could talk to Melvin about his problems, but Melvin was making a speedy recovery that shocked even the nurses and his doctor. And with that speedy recovery, he spent every single moment cupcaking with Stephanie, who basically had invited herself to move in with Ms. Eloise to help out with Melvin as well. Feeling unneeded and out of place, Chris packed up his bags one night, bid Ms. Eloise farewell, and drove down to his mother's house. Melvin understood that there were no hard feelings between them, and actually thanked him for leaving. Now, he could spend 24 hours, 7 days a week hugged up with his boo.

It was nearly midnight by the time Chris arrived to his mother's house, but to his surprise, she was still up. He had called earlier and asked her if he could crash; she reminded him that her doors were always open to any of her kids, and that the key was inside the hanging basket of geraniums over the front porch steps.

"Mama, what you doing up so late?" he asked, dragging his overnight bag behind him.

His mother was curled up in one of the recliners, her reading glasses perched on her nose, her heavily marked up Bible in her hands, and a steaming cup of hot cocoa topped with marshmallows setting atop a saucer. The end table lamp was switched to the dim setting, casting a comfortable glow over the entire front room.

Her house was tidy and smelled like fresh linen—a reprieve to the weird-smelling messy house he'd been living in for the past month. Though her two-bedroom home was much smaller than Ms. Eloise's, it seemed twice as big, being that she lived minus all the clutter. Her front room was very simplistic; a stain-free beige carpet and a soft blue furniture set embroidered in gold. Religious ceramic knick-knacks—little angels kneeling in prayer, Jesus at the Last Supper, the Bible opened to Psalms 23—were sporadically placed across the living room table and the white-washed fireplace mantle.

She looked up when he came in and smiled. "I'm glad you had a safe trip. I don't like you travelling such far distances at night by yourself. It's not safe."

"I'm fine, Mama," he said, locking the door behind him and cleaning his shoes on the welcome mat. "It's past midnight. Why aren't you sleep?"

She sighed. "I couldn't sleep. Some nights are better than others for me."

"What's wrong? You okay? You sick?" Chris asked, flopping down onto the love seat.

She placed a cross-shaped bookmark in the Bible and closed it before setting it on the end table. Again, she sighed. "Baby, your father's been coming to me in my dreams a lot—especially these past few weeks. It's like…" She paused and looked off toward the fireplace. "It's like he's trying to tell me something, but I…" She shrugged her shoulders. "I don't know what he's trying to tell me. But I'm getting all flustered over nothing. I know I am." She easily changed the subject. "Tomorrow's the Fourth of July. You and Angelique gonna spend it together?"

This time, Chris sighed. "I don't know, Mama. I doubt it. She doesn't want nothing to do with me. I messed up big time."

"Hmm." That was her only response, as well as one of the reasons why he respected her so much. She never stuck her nose in any of her kids' marriages. She always said that one of the biggest problems with marriages is that too many couples let too many people all up in their business. So she preferred to stay out of it.

The room grew quiet. Chris's eyes danced around from the different photos on the walls of him and his sisters at various stages in their lives. His mother had walled photos of him from the time he was an infant, wearing a baby blue bonnet, to the time Angelique and he stood in front of the sterling silver candelabra, posing for their wedding picture. His eyes remained glued to Angelique; out of all the years they'd been married, she hadn't aged a bit. She looked as stunning today as she did back then.

Chris brought his thoughts back to what his mother had said earlier. "Does Dad come to you a lot in your dreams?"

His mother rubbed her tired eyes. "When he first died... he came to me in my dreams a lot. Kept apologizing to me. But I hadn't dreamed of him in decades. And now suddenly, out of the blue, he keeps coming to me."

After a few more seconds of silence, he said, "Mama, Dad came to me too. Only once. But it wasn't in a dream."

She lifted her head and looked at him curiously.

"Don't think I'm crazy, Mama, because I swear I'm not. But his spirit came to me a couple months ago, and he was trying to warn me too."

His mother gasped. "Was it about a girl? A girl who paints or draws? An artist?"

Her words caused his heart to miss a beat. A thick crease furrowed his forehead. "No...he said the man. Some man in the shadows. I'm supposed to pay attention to the shadows. But what about this woman? This...this artist?"

"I don't know. He just keeps saying the woman. The woman who draws." She brought the mug to her lips and sipped the hot drink while she looked over the rim, her eyes swimming with worry. "Baby, I want you to be careful. I don't...I don't want you going to Vegas anymore."

"I'm not going to Vegas anymore, Mama. That was just for the escorting gig, and now that that's over with, I have no reason to go back to Vegas. I didn't lose anything over there."

"Yes you did." His mother's voice was soft but stern.

"You lost your morals, your dignity. You lost everything that I had instilled in you from the time you were a young boy. You went up there and lost your mind, baby, and now you've lost your wife."

"Aren't you happy? You never liked her in the first place."

"When did I say I never liked her?" His mother stared at him with questioning eyes. "She might not have been my prime choice for you, but she's treated you like gold from day one. And as long as she's treating my baby boy good, then she's all right with me. And why would I be happy to see you hurting the way that you're hurting?"

Chris dropped his eyes to the floor. He slid off his shoes and peeled off his socks. "Mama, I'm acting just like him, ain't I?"

"You don't have to walk in your daddy's shoes. Make your own path in life."

"I thought that's what I was doing. Until I…fell off track."

"So get back up, dust yourself off, and get back on track."

"God, Mama, you make it sound like I fell out of a tree. It's not that easy to get back on track when she won't even talk to me."

"That girl loves you, Chris."

"*Loved* me," he corrected her.

"*Loves* you," she reiterated with intensity. "You and your sisters always wondered why I kept taking your father back. It's because I loved him. Dearly. And every time he came to me, pleading for me back, I knew that this time, he would change. And he did change—until he got enough liquor in his system. Then it was back to square one. I was a fool," she admitted, nodding her head. "But when a woman loves, she loves hard. She doesn't let go easily. You're the one making it easy for her. You're not even trying."

"I am trying!"

"How so?"

"I try to call her, but she doesn't want to talk. When I come over to pick up Junior, she gives me the cold shoulder—"

"Try harder."

"What do you mean try harder? What else can I do?"

"Sleep on it. If you want her bad enough, you'll figure it out. The sky's the limit, Chris." She sipped down her hot chocolate. "I just put fresh sheets on the bed in the guest room. And there's an unopened toothbrush on the dresser, if you need it. Make sure the lights are off before you turn in."

Signaling that the conversation was over, his mother pushed up from the recliner, her arthritic knees creaking badly. She took her mug to the kitchen and he heard the water come on as she rinsed it clean. He listened to her feet pad down the hallway until her room door closed. As tired as Chris was from the four hour drive, he couldn't fall asleep. Instead of retiring to the guest room, he remained upright on the couch, thinking, wondering. Somewhere in the wee hours of the morning, the thought came to him. Smiling, he snapped his fingers and picked up the phone.

First, he called Melvin. He didn't expect him to answer; he was certain that his boy had his head cocked back, snoring and drooling. He left a message for him, giving him each minute detail of his plan; he informed him that it was very important for him to return his call as *soon* as possible. Then he made another call. Probably because she didn't expect to see his number on her caller ID at this time in the morning, Tori answered on the first ring sounding as though she'd swallowed a toad.

"Tori," he said, excitement lacing his voice, "I need a big favor."

He told her his plan and was happy that she shared his enthusiasm. His mother was right. They sky *was* the limit.

Twenty-Six

Fourth of July was the first holiday ever that we'd spend separately. The thought saddened me, but I refused to let it get me down. Usually for this holiday, Chris would prep the above-ground pool the day before, and then light up the propane grill in the backyard. This was the one holiday besides Christmas that he didn't mind splurging. He'd buy enough food to almost feed the whole neighborhood, and would invite all our family, friends, and neighbors over to make a plate. We'd play throwback music outside, and usually persuaded the attenders to get into place for the "electric slide." And then at night, Chris would light up the sky with some of the most beautiful fireworks I have ever seen. It was always so much fun; a day of laughter and celebration.

Since Dexter was away on a business trip and wouldn't be returning until late that night, I didn't have any plans for the Fourth besides cooking Christopher and me a few hotdogs and turkey burgers on the kitchen stove and then going downtown to watch the fireworks. That's why I was more than thrilled when Tori came and forced me out the house, pleading for Christopher and me to go to the Fourth of July parade with her.

"Don't act like you have something better to do, Angie," she chastised me as she hooked Christopher into the backseat. "And can you put some pep in your step?" she asked, glancing at her watch. "We're already running late."

"How are we running late?" I asked her, sliding into the passenger seat of her car. "The parade lasts from twelve to three, and it's only a quarter to one."

"Exactly. Which means we're missing floats and candy

right now as we speak."

I rolled my eyes at her, but deep inside, I was glad that I didn't have to sit in the house and mope. Tori sped down Market Street like we were truly late for an appointment; twice I had to tell her to watch her speed. The cops stayed hot on the holidays, and there was no point in her winning herself a speeding ticket because of a parade.

Down at Hemisfair Park, law enforcement had blocked the streets off and formed detours for the busy road traffic. There wasn't a vacant park in sight. By the time we found a park fairly close to the 750-foot-tall Tower of Americas, Christopher couldn't sit in his seat a moment longer. He was straining so hard to see out the window, I was certain he'd have a crook in his neck.

Still rushing, Tori snapped her seatbelt open and hurried Christopher out the car. "Come on, come on, Angelique! Goodness, you're moving slower than a granny on a walker."

"What is the rush, Tori? You are acting weird."

"I'm trying to get us a good spot. If not, Christopher won't be able to see over all the people."

"Okay then, fine," I said, almost breaking into a jog to keep up with her. Christopher must've been moving too slow for her too, because she had propped him up on her shoulders.

Tori had one thing right. The street was packed to capacity. We had to muscle our way through the thousands of people who lined the road. I was just thankful that I'd been smart enough to wear flip-flops instead of heels, like some of the women out here. We made it to the roadside just in time to see a group of colorful clowns on stilts walking down the highway. One clown with cotton candy pink hair carried enough balloons in each hand that I was shocked she didn't fly away. Another clown carried an umbrella whose sparkly blue cover was wide enough to keep an entire football team dry from the rain. After the clowns wobbled past, a charity group called The Lord's Table came through pushing 55-gallon barrels that had been designed to look like oversized soup cans on wheels. Inside the drums were tiny baggies full of candy. They tossed the candy out and I managed to catch three little baggies for Christopher.

Next came a sorority team wearing black shorts that they knew were entirely too short and inappropriate for this family event. One girl's booty was so fat, you could see the under-curve of her butt cheeks hanging out the shorts. She wasn't a bad looking young lady, but the men around me didn't know that because not a single one of them was staring at her face. Even though their shorts were distracting, their routine was on point. I found myself wanting to stomp and clap along with them.

Following them up was a fraternity dressed in army fatigue pants and white T-shirts. They outdid the girls because there was such fire, such intensity behind their voices, facial expressions, and perfectly choreographed moves.

"Don't this take you back to our sophomore year at A&M? Remember when we tried out for Delta Delta Nu?"

Tori smiled as she nodded and reminisced. "Girl, I was crushed when we didn't make the team. That lead girl did not like us."

"I was crushed too, but I'm glad we didn't make the cut. You realize that every girl in that sorority ended up with a baby before they graduated. So maybe it was best that we didn't get accepted."

Tori was only half listening to me. For the umpteenth time since our arrival, she glanced at her wristwatch.

"Are we on a timed schedule or something, Tori? Is there someplace you need to be?"

"Look up."

"Look up?" I said.

"Look up," she said again, and pointed up at the sky.

Confused, I shielded my eyes with my hand and looked up, but I didn't see anything but a cloudless blue sky and bright rays from the sun...and a parachute—no, not a parachute, an airplane. No, not one airplane, *five* airplanes—no, not airplanes, those were jets. Five red jets soaring across the sky in a synchronized horizontal line.

"Oh wow," I exclaimed and pointed up. "Christopher, look at the airplanes."

"Ooh, Mommy, airplanes! That's cool!"

212

We weren't the only ones who were transfixed by the airplanes. Just about everyone around us had their eyes shielded or their sunglasses in place as they looked up at the jets that had thick plumes of white smoke coming from their exhaust pipes. Then suddenly, without warning, the jets broke apart and began using their fumes to write in the sky.

"Oh, cool, Mommy!" Christopher yelled. "They're spelling the alphabet!"

At first, I assumed he was right since the first letter I saw forming was an 'A'. But as I continued to watch, I found my chest constricting and it got harder and harder to breathe. These were not some random jets that flew out to write the alphabet. They flew out to write a message in the sky, one that everyone viewed but was meant specifically for one pair of eyes. Once they finished twirling, looping, and flipping upside down in the air, the five jets regrouped and soared away in the same synchronized line they had arrived in, leaving behind four fluffy words:

ANGIE PLEASE 4GIVE ME

My hand flew up to my mouth and my bottom lip trembled as though it was a guitar string that someone had just strung. Wide-eyed, I stared at Tori with complete disbelief written all over my face, then looked back up at the fading words that were blurred by my tears. Again, I stared at Tori, speechless, and she nodded and rubbed my back. From the look on her face, I knew that she knew way more about this than she was letting on.

"That's just the beginning, baby," she said, and started pushing me through the crowd.

"What? What's going on now?" I asked, tears spilling from my eyes as I thought about Chris and what all he had went through to make the skywriting a success. I wondered where Tori was taking me.

She basically pushed me into the road, and I tried to move out the way because a float was coming down the street, but she blocked my retreat.

"Tori, what are you doing?" I whispered through my teeth.

"We're in the way. You're going to get us in so much trouble."

"Will you just calm down? We got this thing all under control."

The float coming down the street bore the banner R&R Cars. I recognized the company because they were the car dealership that Melvin did the bulk of his detailing for. Sitting in the middle of the float was Old Man Henry, the owner of the dealership, stroking an acoustic guitar that was resting in his lap. Beside him stood my husband, dressed in an all-white tux very similar to the one he married me in, and holding a microphone in his hands. His eyes locked in on mine as he motioned for me to get on the float with him. But my legs wouldn't move.

"Go, Angie! Go before you miss it!"

Tori basically pushed me onto the float and Chris's outstretched hand kept me from falling. This was the first time my husband and I had touched in a long time. Old Man Henry began playing the guitar, and Chris held my hand and looked me directly in the eyes while he sang Babyface's "Sorry for the Stupid Things" loudly into the microphone. The attached amp amplified his voice so that everyone could hear him. The float eased by ever so slowly as he sang to me, dropping on his knees in front of all those thousands of people, and apologizing not only for himself, but for all the stupid things that men do to women even when they know what they are doing is wrong.

By the time Old Man Henry strummed the last chord and Chris hit the last note, my face glistened from all the tears I'd shed. Still on his knees, Chris said into the microphone, "Angie, I hurt you. I betrayed your trust. And I was wrong. If you despise me for the rest of my life, I feel like I deserve it. But in front of all these people, I'm on my knees begging for another chance, baby. Give me one last chance to prove to you that I can be the husband that you need me to be. Forgive me, baby."

My throat was too choked to speak. I didn't know what to say. And then the crowd started chanting, "One more chance! One more chance! One more chance!"

It amazed me that these complete strangers had formed a force field behind my husband, rooting for him—no…rooting for us. I looked down at Chris and giggled. "Get off that filthy floor, baby. You're ruining your suit."

Still, he remained on his knees. "Is that a yes? Please, Angie, tell me it's a yes."

I smiled until my cheeks hurt. "*Sí,* Chris. It's a yes. Yes, yes, yes!"

Before I knew what had happened, my feet were swinging in the air and Chris had his steel arm around my waist, nearly crushing me from holding me so tight. His lips descended on mine as the crowd clapped and cheered with our float floating away. Chris held my face and kissed me ever so gently. I could taste my fresh tears on my lips and knew that he could taste them too. God, how I had missed him. I missed how he tasted, how he smelled, how good he felt in my arms. I clutched the front of his tux in my hands, not wanting to let him go. This felt like a taste of heaven.

After the parade was over, Chris and I left Hemisfair Park hand in hand with Christopher up on his father's shoulders, and Tori following closely behind us.

"How in the world did you pull that off?" I asked.

"I came up with the idea, Melvin put it in motion, and Tori made sure you arrived. So I can't take all the credit for it."

So Melvin had helped put this thing in motion? Maybe he wasn't as much as a nuisance as I thought he was. I kissed Chris again and told him to personally thank Melvin for me. Then I thanked Tori for finally being able to keep a secret from me so she wouldn't ruin the surprise. This was perfect. This was how things were supposed to be. That night, we brought Christopher downtown again to watch the fireworks. Then we returned home and made our own fireworks.

Twenty-Seven

Our honeymoon years were back. Forget a Cloud 9—I was on Cloud 99. Many mornings I woke up and pinched myself, certain that I had to be caught in a happy-ever-after dream that refused to end. Some women say that "once a cheater, always a cheater." But I knew firsthand that that wasn't true. Men can change. A woman can't change a man, but if a man loves a woman enough, he'll be willing to change for her and for himself. Chris was a changed man, and no one could tell me differently.

My husband got his job back at TCP Robotics. They didn't give him back the engineering position that he'd had originally, but they promoted him higher. He left TCP as an engineer, and returned two years later as the executive director of aerospace engineering. It was a salaried position in which he made $190,000 a year. The great thing about his new position was that he didn't have to work half the hours he used to work as a computer engineer. He went to work at eight in the morning and was home by two. The only days that he had to work late were Wednesdays, but Christopher and I could deal with one long day out the week. With his salary at TCP and mine at Lumpkin, we'd be able to pay off our house and cars within a year's time. Not only were our finances back under control, but we'd even started marriage counseling. And also, we'd started working on that second child again. It finally seemed like things were back on track.

And Dexter was happy for me—truly happy for me. He respected my decision to take my husband back and make things work. Not only did he step back and grant me space, but he informed me that if I ever needed him for anything, he was just one phone call away. I appreciated him being so understanding.

July rolled away, and we were still in the honeymoon stage. August came knocking, and we were still acting like newlyweds. It seemed like we blinked our eyes and September arrived. It was time to enroll Christopher for first-grade at Dunberry Elementary School. Not only did we enroll him for school, but we also enrolled him for an afterschool program so he could spend more time with peers and participate in extracurricular activities. I couldn't believe our little boy was growing up so fast. If time continued to move at this rate, I knew I'd go to sleep, wake up, and my little boy would be a grown man on his way to college.

One Wednesday in mid-September, I was driving home from work, listening to the throwback station which was playing a string of songs dedicated to the nineties. The radio started playing Christopher Williams "I'm Dreamin'." I blasted the song and started singing along with him. I knew exactly how he felt. I felt like I was dreaming too, and if I was, I just wanted people to let me sleep until my dream was complete.

***

A brown package was waiting for me on the front porch steps. The package was addressed to me, but I hadn't recalled ordering anything online. Curious, I picked up the book-sized box and carried it into the house, placing it atop the island.

The house was quiet with Christopher staying over in the afterschool program. I still hadn't quite gotten used to the stillness and quietness of the house without him here. Chris would be working late, so I knew there was no rush in making dinner, but I wanted to go ahead and get it over with. The thighs I had left in the sink had thawed completely. I rinsed them off, seasoned them, and chopped up onions and red bell peppers and layered it on top of the meat. Then I covered the baking pan with aluminum foil and turned the oven on low.

The house was spotless, so there wasn't really anything for me to clean. Even Christopher's room was tidy, besides the few toys scattered here and there and the books tossed haphazardly on his bookshelf. I straightened up the bookshelf and picked up his toys. By the time I finished, I could smell the chicken all the way up the stairs. Returning to the kitchen, I was about to put on a pot of rice when the package caught my eye. I had almost forgotten about it. I picked up the box and put it near my ear, then shook it. It made no sounds and it was rather light. Was it a book? A CD? A surprise gift from Chris? Dexter? Jewelry? A tennis bracelet? A gift card?

Unable to curb my curiosity for a second longer, I used the paring knife to cut into the cardboard. Inside were two sheathed DVDs and a folded card on heavy stock paper. Frowning, I read the words on the card:

Angelique,
What did you ever do to deserve me hating you so much?
Well, sweetheart, I can show you better than I can tell you.
Yvonne

When I read my mother's name, I dropped the card like it had burnt my hands and stared at the two DVDs, unable to move or barely breathe. My heart was beating too fast and I clutched at my chest, breathing as though I'd just finished running a marathon. My mind screamed for me to trash everything: the box, the DVDs, the envelope. Just stuff everything in the garbage disposal and be done with this hateful woman. But I couldn't. I knew there was something on those DVDs that I needed to see.

Almost robotically, I removed the two DVDs from their protective covers and walked slowly into the living room, approaching the television set the way a condemned man would approach the death chamber. The television buzzed as I turned it on and popped in the first DVD. At first, the screen was pitch black. Moaning and groaning filled the speakers, but I couldn't see anything. I stepped closer to the TV, squinting my eyes as though by doing so, it would help me see through the darkness. Continuing to squint, I noticed that the screen wasn't as dark as I originally thought. There was just enough lighting casted on the bed that I could see two figures under the sheets. The man was on top, bucking and gyrating his hips; the woman was beneath him, her nails digging into his back.

"You nasty freak!" I exclaimed. I couldn't believe my mother was so classless that she would send me pornos through the mail.

I was just about to turn the disc off when the woman's voice said, "Chris...ooh, Chris. Mmm, Chris. Yes, yes, Chris."

My stomach flip-flopped as I stood there, hoping I'd heard wrong. Was that woman calling out my husband's name? Was that truly Chris in the bed, giving that woman some of the best sex in her life?

"No," I said aloud, "there are thousands of Chris-es in the world. It could be anybody."

And then what was undoubtedly Chris's voice: "Raleigh, shit, it feels too good. You're too wet, too tight. God, I'm 'bout to bust."

Trapped in a real-life nightmare, I watched the obscure picture and listened to the familiar sounds of my husband busting—inside another woman. Vomit rose up in my throat. I clutched my stomach and stopped the DVD, unable to watch a second more. Without hesitation, I popped in the other DVD; whatever was on this disc couldn't compare to the horrific scene I'd just seen and heard. This time, the screen was well-lit. Again, the camera was angled at the King-size bed. The bed was untouched; the pillows fluffed, not a wrinkle in the covers. From the surroundings, I gathered that this was a hotel room—an upscale hotel room.

Once again, I heard moaning and groaning before I saw anything and prepared myself for the worse. My husband came into view; although I could only see his heavily muscled back, I'd seen him naked enough that I could pick his back out of a lineup. Because his pants were bunched at his thighs, his buttocks also showed. He had some woman pressed up against the wall, hitting her from behind. His strokes were hard, pounding, rough; and the woman screamed out like he was actually hurting her. Yet from time to time, she taunted him, "That's all you got? With that big cock of yours and that's the best you can do?"

In response, Chris would bend her over further and hit her

even harder.

I had seen enough; I was sick to my stomach. Just as my finger neared the stop button on the DVD player, I heard the woman say, "Let's get in bed, Chris. I want you to sex me like you sex your wife."

Transfixed to the screen, I watched in horror as Chris picked up the petite woman by the waist and all but slung her into the bed. For the briefest second, I watched as the woman laid back on the bed and looked directly at the camera and winked before pulling my husband on top of her. They commenced to rough, animalistic sex, but I didn't need to watch it; I had seen all I needed to see.

I turned off the television and tried to return to the kitchen, but my knees gave out on me. My head spun out of control and the smell of the chicken in the oven made me nauseous. I found myself crying and nearly hyperventilating, having what felt like yet another panic attack. This could not be happening to me. Not again.

On hands and knees, I crawled over to the couch and buried my face into the cushions. Sobs tore through my body like labor pains. How could he do this to me? What had I ever done to deserve this? Now I knew the truth. Chris never loved me. There was no way he could do what he'd done and actually love me. He doesn't love me and he doesn't respect me. People treat bums on the street better than he'd treated me.

Why hadn't Chris been upfront with me? Technically, he hadn't lied about the situation. He had admitted to having sex with two women in Vegas. But the first woman—he wasn't just having sex with her. He was making love to her—the same way he had made love to me! And the second woman? Again, sobs racked my entire body. My mother? The woman who bore me? And he had screwed her so flippantly, like he was a porn star performing on a flick.

I didn't know who Chris was anymore. Without the gritty details, I could have lived in my 'happily ever after.' But with the reality tossed so crudely into my face, I couldn't cover my eyes and ears and pretend like I hadn't seen what I saw. There were a lot of things I could forgive Chris for—a lot of things I *had* forgiven him for. But screwing my mother was not one of them. This time, as much as I hated to make this decision, I knew that I could not stay married to a man who had crossed the line.

My knees burned and ached from being stuck in the carpet for so long, but I remained kneeling against the couch and put my hands together to pray. I prayed for God to give me peace and endow me with strength. Once I felt my strength renewed, I picked up the phone and dialed my lawyer. Whether he wanted to or not, Chris and I were getting divorced. And this time, I meant it.

Twenty-Eight

Back at work, I kept a smile glued to my face, even though I was dying inwardly. My personal life was just that—personal. I was not about to bring problems from home to my job and allow them to negatively affect my work performance.

As I sat at my desk, typing up a correspondence email for the head of the advertising department, I thought about what had transpired in my house two days ago. Chris had come home completely drained from his day at work. He didn't even recognize the thunderstorm brewing on my face. Somehow, I had managed to keep my cool and feed Christopher the Chinese food I had ordered—the chicken in the oven had burned beyond recognition—before putting him in the tub, and then tucking him in bed.

Once I finished with him, I returned to our bedroom and asked Chris was he up to watching a movie with me tonight.

"No, baby," he had declined, giving my thigh a light squeeze. "Baby, I can barely hold my eyes open. And you know I have to get up early in the morning."

"Just watch two minutes of it, baby. That's all."

"Two minutes?"

"Two minutes."

"Okay," he had agreed through a yawn and sat up in bed, stretching his eyes wide to try to keep them open.

That's when I had popped in the DVDs, one after the other. And the sleep that had initially clouded his vision disappeared like an ace of spades in a magician's hands. Then came the explanations, the constant reminder that he had already admitted to me about his infidelity in Vegas. He swore up and down that he didn't have the slightest idea that Yvonne was my mother. He would never intentionally hurt me like that. As far as the "love scene" with Raleigh, he couldn't quite explain why he'd done what he did. He'd gotten caught up in the moment. It was a mistake. He wasn't thinking straight. And then there was the slew of apologies and the pleading for me not to do this to him again. Not to do this to *him* again? The nerve!

The night ended with him packing up the majority of his things and heading back to his mother's house. I couldn't sleep in the bed without him. It was too big, too spacious…too empty. So I descended downstairs and turned the couch into a bed. I had stayed up nearly all night long, praying to God and wondering if I was making the right decision. And then the next day, I had taken the two DVDs to my attorney's office, played them for him, and filed for a divorce.

"Good morning, Mrs. Hines."

Dexter caught me by surprise. Usually he knocked before entering. If he had knocked, I was so caught up in my thoughts that I hadn't heard a thing. As always, he looked dashing in his black dress pants, slate gray collared shirt, and gray and pink tie. Not many men could pull off pink, but he did it effortlessly.

"Just dropping in to check on you. Hadn't heard from you in a while."

"I'm fine," I lied, and plastered a smile to my face.

"I like what you've done with *Nice & Naughty.*" He was referring to our top-selling men's pornographic magazine. "Up until you came along, it's only been available in adult stores. I like how you worked with the different store chains and got it into the sporting good stores. That was an excellent marketing strategy, and we're already seeing an increase in sales."

"To be honest, I just thought it was the logical thing to do."

Dexter invited himself to sit on the edge of my desk. He stared in my eyes so long that I had to look down at my desk. "Look at me," he requested in a low voice, and I did. He touched my chin. "You're hurting, baby girl."

Immediately, my bottom lip betrayed me; it trembled

uncontrollably and my eyes welled with tears. Dexter touched my shoulder and his touch was my undoing. I didn't realize how loud I was weeping until Dexter locked my office door, came around the desk, and pulled me into his arms. I needed this hug. I was so very tired of trying to hold everything up, trying to be strong. I needed someone to allow me to be weak, vulnerable. To lift and sustain me while my walls of pretense came crashing down. Dexter held me and I soaked the front of his shirt with my tears.

He didn't ask me what happened. Just kept rubbing my back, smoothing my hair, and promising me in a soothing voice that everything would be okay. Even though he didn't ask, I told him everything that had happened, from the moment I saw the package sitting on my doorstep until the time Chris backed out the driveway, headed to his mother's house once again.

"Why'd you even come to work today?" Dexter asked, still comforting me with his voice and touch. "You could've called in and took the day off."

"And do what? Sit home and drive myself insane thinking about what happened?" I chomped on my bottom lip and shook my head.

Dexter pulled a box of Kleenex from my desk drawer and gently wiped the tears from my face. I was glad I hadn't worn mascara today or I would look like a raccoon who'd been in a rain shower. It was bad enough that my nose was running. "Thanks, Dexter," I said, taking the tissue from him and wiping my nose. "This is kinda embarrassing."

"No, this is life. You have to take the good with the bad, the pretty with the ugly."

"Do you think I'm making the wrong decision? To divorce him?" I had asked Tori the same question yesterday after leaving the lawyer's office. She didn't give me a definite answer. For one, she felt like I was too emotional to think rationally. And for two, she reminded me that Chris would never have knowingly slept with my mother. Knowingly or unknowingly, that did not change the outcome of the situation. Chris had slept with my mother and the image of them screwing would forever be tattooed and engraved in my mind. Tori did say that whatever I chose to do, she had my back and supported me wholeheartedly.

"I can't tell you if your decision is wrong or right. Only God knows the answer to that. But I will tell you this." He stood to his feet and stretched. "I want you to take the rest of today off. And tomorrow too. It's just added stress that you can do without in your life right now."

No, he was wrong about that. This job wasn't added stress that I could do without in my life. Christopher Hines was added stress that I could do without. I was so sick and tired of the up and down roller coaster that our lives had become. I was so sick and tired of my son having to go through this turmoil with us. He deserves better than this, and so do I. Whether I was making the right decision or not, one thing I was certain of: I could not remain married to a man who every time I looked at him, I saw him bucking, grunting, and gyrating on top of my mother, freely and willingly giving her the long deep strokes that belonged only to me. I couldn't do it.

"I've already acquired a lawyer," I told Dexter. "The divorce proceedings are in process."

Dexter stood behind me, squeezed my shoulders, then gave them a deep massage that felt delicious. It seemed like all my stress had bunched in the muscles around the base of my neck, and his strong hands were easing that tension away. My head fell back and I sighed contently.

"Baby girl," he said while he continued the massage, "whether you divorce your husband or stay with him, I'm still going to be here for you. But I wouldn't feel right without letting you know the whole truth."

With my head still tilted back, I opened my eyes and looked up at him, waiting for him to continue speaking.

"It wasn't all your husband's fault. Like you've already said, he didn't even know that Yvonne was your mother. But she knew. The whole time, she knew that was your husband. She set him up."

"I don't believe it." Immediately, I pressed my hands against my stomach, feeling sick all over again. I had too many revelations and secrets unveiled lately, and I wasn't sure if I could handle anything more.

Dexter continued, "I work for your mother."

"You work for my—"

"Don't interrupt me. Let me finish." While he talked, he continued massaging my shoulders, but suddenly the massage didn't feel as good as it had just seconds ago. "I had no idea that Mrs. Whitmeyer was your mother. Not until I saw the picture of your husband." He pointed at the family picture on my desk, which I had flipped face down upon entering my office. "When I saw that picture, a lot of things started making sense. Like why she had paid Giovanni so much money to locate your husband and plant the escorting idea into his head, and why she paid so much money to spend two nights in Vegas with Chris."

"So all this time you knew?" I exploded on him, pushing his hands away from me. I glared at him as though he was just as guilty as my husband.

He cleared his throat, walked around the desk with his arms crossed. "After your first day working as a marketing director, I knew."

"Then why didn't you tell me?" I asked, feeling as though he'd just poured salt into an open wound.

"Because Mrs. Whitmeyer told me that if I so much as breathed a word about this to anybody, she'd terminate me. You got to understand, baby girl, that your mother is a very powerful woman. She owns Lumpkin Enterprises and everything that falls under the umbrella of this business. Your mother is at the top of the sex industry, and one word from that woman can make or break a person. I didn't want to lose everything I've worked so hard for. So I kept quiet. But I hate seeing you hurt like this. That's why I had to tell you the truth."

Dexter reached over and took my hand, then brought it up to his lips and kissed each knuckle. His lips felt soft, warm, comforting. "Please, don't hate me for this."

I didn't hate him. I couldn't hate him if I tried. Yet and still, one question kept nagging at me. "Why, Dexter? Why'd she do it? It was so cold, so cruel. Why'd she do this to me?"

"That, I don't know. You'd have to ask her yourself."

My office phone rang, but I was too numb to answer it. Dexter took the call, and while he spoke to the person on the other end, I sat there quietly, absorbing all this bitter information. But why? The question concerning my mother refused to stop nagging at me. Why would Yvonne go to such great lengths to pull Chris into the escorting industry? And furthermore, why would she record him having sex and send it to me, blatantly rubbing it in my face? It was like she was trying to hurt me, intentionally attempting to destroy my marriage. But why? What had I ever done to her?

When Dexter hung up the phone, I said softly, "Dexter, do you love me?"

He seemed surprised by my question. It took him a minute to find his voice, but when he did, he whispered, "Immensely." There was an intensity in his eyes, his voice, that caused a warm feeling to swirl in my belly.

"If you love me as much as you think you do, then do me a favor."

"Anything. Just ask."

"Call my mom and ask her to meet you at the White Rock Café in an hour."

"I can't." He shook his head. "I have a business conference in an hour that I have to—"

"I told you to ask her to meet you there. I didn't say you were actually the one who was going."

"Angelique…"

"Dexter, please…"

He still seemed unsure. We both realized how dangerous this situation could possibly be. But I needed to know the truth straight from the horse's mouth, and this was the only idea I could come up with. Dexter didn't seem too excited about my idea. So I decided to give him a little motivation. I walked over to him, held the side of his face, and kissed his lips gently. Sparks shot through me, and I knew he felt them too. He groaned into my mouth and kissed me back, tilting my head to the side to deepen the kiss. By the time we broke apart, my heart was knocking in my chest and Dexter looked like he was in pain. The bulge in his pants could be seen from a mile away.

We both didn't quite know what to say or do after that kiss. Dexter recovered first. He slid out his cell phone and dialed my mother's number. "Mrs. Whitmeyer," he said, "you got a minute? Yeah, it's kinda important."

***

En route to White Rock Café, styling and profiling in Dexter's Bentley, I called Tori and asked her if she could pick up Christopher from the afterschool program. She wanted details, so I told her my plan and how Dexter had helped me set my mother up. Tori made me promise to call her as soon as the meeting was over and let her know how things transpired. I also told her about the electric kiss in my office.

"You better slow your roll, Miss Thang. Things with you and Chris are still smoldering and you're already locking lips with another man."

"I didn't plan on kissing him. It just kind of happened."

"Can he kiss?"

"Can he?" I sucked in a breath threw my teeth, remembering the touch of his lips on mine.

"I'm not hating on you," Tori said, laughing at me. "I like Dexter. He'd make an amazing husband and an excellent father. But I still want you to take things slow. You and Chris still have some loose ends to tie together. And you never know. You might find it in your heart to forgive him—"

"You're right," I told Tori. "I'm sure one day I will be able to forgive Chris. But I will never ever forget what he did to me. And because of that, I'm done. I'm through with this marriage, and I'm through with him."

"Like I told you before. Whatever you choose to do, I got your back. Because at the end of the day, your happiness matters more to me than anything else. I'll get little man for you, and make sure you call me after the meeting."

When I pulled up at the coffee house ten minutes early, underneath the signage, a marquee stated: OUR COFFEE WAS ROASTED TODAY, WAS YOURS? I cracked a faint smile when I read it. The parking lot was half-full. I found a parking spot close to the entrance, snatched my oversized designer purse off the passenger seat, and got out the car. Using the keyless remote, I locked the doors, took a deep, calming breath, and went inside.

A quick scan of the room revealed that Yvonne was nowhere in sight. So, I ordered a cup of iced mocha and took a seat in a corner facing the window so that I could see Yvonne when she walked up. The sweet scent of cinnamon and buttercream icing, chocolate muffins, and caramel latte cheesecake tempted me, reminding me that I still hadn't eaten a thing all day. As hungry as my belly was, I didn't have much of an appetite. However, I ordered an icing-covered cinnabun and nibbled at it while waiting for my mother to arrive.

Outside the window, I noticed an elderly couple walking hand in hand down the sidewalk. It was a touching sight to see. Both were white headed, both had humps in their backs, and both walked slower than refrigerated molasses. They looked so much alike that it was obvious they'd been married for years. Sighing, I looked away and checked my watch. It was two o'clock and Yvonne still wasn't here. I wondered if she'd caught on to the fact that this was a setup and wasn't going to show up. But as soon as the thought crossed my mind, I saw Yvonne whip her sleek silver Audi into the parking lot, completely indifferent to the pedestrians who were in her way.

I pursed my lips and watched as she floated on her broomstick across the lot. I looked in the direction of the doorway and saw Yvonne standing there dressed in a tangerine orange halter dress that complemented her toned arms and smooth shoulders. The perfect outfit for these warm September breezes. Even from across the room, I could tell that she'd had enough plastic surgery and Botox injections for every woman in the café. Her eyes danced around the room and she frowned. She flicked out her cell phone, probably to call Dexter, but I stood up and yelled her name, then waved her over.

Shock registered on her face and she remained at the doorway, as though she was contemplating making a run for it. I half-expected her to run, just like the coward that she was. But surprisingly, she pocketed her phone and prissed over to my table. As she approached, the faint scent of White Diamonds perfume wafted in the air, interfering with the aroma of freshly roasted coffee.

"Let's go upstairs," I suggested.

Her eyes looked at me distrustfully. "Dexter's upstairs?"

"No, Dexter isn't here."

"He isn't?" She glanced out the glass window in the direction of the Bentley. "But his car is outside."

"He let me drive it."

Her eyes narrowed as she realized she'd been tricked. Again, I expected her to turn on her heel and speed out of the place. Instead, she stood her ground, staring at me through eyes that had become slits. She seemed reluctant to follow me up the stairwell and decided to buy a blueberry wheat muffin first. From the look of things, she could use two or three of those blueberry wheat muffins. My mother had never been so small in her life. She had to be a size two—a three at the most. I wonder how she'd lost so much weight and figured the surgeon's scalpel had helped with that as well.

With her muffin resting atop a ceramic saucer, she followed me upstairs and we found a quiet spot to sit and talk. The handful of patrons were caught up in their own conversations, sipping on their drinks, eating pastries, and not paying any attention to us.

"I never did like surprises," she said testily. "What's this about, Angelique?"

Puh-lease. Like you don't know. With a straight face, and conscientious about not raising my voice, I said, "You slept with my husband, then mailed me the DVD. I think that's worthy of a conversation."

She smirked.

My hand itched to slap her. "I know you knew who Chris was when you seduced him. Why'd you do it?"

She looked around the room, seemingly more concerned with what the patrons were doing than finishing our conversation. Finally, her eyes returned to mine. "You stole my husband, so I thought I'd return the favor." She gave such a wicked laugh that I felt my insides quiver.

"What are you talking about?" I wanted to add: you crazy

bitch.

She licked her glossy lips. "Before you came along, my life was full and complete. I had all the children I wanted, and my husband adored me. Then my husband decided that he wanted us to try for a little girl. I didn't want that, but he pressured me into it. I succumbed to his request out of fear of losing the man that I loved."

My lower lip trembled, so I lightly bit it. I didn't want to give her the satisfaction of knowing that she was getting to me.

"When you were born, your *papi* directed all of his love and attention toward you, his precious little princess." She sucked air between her teeth. "I resented you."

Her words stung like alcohol on a fresh wound. "Why didn't you love me?" I had to know. The words flew out of my mouth before I had a chance to stop them.

"When you were growing up, you were stubborn, and you used to challenge me all the time. You'd listen to whatever your *papi* had to say with no problem. But me," she rested her hand on her chest, "you'd defy me every step of the way. You constantly tested me and tried my patience. I know some people might think I was wrong, but I got frustrated and backed off from raising you. Instead of stepping up to the plate, I gave up." She dropped her hand. "The truth is…I couldn't handle you, because you were so much like me."

The more she spoke, the more convinced I became that Yvonne and I could never have a relationship. I didn't respect her as my mother, nor did I like her as a person.

"But I was your child. How could you give up on me like that?" I don't know why I cared, but I did.

"Don't you dare judge me," she snapped. "I married your *papi* when I was eighteen years old. I loved him with my whole heart and soul. Because I rejected you, he turned his back on me. We had a good marriage until you came along. You ruined everything! You stole his heart. He would never admit it, but I knew he loved you more than me."

"That wasn't my fault," I defended. "I was just a child."

"So what!"

My eyes grew wide. I had to sip my drink to keep from throwing it in her face. "You need to calm down."

"Why should I?" she challenged me. "I was a good and faithful wife. But you know what? And this is truly the icing on the cake."

I tilted my head to show her that I was listening.

"When your father died, he had two insurance policies." She held up two fingers. "His work policy was worth $20,000 and that went to me." She dropped her hand. "I had to use some of that to bury him with. But here's the kicker." She chuckled in a disgusted way. "His private policy was worth half a million dollars."

I gasped. My brothers and I hadn't received a dime of that money. I swear...if she tells me that she spent that money, I'd be willing to catch a murder charge.

"I didn't touch that money, if that's what you're worried about. I couldn't touch it if I tried." And I was sure that she had tried. She seemed reflective when she said, "Not only did I give him the best years of my life, but I bore him six children. *Six* children. He acted like none of that mattered. Not me, nor your brothers. Because when he passed, he left all that money to you." She stared me in the eyes with such disdain that the fine hairs on my arm stood at attention.

"What?" I couldn't hide my shock.

"Oh yes," she said sarcastically. "His precious little princess got it all. I was the one with him during the struggle and never once complained. I didn't care about how much money he made, or didn't make. But it was a real slap in my face for him to leave all his money to you."

Stunned, I asked, "Well...where's the money? What happened to it?"

She sighed in frustration. "Nothing. Nothing happened to the money. You'll get it all on your thirtieth birthday. How 'bout that?"

I did a quick mental calculation. My birthday was only three months away, the day before Christmas to be exact. I tried my best to wrap my brain around what she had just said, but it was all so unbelievable. At least now I knew why she hated me.

"So you set out to destroy my marriage because my daddy left me all his money?"

"No, sweetie pie." She patted my hand and I recoiled from her touch. "I set out to destroy your marriage so you would know how it feels to hurt like that. So you could empathize with my pain. And you made it easy for me. Since you're so much like me, you dropped your morals for money. And Dexter went crazy over you. When he started talking to me about the sexy stripper Angelique and how he couldn't keep you off his mind, I looked into it and found out that his Angelique was my Angelique. And that's what set my plan into motion."

I wanted to knock some of those pearly white teeth out of her head.

"From there, I used some of my inside sources to collect information. I found out that you and your husband had lost your jobs and you both were desperate. You were so desperate that you took off every piece of your clothes and worked that pole like you were born to do it. And your husband was so desperate that when I dangled the escorting job in front of his face, it was an opportunity that he couldn't pass up. It all came together so effortlessly."

I took a sip and choked on my drink, unable to swallow the liquid that suddenly tasted sour and stale. "But I-I don't understand. Why did you feel the need to sleep with Chris? Wasn't it enough to humiliate me by having me strip in one of your clubs? Or having him…having him have sex with…with that other woman."

"Of course not. You really think I'd pass up the opportunity to ride the cock that's given my daughter so much pleasure?"

That's when it happened. My arm moved on its own accord and I threw my drink in her face. The pale liquid saturated her expensive weave and sloshed down her forehead, beading on the edge of her eyelashes. She gasped like she was drowning and jumped up from the table, looking at me incredulously. It took every ounce of restraint not to crack my glass over her head.

"You're the biggest bitch I've ever met," I huffed, pushing away from the table and standing to my feet. "I hate you. You're dead to me."

She patted her face with a napkin. "The feeling's mutual, sweetheart."

As I walked away, completely ignoring the flabbergasted looks from the seated customers, as well as the store manager's stuttered attempt to ask us to evacuate the premises, Yvonne called out, "It seems like you got the last laugh, doesn't it? But Mommy always wins, Angelique. Remember that. I always win."

Turning on my heel, I marched back to the table.

"M-ma'am…" the store manager stuttered, and I glared at him, daring him to speak another word.

Eyes followed me as I marched to the table and sat my purse down. I leaned over so that I was eye-level with my mother and said through my teeth, "Well, Mommy didn't win this time. Did she?"

"I didn't?" she asked with her eyebrows high and a smile dancing on her lips.

"No, she didn't," I continued without breaking eye contact. "You see, what Mommy forgot is that while she's trying to make her way to the top, using Dexter to run her sex businesses so that it doesn't soil her 'political' character, Mommy forgot to think some of her plans all the way through."

"You think so?" Yvonne said, a nasty smirk replacing her flippant smile. She leaned so close that I felt like I was going cross-eyed while I tried to continue looking at her. "Well, let's see. I planned to marry a rich man, and I did. He has more money than you and your husband will ever have in your entire lifetimes combined. I planned to build a lucrative enterprise in the sex industry, and I've been rather successful with that. I planned to seduce your husband, and sweetheart, my kitty is still throbbing from the way he put it on me. And I planned to ruin your marriage. Guess who filed for a divorce?" She pushed up out of her chair and stood to her full five feet and six inches, with heels. "So if you ask me, I seem to have thought my plans out and executed them fairly well."

Her hurtful words had made their mark. But I wasn't backing down. "Yes, Mother," I continued without missing a beat, "but what you didn't plan on, sweetheart, was for the sex tape of you getting your freak on with my husband going viral all over the Internet." My threat was nothing more than a bluff; I didn't even have the DVDs anymore. My attorney had the originals and Chris had burned a copy of each. But my mother didn't need to know that.

Her face lost every shade of color and she staggered before falling back into her chair. I smiled triumphantly. "Once the world sees the true side of Yvonne Whitmeyer, you can kiss your political career goodbye."

Looking like she'd been tased, Yvonne whispered, "You wouldn't."

"No? You don't think so?"

Finally, she snapped back to reality and that evil glint returned to her eyes. Her voice barely audible, she issued her threat. "If that DVD goes viral, it'd be a shame to see your son, Christopher Hines, Jr., first-grader at Dunberry Elementary School, come up missing. Such a precious boy to lose at such a young age."

That did it for me. I slapped Yvonne so hard that she fell out of her chair. I rubbed my hands together to soothe my stinging palm. That bitch had threatened the wrong little boy. Unlike her, I'd throw a brick in church about my child. She was lucky I didn't break my foot off in her ass.

"You better keep my son's name out of your mouth."

She touched the side of her face and got up off the floor.

I stared her down. "If you even see my son on the street, you'd better run the other way. I promise you this on everything I love if you ever come near my son I'll kill you, bitch."

My handprint had left its mark on her cheek and she continued to rub that spot.

Still rubbing her reddening cheek, my mother looked me in the eye and said through a snarl, "I hate you. I should have aborted you when I had the chance. I wish you were never born."

After an extended pause I said, "I forgive you, Yvonne."

She looked at me like she had caught me smoking crack. "I said I *hate* you."

"And I said I forgive you. For not loving me the way I needed to be loved. Because I finally figured it out. How can you love someone when you have an empty place where your heart should be? My only prayer for you is that when your Day of Judgment comes, may God have mercy on your soul."

With my head held high, I squared my shoulders and walked out of the White Rock Café. Inside Dexter's car, I thought I was going to cry. I even pulled napkins out of his glove department to catch the tears. But my face remained dry. My eyes didn't even glisten. It was as though God had just freed me from the pressure, the stronghold, the burden that had held me down my whole life. I was finally free. No longer did I have to look back or revisit the pain. God had given me permission to release my mother, and I felt light enough to fly.

I knew that getting over Chris would be one of the most difficult and daunting tasks I'd ever have to do. But I knew that God would give me the strength to survive. A divorce was not the ending of my life. It was the beginning of a new phase in life. With Tori and Dexter supporting me, and Christopher loving me, I knew I'd make it just fine. I'd just have to take each day one moment at a time.

Twenty-Nine

At the back of his mind, Chris always thought that his marriage was still savable. Angelique and he had been tested through the fire plenty of times, but each time, they had overcome. There was no doubt in his mind that they'd be able to rise above this repulsive situation with her mother. What the devil had meant to tear them apart, he was certain that it would work in their favor to bring them even closer together. Angelique just needed time and space, and then she'd eventually come around—he was sure of it.

Reluctantly, he had moved back in with his mother and submerged himself in his work to maintain his sanity. He viewed each day as one day closer to him and his wife getting back together. Or at least this was what he thought until he went to check the mail one day. Inside was a thick white envelope from an attorney's office addressed to him. As soon as he saw the envelope, he knew it was all over. A breeze blew hard, as though it was trying to blow the envelope out of his hands, and he kind of wished it would blow away. He didn't open it until he was seated at his mother's kitchen table. His mother was at the church, helping with the food bank, and he was relieved that he was home alone. He didn't want anyone else partaking in his pain, his misery. Just as he expected, the thick envelope contained divorce papers. Optimism that he'd firmly held on to for this long finally dissipated. If Angelique had gone as far as to hire an attorney and file for a divorce, he knew that this thing was final. There was no turning back from here.

He called Angelique, but it was pointless. She didn't want to hear his tearful pleas or begging. All she wanted to talk about were the technicalities of the divorce; things like custody rights and separation of assets. He called Melvin instead. Melvin agreed to hang out with him, which would be his first time really going out since having the stroke. They went to a sport's bar and watched the football game. It was boring. Melvin couldn't drink with him because of his medications, and if Chris heard one more word about Stephanie, he was going to croak over. Chris cut their outing short and returned to his mother's house. He crawled in bed and stayed there for the next few days.

His mother thought he was coming down with the flu. She knew that Angelique and Chris were experiencing marital problems, but she had no idea that Angelique had filed for a divorce. Chris wallowed in bed, sipped on the chicken noodle soup his mother brought to him, and thought about his wife, as well as all the events and poor decisions that had brought them to this point.

Unable to stay out of work a day longer without the possibility of losing his job, Chris returned to work with a full beard. He knew he looked a mess but couldn't care less about his physical appearance. He was supposed to get off at two, but he worked over anyway. There was nothing to look forward to except crawling in the twin-size guest bed and staring at his mother's floral print walls. It was nearing seven o'clock and the maintenance man peeked in Chris's office, reminding him that he would be locking the building up within the next ten minutes.

"Okay, Mr. Vince," Chris called out to him. "I'll be out in five minutes."

The gray-headed man nodded, gave him a toothless smile, and went back to whistling as he paced the hallways, checking for any other scragglers. Chris liked Mr. Vince; he was a hardworking man who was always smiling, whistling, and telling stories about the good ol' days. It made no sense to Chris why Mr. Vince would come work for a company whose very foundation was built upon the creation of new technology when he couldn't stand anything battery-operated but a car. The man didn't use a microwave, arguing that that was the problem with people in the world today. They want things done instantly, which is why "young folks"—

which according to him is anyone younger than the age forty—
don't know nothing about patience nowadays. He absolutely
despised cell phones and text messages and promoted face-to-face
conversation and written letters instead.

"When you dead and gone, what you gon' leave behind
yo' chilluns? Text messages and posts on Facebook? Emails? Why
don't you leave behind some letters that you wrote wit yo' hands?
A handwritten letter mean so much more than some compooterized
text."

And that's when the idea came to him.

Chris sat up in his chair, his eyes shining bright as though a
light bulb had literally lit inside his head. *That* was the answer. The
emails.

It wasn't fair for Chris to lose his whole entire marriage,
based upon a trap that Mrs. Whitmeyer had set up specifically
for him while she got to walk away scot-free, no repercussions
whatsoever. It had nearly slipped his mind that that day, a long
time ago, when he had sat at her office computer, reading that dry
escorting manual, he had done a little dallying around himself.
She had forgotten that computers were his life. He could just about
build his own computer from scratch. That's why for him, breaking
through her password-protected files was as easy as boiling water.

He had been curious about who her husband was, hacked
into her email account, and had found correspondence emails that
they had sent back and forth. He'd nosily read them, but quickly
closed out the program when he realized that their boring emails
were about as exciting as the handbook manual. However, from
the emails, he learned that her husband, Wallace Whitmeyer, was
not only an oil tycoon, but he was an assistant pastor at a church
located in southern Texas, just two hours away from San Antonio.
That information had shocked the hell out of Chris. There was no
way that Wallace Whitmeyer could have married Yvonne while
being fully knowledgeable of her true profession.

Fingers moving speedily across the keyboard, Chris did
a people search for Wallace Whitmeyer, and within seconds, he
had located Mr. Whitmeyer's email address, phone number, and
personal mailing address. Chris printed off the information, then

called out to Mr. Vincent that he was gone. He returned to his mother's house and searched through his things for the two burned copies of the incriminating DVDs. He found them and selected the one of him and Mrs. Whitmeyer. Then he pulled out a sheet of paper and began writing. In his letter, he told everything, leaving out not a single detail, not even the tiny black mole on the left side of Mrs. Whitmeyer's butt cheek. Mr. Whitmeyer deserved to know the truth. If Chris's marriage was going up in flames, then he'd make sure that Mrs. Whitmeyer's went up in flames too. They would go down together.

Early that next morning, he went to FedEx and sent off the letter and DVD. For the first time since receiving the divorce papers in the mail, he realized that he finally had a smile on his face.

***

The weekend before Thanksgiving, Chris found himself in Las Vegas yet again. He didn't tell his mother that he was going because he was certain that she'd worry herself silly until he returned. He didn't want to put that kind of stress on her. So he simply told her that Melvin and he would be hanging out for the weekend and he wouldn't return until late Sunday night—which, technically, was not a lie.

She had kissed his cheek and held him like she'd never see him again. "Take care of yourself, Chris. I love you."

"I love you too, Mama," he had said, and left quickly because he was running late and he didn't feel like hearing Melvin's mouth.

Before stopping by to scoop Melvin, Chris felt the overwhelming desire to stop by Angelique's house to see Christopher. As always, his son was excited to see him and bounced into his arms.

"Daddy, can I spend the weekend with you?" he asked.

Chris hugged his son, but shook his head. "Not this weekend, little man. Daddy's going on a little trip. But I'll be back Sunday, and if I don't get back too late, maybe you can come over and eat Sunday dinner with me and Grandma."

"Can I, Mommy? Can I?"

Angelique shrugged her shoulders. "I don't see a problem with it."

Seated at the dining table and fingers dancing across her laptop, Angelique looked stunning in a pair of jeans and a low-cut black shirt, her hair pulled tight atop her head. He made small talk with her, but couldn't stay long. He was already pressed for time. "Where're you headed?"

"To support my boy, Melvin. He's performing at a club big enough to hold two thousand people."

"Wow. That's impressive. Where's the club at? In Vegas?"

Chris dropped his head, but didn't say anything.

"Hmm. Have fun."

"Angelique, it's not even like that—"

"Chris, honestly, it doesn't matter to me. You're a free man now. You don't have to answer to anybody but the Man above."

"Can I have a hug?"

Usually, she ignored him when he asked this question. But this time, to his surprise, she walked over and not only gave him a hug, but kissed his cheek. She wiped her lipstick from Chris's cheek and smiled. "Have a safe trip, Chris. And tell Melvin to break a leg."

As much as he wanted to stay for a little while longer, he knew he needed to get going. He kissed Christopher again and waved goodbye to Angelique. Then he sped over to Stephanie's place. Stephanie and Melvin were already outside waiting on him. Of course Melvin had a thousand things to say about him being late, but they made it to the airport on time.

Chris still couldn't believe Melvin had landed the comedy gig. He had entered into a contest online and was one of the three winners chosen to perform at the casino inside the Windsmore Hotel. Chris was so proud of his friend and how he refused to let anything keep him back from going for his dreams—neither a life-threatening stroke or a heart attack was enough to stop the man. His perseverance inspired Chris.

For the three and a half hour flight, Chris found himself thinking about Angelique. They'd been apart for two months now, but it felt more like two years. He had requested that they spend

Thanksgiving together as a family, but Angelique declined his suggestion. She already had plans. She was spending Thanksgiving with Dexter so she could meet his family. In other words, she had moved on with her life; and as difficult as it was going to be for him to let her go, he realized that eventually, he had to move on with his life as well. She'd always hold a special place in his heart.

Once their plane touched down at the McCarran International Airport, they deboarded, took their luggage from claims, and waved down a taxi to take them to their hotel room. They had separate rooms that were attached via the bathroom. Melvin had forewarned him to bring ear plugs because Stephanie and he would be getting it in all weekend long and, according to Melvin, Stephanie was a "screamer."

"Why don't you call Raleigh while we're up here?" Melvin suggested, elbowing Chris in the side. "You said she lives on the outskirts of Vegas. It wouldn't take her no time to get here. You said that thang was on point, so get you some more. Coochie gives you energy, and you look like you could use a little bit of that right now."

Chris retired to his room and laid back on his bed. No, he wasn't going to bother Raleigh. She had his business card, which meant she had his number, and his phone had yet to ring. It was obvious that what they had shared was nothing more than a one-nightstand, and he was okay with leaving it that way.

As if on cue, his cell phone rang and lit up with an out-of-state number that he knew by heart. He knew of the saying that you could talk or think somebody up, but it amazed him that he could be thinking about her at this very moment, and then out of all the months of silence from her, she finally called.

He answered the phone, a smile in his voice. "Raleigh?"

"Yeah, it's me," she said, laughing. "You sound surprised."

"I'll admit it. I am. I never thought I'd hear from you again."

"Same here, stranger."

Chris sat up in the bed. "So how have you been? How's life been treating you?"

"Okay, I guess. I miss you."

"I miss you too, Raleigh." And he meant it. He was hurting and right now, he would've given anything to hold a woman in his arms who actually cared about him and his situation. "When can I see you again?"

"I was going to ask you the same thing."

"I'm here in Vegas. My plane just touched down about an hour ago."

"You're lying! What hotel are you at?"

"The Windsmore Hotel."

"The one on Sands Avenue?"

"That's the one," he said with a laugh. Her excitement was catching. "But don't come right away—"

"Why? Is your wife there?" Her excitement deflated.

"Truthfully," Chris said after a brief pause, "my wife and I are going through a divorce. To cut a long story short, she found out about the whole escorting job and she filed for a divorce."

"I'm sorry, Chris."

"Don't be. Everything happens for a reason." Chris cleared his throat and sat back against the pillows. "I'm up here with my best friend. He's performing at the casino downstairs tonight. He does comedy. The show starts at seven. Can you make it?"

"Definitely."

"I'll see you then. And Raleigh?"

"Yes?"

"It's nice hearing your voice again."

He could hear her smile. "See you in a little bit, Chris."

Chris ended the call with a huge smile glued to his face. The smile was interrupted when he heard a consistent thump against the wall and Stephanie's tiny screams coming through the thin plaster. "Hey!" Chris yelled, banging on the walls. "Calm that shit down! Nobody wants to hear that!"

"I forewarned you," Melvin yelled back. "I told you she's a screamer."

Thirty

"A'ight, so a man walks into a bar and sees a woman sipping a martini…"

"Oh my God," Chris and Stephanie whispered at the same time. They both dropped their heads and looked away. Chris knew his friend was about to embarrass the hell out of himself in front of this Las Vegas crowd. Up until this point, Melvin had been on a roll.

"Look at y'all," Melvin said, pointing at the hundreds of people filling the tables as he wiped sweat from his forehead. "Y'all thought I was about to tell a bar joke. No siree. I tricked y'all ass. Save the bar jokes for the white comedians—they actually make that shit funny. But black folks like real jokes. If y'all wanna hear some real jokes, let me hear you say 'Black boy, tell us!'"

"Black boy, tell us!" the crowd hollered back at him.

Chris and Stephanie shared relieved looks, and then Chris glanced back at the entrance door to the club for the umpteenth time. Raleigh should've been here by now. It was twenty minutes past seven. She had called him at a quarter til and told him that she was having car trouble. He asked her if she wanted him to go meet her, but she refused the offer, insisting that she'd be fine.

"She's coming Chris, just be easy," Stephanie said, giving him a knowing smile. "You must really like this girl. I've never seen you look so antsy before. And you look very dapper too."

He gave her a piece of a grin but dismissed her comments with a shake of his head. He'd never admit it to Stephanie, but he had paid special attention to his wardrobe tonight, specifically for Raleigh. Since the dissolution of his marriage, he had dedicated his time to his son, TCP Robotics, and the gym. Over the past few months, he had visited the gym so often that they offered to put him a bed in the dance room. He basically lived at the gym, using the work out equipment to build up his arms and chest, and running five miles around the gym's track every day. The strenuous workout was not just to chisel his physique. Working out at the gym until he could barely move a muscle was his way of numbing the pain.

Tonight, if Raleigh allowed him to, he'd relieve his pain in a different way. He sipped his Scotch, then refocused his attention on the stage.

"Y'all want some real jokes? A'ight cool," Melvin said, moving the microphone cord out his way. "Joke number one, and this shit ain't funny: take your black ass to the doctor. I don't care if you have to use Medicaid, Medicare, the free clinic—take yo' ass to the doctor and get a health checkup. Real talk, I just had a stroke and a heart attack a few months ago from heart disease. That shit ain't nothing to play with. I had to learn how to walk again, talk again, everything. Ain't nothing like a real heart attack—you feel me?

"We have fake heart attacks all the time. Show of hands: how many of y'all been driving with no insurance and revoked tags, then you look in the rearview mirror and see a cop car behind you? Heart attack. Fellas, how many of y'all had an AIDS test done, knowing damn well you done hit one too many raw, and then the nurse call you to the back to read you your results and her face looks like this—" He made one of those 'I hate to break the news to you' type of faces, and the crowd fell out laughing. "Heart attack. Fellas, how many of y'all done been in a committed relationship, and you accidentally left your phone at home and forgot to lock that bitch? Heart attack, stroke, seizure—everything in the book!"

Chris had to stand up with the rest of the crowd and applaud his boy. Melvin had the crowd rolling. But he didn't stop there. He pointed Stephanie out and asked her to stand. "Y'all see that right there? That's my fiancée. Me and my baby getting married in two months. January twentieth, that's gonna be my wife. She's beautiful, ain't she?"

And she did look gorgeous in a form-fitting red dress that stopped just above her knees. She had on red bottom heels and a beautiful red, double gardenia in her hair. She looked stunning, but being around all that red made Chris feel uncomfortable. Red reminded him of that grisly scene he'd stumbled upon just a few hours after his father committed suicide. The crowd clapped for her, and Stephanie smiled and blew Melvin a kiss before graciously retaking her seat.

Melvin continued, "Marriage is a mu'fucka, you hear me? You don't believe me, ask my boy Chris," he said, pointing at him.

With a bored look on his face, Chris stuck up his middle finger and Melvin cracked up on the stage. "No, but for real. Real talk. Watch this. Round of applause from all the single people up in here." Melvin held out his microphone toward the crowd, and Chris was nearly deafened as the majority of the people in the room clapped, roared and hooted. Melvin said, "Now, round of applause from the married people in here." It sounded like about three people in the whole room clapped, and they didn't seem too enthused. "Listen to that pathetic shit," Melvin said and started laughing. "The only person excited about being married is the woman. The man clapping 'cause he know he gotta clap. If he don't, when he go home tonight, his wife's gonna be in his face talking about, 'Why the fuck you ain't clap? Something wrong with yo' hands? You betta be glad I married yo' sorry, tired, good-for-nothing, can-barely-feel-it-when-you-got-it-in ass anyway.'"

Laughing so hard she nearly peed herself, Stephanie stood up from the table and said she needed to use the ladies' room. Chris watched Melvin finish up his performance, and he stood and clapped for his boy, then cupped his hands around his mouth and hooted the loudest. He had to admit, he was a little upset that Raleigh hadn't made it in time to see his best friend perform.

Melvin walked over to the table and Chris engulfed him in a bear hug, thudding his back. "You did your thing, man. I'm proud of you."

"Where's my baby?"

"She just left to use the bathroom."

"Where's your baby?"

Chris glanced back at the door again. He dropped his shoulders and sighed. "Your guess is as good as mine."

"So how'd I do?"

"Man, you blew that thing out the water. It was funny from beginning to end. You scared me when you were about to do that bar joke though."

Melvin held his stomach and laughed. He didn't have a belly to grab anymore. Those months of rehabilitation and monitored meals had helped him shed weight until he was just a few pounds heavier than Chris. Stephanie loved him while he was big, but Chris was sure that she liked him even better now that he'd lost weight. Chris had to give it to him. He looked like a new man with his new body, and Chris even noticed that Stephanie wasn't the only woman who had her eyes on Melly Mel.

Chris's cell phone rang displaying Raleigh's number. "Hello? Are you close?"

"Chris, help me!"

"What's wrong?"

"What's wrong?" Melvin asked.

Chris waved for his friend to be quiet and tried to listen to Raleigh through her hysterical voice. "Chris, I was taking the back way to the casino and my car cut off in this alley. It won't crank. There are strange men walking around. I'm within walking distance of the casino, but I'm scared to get out! They might rape me or hurt me or something. Come get me, Chris!"

Chris was already on his feet, ignoring Melvin's persistent question of 'What's going on, man?' "Stay in the car," Chris told her. "Lock your doors. No matter what, do not get out that car. Do you understand me?"

"Yes. Chris, hurry. Please, I'm scared."

"What street are you on? How do I get to you?" She gave him the rather simple instructions and Chris reminded her again to stay in the car and keep the doors locked. If anything happened to her because she was coming down to Vegas to see him, he would never be able to live with himself.

"Chris, man, tell me what's going on."

"It's Raleigh," Chris called over his shoulder as he headed out the casino and into the cool night air. "Her car broke down in an alley, and she's right up the street. Some men are around her and she's scared to get out."

"I'll come with you."

"No!" Chris demanded. "Go back in there with Stephanie. I don't want you missing the other comics—"

"I don't give a damn about the other comics. I gotta make sure you a'ight, you feel me?"

Chris didn't waste time arguing with Melvin. He ran down the cement sidewalk that was congested with hordes of people dressed in barely any clothing despite the chill in the air.

* * *

Melvin was hot on his heels, but Chris didn't know that. Though he tried to keep up with his friend, the effects of his stroke were working against him while the strenuous workout in the gym was giving Chris amazing speed and stamina.

Chris ran with only one focal point: finding Raleigh and rescuing her before those men hurt her, tried to rob her—or worse, tried to rape her. He was so focused on the task at hand that he didn't pay attention to the shadows. He was so focused on locating Raleigh that he didn't pay attention to his father who had materialized out of thin air and was racing beside him, his face contorted in fear as he screamed his son's name.

"Chris, the shadows!" his father yelled. "Open your eyes, son! Pay attention! Chris! Chris!"

Chris rounded the corner and turned on the alley that Raleigh had said she was on. He saw the small red Kia, its headlights shining directly in his face. But what he didn't see was the short, stout man step out of the shadows. He didn't see the starlight reflect off the man's gold-green front tooth. And he didn't see the blue moonlight momentarily illuminate the barrel of the revolver. Neither did he see his father jump in front of him, his arms outstretched in a futile attempt to save his son from the inevitable.

Even though Chris saw none of these things, he felt the burning white-hot pain as the bullet twirled through his father's misty body and tore through Chris's solid chest. He felt the sidewalk scrape the skin off his chin and forearms as he collapsed in the street and slid to a halting stop. He tasted the grit and dirt in his open mouth as he screamed in agony and clutched the right side of his chest. Red blood seeped over his fingers as he held the wound that spurted and gushed to the beat of his heart.

His father bent over him and pressed invisible fingers over the wound, trying to stop the flow of blood. Charles looked up to heaven and implored God on behalf of his son: "Please, Master. He's too young to die. Don't let him go out like this. Save my son."

Red frothy blood burbled out of Chris's open mouth.

Ahead of him, Raleigh watched him fall to the ground, cranked the car, then threw open the passenger door. "Get in!" she yelled at the gold-toothed man.

"And run over his ass too," the man said, glaring at Chris's twitching body. "Think he's gonna punch me in the mouth and not get what's coming to him."

Instead of running over him, Raleigh maneuvered the car around his body. She stopped the car, kept it running, but put it in park.

"What the hell are you doing? I know somebody heard that gunshot. We gotta get the hell out of here before the cops come!"

"Just chill. It'll only take a second." Raleigh stepped out the car and walked over to Chris's twitching body. His eyes were still open and the life hadn't left his body just yet. But judging by the amount of blood that was spilling from his chest, she knew he only had a few minutes left to live—if that long.

She knelt beside him and touched his face. "No hard feelings, okay, Chris?" She shushed him as he tried to make some sound, and she shook her head. "Nobody told you to send that DVD to Mrs. Whitmeyer's husband. He's filing for a divorce. You didn't think she'd pay you back for that? Now look at me," she said, lifting up her hand and smiling. "Because I agreed to go through with this, she's already got my *Naked* portfolio accepted for an exhibition at the Southern Nevada Museum of Fine Arts.

Now who in their right mind would've passed up that deal? And the only thing it cost me…was your life." She tapped his nose, then stood up, still looking at him and shaking her head. "The things we do when we get desperate."

The sound of approaching sirens filled the night air.

"If you don't get in this damn car right now," the gold-toothed man screamed, "I'm leaving you. You going down by yourself!"

Raleigh glanced at Chris one last time, then got back in the car and drove off without looking back once.

As the red Kia merged with the busy highway traffic, Melvin finally neared the alley. He'd heard the gunshot and had been praying with every step that Chris was okay. Heaving, out of breath, and so wore out that he didn't think he could take another step, Melvin finally made it around the corner. When he saw his friend lying in a pool of blood, his knees went weak and he fell to the ground.

"Help!" he screamed, his voice echoing in the empty alley. His echo mimicked him, taunted him. "Please someone. Help! Help! He's dying!"

Chris's father was still kneeling beside his son, praying for a miracle. But he could clearly see that Chris's vision was starting to fade and his breathing was slowing to a stop. Flickering like a flame that someone had blown too hard, his father's spirit stalled. And then the flame went out.

Reading Group Discussion Questions

1. Do you think that if Chris would've given his father a chance to fully warn him about what was to come without constantly interrupting him, that it could have possibly changed the outcome of the story? Why?

2. How did you feel about Angelique's reasons for becoming an exotic dancer? Explain your answer.

3. Dexter seemed to genuinely care for Angelique. Do you think they should've pursued a relationship? Why or why not?

4. Angelique didn't have a relationship with her mother. Do you feel Angelique handled the situation between Chris and Yvonne appropriately? Explain.

5. How did you feel about Chris and Angelique's love? Were you for them or against them staying together?

6. Did Raleigh's hidden agenda catch you completely off guard, or did you already have your suspicions about her? Explain why you were or were not suspicious of her. Were you disappointed that their short-lived romance ended the way it did?

7. Melvin had no reservations about openly verbalizing his dislike for Angelique. He said a lot of things about Chris's marriage, including: Angelique is a gold-digger, the marriage is a farce, Chris is only toughing it out for his son's sake, Chris is willingly turning a blind eye to the "truth." Do you think any of

Melvin's accusations were founded, or do you think his anger and resentment toward Angelique stemmed from jealousy? Explain.

8. Chris tells a lot of lies to his wife in order to cover up what he's really doing. Not only does he lie about working at Womack's IGA store, and lies about going to Ms. Eloise's house, but he also lies about escorting and fabricates the non-existent Diamond-Elite Business Solutions company. Do you think if he would've told his wife the truth from day one, that she would've been more understanding of his situation, being that she took on a similar job for similar reasons? Why?

9. Angelique clearly loved her son. Do you believe people can have questionable career choices and still be effective parents? Why or why not?

10. In his younger years, Chris had a reputation for being a ladies' man. Do you believe a cheater can change, or once a cheater always a cheater? Explain.

About the Authors

Nicki Monroe is a graduate of the University of Alabama in Huntsville. She's a lover of life. She has a passion for all things fun, exciting, and adventuresome. She's well-traveled and works as a professional ghostwriter and college instructor. She has written fiction and non-fiction books for traditionally published authors, self-published writers, and publishing houses. Although she spends most of her time writing or reading she's a devoted wife and mother to her daughter who has the "Only Child Syndrome." Visit Nicki on the web at www.nickimonroe.com or e-mail her at nicki@nickimonroe.com.

Author of Confessions of a Diva, Jessica Barrow-Smith is a North Carolina native who holds a degree from Campbell University and National University of La Jolla, California. As the founder of S&B Manuscript Editing & Critique, she has had the opportunity to perform editorial services for authors spanning from California to the United Kingdom. She is also an English Instructor and the recipient of the Josephine-Gardner Creative Writing Award and the Wallace-Vale Award for Excellence in English. Whenever she's not writing or reading a book—or grading papers—she likes to spend time hugged up with her husband and children.

Coming soon to a bookstore near you...

The saga continues in Book #2 in the Desperate Series. Be sure to pick up your copy.

CPSIA information can be obtained at www.ICGtesting.com
Printed in the USA
LVOW08s0957010913

350482LV00001B/192/P